SHADOW ANGEL

BOOK TWO

SHADOW ANGEL

BOOK TWO

LEIA STONE & JULIE HALL

USA TODAY BESTSELLING AUTHORS

Save my mom.
Save the souls.
Save the world.

No pressure.

BOOKS BY JULIE HALL

JULIEHALLAUTHOR.COM/BOOKS

FALLEN LEGACIES SERIES

Stealing Embers

Forging Darkness

Unleashing Fire

LIFE AFTER SERIES

Huntress

Warfare

Dominion

Logan

Julie's books have won or finaled in 21 awards.

To our readers.

CHAPTER
ONE

I stared at the crack in the stone wall and the empty dread settled deeper into my bones.

Two weeks.

I'd been basically living in the sanctuary for two weeks staring at this crack and hoping that Gage would walk out of it alive. But… he was gone. I'd told myself that today was the day, that if he didn't come back, or the portal didn't magically restore itself, I would let him go.

A sob formed in my throat, and I stood, once again reaching out and pulling for my power. Purple arcs of light flared from my palms and licked the wall where the portal once stood, but nothing happened. It appeared that my portal making powers were limited and creating an opening to Avalon was not in the cards for me.

The back door opened, and I sighed, already knowing who it would be.

"Tatum," Aurelia called behind me. There was so much pity in her voice. I didn't want to hear what she had to say. "I think it's time to say goodbye."

How did you say goodbye to someone when you weren't sure what had actually become of them? There was no closure, no body, nothing.

"He could still be alive. He could still come back," I said quickly, not turning to face her. She was a Portal Master, and even with her help we weren't able to restore the portal to Avalon. It was just here one day and then it wasn't. Was this my punishment for throwing a Shade into the heavenly city of Avalon? They cut off our access to it? Or maybe Gage's dark magical energy just broke the thing? I'd racked my brain for countless hours trying to figure out how to fix it and I'd come up with nothing.

"He could..." Aurelia hedged. "But I think it's time we focused on your studies. You have a great ability, but it needs to be shaped and molded so that you can live up to your potential."

Yeah, and my "life mission," which was a giant mystery since Cael hadn't even told me in detail what that was because he'd claimed the time wasn't right... whatever that meant. I only knew that my mission involved defeating Apollyon, which I was super on board with after he'd crashed my Ascension Ceremony. But since I'd broken the only way to get to Avalon to ask Cael about my mission and when the time *would be* right, I might never know what I was supposed to do.

"Your mother is counting on you too, dear," she said softly, and my body went rigid. A month ago I didn't even know my mother was alive, and now I'd not only met her but learned that she was trapped in the Netherworld.

Aurelia was right, I needed to focus on getting my mom back too. I'd promised.

I turned slowly, finally facing the master Lumen. She was dressed in battle leathers, hands clasped in front of her as she looked down at me with compassion.

This was beyond hard. I wasn't just grieving over the loss of Gage, but the loss of potential. For the person I knew he could have been. Of what *we* could have been had we had the chance.

"I know. I need to let him go," I croaked.

She nodded and a single tear fell down my cheek. I'd sobbed myself to sleep the first three nights. But now I was running out of tears. Gage Alston was gone, and I needed to pick up the pieces of my life and move on.

Looking back at the crack in the wall one more time, I nodded.

Goodbye, Gage. I tried. I really tried to save you, I said, and then spun and left the building with Aurelia, leaving a piece of myself behind in the sanctuary.

It felt strange knocking on Gran's door. Our relationship had been strained the last two weeks, and it wasn't just because I'd hardly left the sanctuary since the day of my Ascension. It was also because we hadn't had a real conversation since she'd dropped the bomb on me that Apollyon was my father. Learning the truth felt like a betrayal, especially considering how close we'd always been, and a small part of me resented Gran for not telling me about Apollyon sooner. It wasn't fair of me. I knew it wasn't. Gran was literally incapable of telling me the truth because of the curse Arthur had placed on her, and the times she'd tried had only made things worse for her, but a kernel of bitterness had taken root in my heart that day which kept me from her ever since.

But all that ended today. It wasn't just time for me to let Gage go, it was also time for me to let go of the resentment I held against Gran. She'd been a victim of Apollyon and Arthur as much as I had, even more so. She bore the weight of an actual curse on her shoulders for seventeen years just for being part of my life.

The door swung open, and I almost took a step back when my gaze landed on Gran standing in the entryway. Her hair hung in loose waves that barely grazed her shoulders. Only a single streak of gray mixed in with her brown strands. Her brown eyes sparkled with life that wasn't there months ago. Gran was always hunched, so I was used to looking down at her when we stood toe-to-toe, but her frame today was strong and straight, and I found she was actually eye level with me.

Gran was in her early sixties, but as long as I could

remember she looked ten years older. Now that the curse was lifted from her, she looked ten years *younger*. In fact, she looked younger than I ever remembered her being. The change was shocking, and I was so relieved the curse was gone.

"Tatum," Gran said as I stood in shock in front of her. "Come on in, dear."

She ushered me into her studio apartment. Drea had told me she'd been moved from the healing center into the family housing building next to the dorms last week. I barely noticed the room because I was so distracted by Gran's physical transformation, but even from a brief glance around I could see she'd already started to make it her own. That made me happy.

"Gran, you look…" Words failed me, but she picked up on what I was trying to say and grinned.

"Watchers are known for aging well," she said, but then the smile slipped off her face. "The curse was hard on my body as well as my mind."

She fell silent for a moment; her eyes took on a faraway look as if she was thinking back over the years that she'd lived under that damned curse. My heart broke in that moment and an unbridled rage toward Arthur washed over me.

I'd been so consumed with myself I hadn't really stopped and considered what Gran had gone through. What she'd had to endure.

Gran shook herself a little, snapping out of whatever

remembrance she'd fallen into a moment before. "But that's all over now, and I feel better than I have in years."

Without warning, I reached forward and crushed Gran in my arms, squeezing tight, no longer worrying about hurting her frail frame. My heart was heavy with regret that I'd kept her at arm's length these past couple weeks. Yes, losing Gage had been soul-crushing, and I'd be the first to admit I hadn't been fully in my right mind lately, but this was Gran. My gran. I never should have held her responsible for Arthur and Apollyon's deeds. It was stupid and selfish of me.

"Oh, Gran, I'm so sorry. Will you forgive me for being so distant lately?" I asked with my face pressed to her shoulder. She rubbed circles on my back like she used to do to calm me down when I was little, and my agony lessened with each rotation.

"Oh, honey, there's nothing to forgive. I knew you needed some time. But I have missed you."

"I've missed you too," I managed to croak through my emotions.

Gran held me until tears lined my eyes and I started hiccupping. We both laughed and she pulled back with a smile. "Go sit down, I'll make you some lemon tea and bring you a spoonful of honey for that hiccup. I have a fresh batch of chocolate chip cookies too."

Gran might look different on the outside, but she was the same Gran I knew and loved.

"Cookies?" I said and then returned her smile with a wobbly one of my own, and another hiccup. Normally, Gran making cookies in the oven would have sent me into a panic, but now that the curse was broken I was no longer afraid of her burning the house down.

Gran chuckled and shooed me over to the same bistro table that had been in our last apartment, the one Drea and I had set up in here a few weeks ago. I ran my fingers over the table, remembering how many meals Gran and I had shared on it and smiled. I was holding my breath, trying to get rid of my hiccups, when she returned a few minutes later. The tea tray she held was loaded with a teapot, two teacups, a plate of cookies, a spoonful of honey, and a small silver key. I popped the honey-covered spoon in my mouth, sucking the sticky sweetness off as I stared at the key. It was short and the teeth were a bit blocky with a deep notch in the middle. The top half was chunky black plastic. It looked familiar, but I couldn't say why. I also didn't know why she'd put it on the tea tray of all places.

"What's that?" I asked, blessedly hiccup free.

Gran pushed the key across the table toward me. "That is yours," she said.

"Umm, thanks? What's it for?" Gran was being cryptic and even though I knew she wasn't cursed anymore I worried about whether or not she was making sense.

She snatched up a cookie, taking a bite. "I've held on to that key for years. Arthur's curse prevented me from telling you about it or giving it to you, although I tried many times."

That's why it was familiar. It was always hanging from Gran's keychain. I'm sure I asked her about it at some point, but never got a straight answer.

I picked it up, turning it over in my hand. I ran my thumb over the teeth and then flipped it over, noticing that there weren't any markings on the metal. Gran had possessed it so long; I'd barely given it a second thought. Since she was giving it to me now, I assumed it opened something special and she wasn't just handing down a keepsake.

I glanced back at her, waiting for her to go on.

"Your mother gave that to me the last day I saw her. It goes to a safety-deposit box downtown. I was supposed to give it to you when you turned thirteen, but of course I couldn't, due to the curse." She took a deep breath, and I leaned back in my chair.

My mom. It felt like a blade stabbed my heart then. That key was another reminder of what my obsessive portal watching had stopped me from doing. I should have been preparing for my mom's rescue, but Gage's loss hit me so hard I'd put it out of my mind. Staring down at the key I thought about how many years Gran had held on to it and I was flooded with regret over not making my mom a priority.

I heaved a sigh, and even the breath in my lungs felt heavy.

A safety-deposit box? I wondered what was inside. I looked back up at her trying to keep an open mind and take in everything Gran was saying.

"Tatum, your mother knew the day she dropped you off with me that she may not be coming back. She didn't tell me that in so many words, and I didn't realize it at the time, but looking back I can clearly see she left that day with a mission. One she wasn't confident she'd accomplish. I don't know what it was, and it's apparent now that the whole car accident was just a cover-up for whatever really happened to her, but I think you may find some more answers in whatever she put in that safety-deposit box."

"You don't have any idea what she left me?" I asked.

Gran shook her head. "After her accident I tried to access it, hoping to find out if it led to any clues as to why she left in a rush. But it's in your name and they wouldn't let me. I would have brought this to you earlier, but I just remembered it this morning. There are some memories that the curse stole from me that are still coming back in bits and pieces. Some things are still scrambled. I have the name and address of the bank though, so you can go check whenever you're ready."

Holy crap. Excitement and nervousness thrummed through me in equal measure. I was torn between jumping out of my seat and running to find out what my mom left me, and staying glued where I was, terrified I'd find out something even worse about myself.

"Thanks, Gran," I said, and then reached across the table to squeeze her hand.

The indecision I felt must have been splashed across my face, because Gran set down her half-eaten cookie and grabbed my other hand. She waited until she had my full attention to speak. "I know that finding out about Apollyon being your father was a shock. I can't tell you how much I wish I could have prepared you for all of this sooner." She waved her hand indicating the room, but what she really meant was all the Watcher stuff. "And I know you're probably feeling a little insecure about it all, but I want you to know that you are still you. It doesn't matter who your parents may be. You are still Tatum Powers, the strong and compassionate girl I raised. That was true last month, and it's true today. No matter what you've learned in the last month, or what secrets you might uncover with that key, nothing will ever change who you are."

She'd hit the nail on the head. That was exactly what I was apprehensive about. I might be a full-fledged Lumen, but there were still pieces of Apollyon living inside me. Even Cael had said only I had specific abilities to defeat Apollyon, and I was smart enough to understand what he meant by that.

I so badly wanted to believe Gran was right, that I was still me no matter what, but what if she was wrong? What if the same darkness that festered in Apollyon's dark heart lived in mine too?

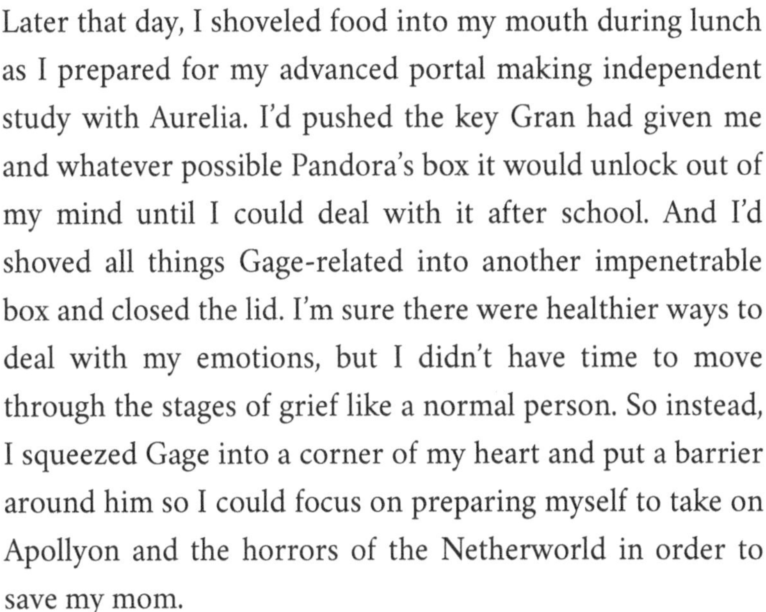

Later that day, I shoveled food into my mouth during lunch as I prepared for my advanced portal making independent study with Aurelia. I'd pushed the key Gran had given me and whatever possible Pandora's box it would unlock out of my mind until I could deal with it after school. And I'd shoved all things Gage-related into another impenetrable box and closed the lid. I'm sure there were healthier ways to deal with my emotions, but I didn't have time to move through the stages of grief like a normal person. So instead, I squeezed Gage into a corner of my heart and put a barrier around him so I could focus on preparing myself to take on Apollyon and the horrors of the Netherworld in order to save my mom.

I couldn't do anything for Gage, but I could help my mom. I didn't have a hope of succeeding if I was distracted, so all my attention needed to be focused on that one task. *Save my mom.* I'd deal with grieving for Gage properly and opening Pandora's box later, possibly with a therapist.

Lumen Academy had given me a leave of absence due to what happened with Gage, but now they'd thrown me in full throttle. I was set to take the Junior Hunter Skills Test tomorrow, and then Aurelia said she would advance me to junior hunter.

Aurelia promised me that once I advanced to junior hunter she would start to plan a mission with me to the Netherworld to rescue my mom. She'd said that because it was dangerous, she'd have to ask people to go on a volunteer basis only. She also mentioned that after a lot of the hunters saw how hard I worked trying to close the portals during the attack on my Ascension Ceremony, she didn't think we would have a problem finding enough volunteers.

"So we fight in teams." Drea held her open notebook out in front of her and rattled off things she knew that I would need to know for my test. Drea and the rest of the Angel Gang had been amazingly supportive through this entire Gage-missing fiasco. Sometimes I'd burst into tears, and they pretended not to notice. And not that I'd left the sanctuary very often, but the few times I'd emerged they'd put off their plans, sometimes just sitting and watching a movie with me instead of going out. I think Skye even canceled a date once, which was huge for her.

"Every team has a leader and a scanner," I spoke through a mouthful of food as I thought of Drea, and Marlow with her device. "There's also a flyer and at least two warriors."

"I'm the flyer." Jacob winked at me from across the table and I couldn't help but roll my eyes and offer him a smile.

"I'm the warrior, along with Dash." Skye puffed up her chest, which caused Drea to laugh.

"Well, we're all warriors, but yes, in an attack Skye and Dash take defensive point first," Drea said.

Dash had headphones in with his hood up and poked at his food as he looked out onto the New York skyline. My heart pinched as I remembered how he'd picked up Gage's feet and asked me where we were flying him without hesitation. I shook the memory from my head, cramming it deep down into that box.

Move on, Tatum. Just move on.

"Do Shades work in teams like this as well?" I asked.

Drea shook her head. "They'll work in groups to defend open portals, but they don't have dedicated teams like we do. It takes a lot of trust to form an effective unit, and trust isn't something Shades cultivate within their ranks."

From my own experience with Shades and at their academy, that made sense. There was an air of distrust that always seemed to be present, as if people weren't truly friends, but rather temporary allies. It was obvious that Gage had been a lone wolf.

I gritted my teeth. *Stop thinking about Gage, Tatum.*

"Demon levels?" Marlow quizzed, helping me shift my thoughts back where they belonged.

I rattled off the levels and characteristics and they all grinned.

"Okay, guys, I've got Angel Script class." I stood and popped the last tater tot in my mouth. The thirteen-year-olds in my class thought it was hilarious that I had to sit with them and learn for the week. I was like a baby having to learn about a new world.

"See ya la—" Drea's voice cut off when everyone's phones began beeping with a demon alert. I'd gotten used to this, seeing them get these alerts and run out on calls. I wasn't allowed to go until Aurelia approved me, and she thought with Gage and everything that I wasn't ready.

Drea stood, looking down at her phone. "We've got a bunch of level twos and threes in Central Park."

The team chewed the last bites of their food and then pushed off the table to join their leader.

Drea looked at me with a grin. "My mom just texted that you can tag along."

"Yes!" I screamed a little too loudly, causing some of the other hunters to stare.

This was *just* what I needed to get my mind off of Gage and my mom.

"Armory!" Drea grabbed her backpack and slung it over one shoulder as we bolted out of the Academy. My heart pounded in my chest as we jogged the few floors down the steps. This would be my first ever demon call.

Normally, Drea and the team got called out after school hours. For dispatch to pull them from class, there had to be a good reason.

By the time we made it across the courtyard and to the armory, I was surprised to see it packed full of hunters. They were all stowing weapons, either on their arms through their magical tattoos or on their person.

"What's going on?" Drea asked one senior hunter.

"Coordinated attacks all over town. They're drawing us all out." He looked concerned but just continued to pull swords and daggers from the wall. I'd never seen the armory look so empty. The giant barnlike room with floor-to-ceiling walls was normally full of glinting gold and silver, but now was nearly bare.

Coordinated attacks? That didn't sound good.

Marlow walked up to me, grinning. There was a giant sword in her hands. "Weapons storage mini lesson. You ready?" she asked.

I swallowed hard and then nodded. I'd wanted to learn how to store the weapons as tattoos since I'd first seen her pull one off of her arm on the subway.

"Activate your angel marks," she said.

With only a thought, the white swirls and arcs appeared on my arms. She pointed to a swirl with three dots on my wrist and then an identical mark on my elbow. "Transfiguration magic. You touch the tip of the weapon to the mark." She pressed the sword to a matching mark on her forearm and it slowly sucked into her arm, turning into an inky tattoo of the sword.

"So cool." I stared in awe.

Jacob slid up next to me and bent down, attaching something to my ankles.

"Whoa, okay," I said as two bracelets clicked and a buzz of power shot up my legs.

"Sorry, no time to train you, but all Lumens with wings wear these. Basically, if your wings are out, then the second your feet leave the ground you will become invisible to humans. Watchers and demons can still see you though."

Holy crap, did he just say *invisible*?

"Have you been wearing these the entire time?" I looked down at the thin silver anklets and he grinned. No wonder humans didn't point and stare when Jacob was flying over the city. They couldn't even see him!

"Yep." He popped the "p."

Invisible. Okay. At this point not much could surprise me.

"Avalon tech," Marlow said with a wiggle of her eyebrows.

"We gotta roll! A horde of lower level demons has been reported." The urgency in Drea's voice spurred me into action.

I reached out and yanked a cool weapon from the wall. The curved blade shone in the overhead lighting and reminded me of a single sharp claw. The handle had indents for an easy grip, and even a round hole at the end to slide my index finger through.

"Karambit, nice choice," a male said as he passed by and looked down at the weapon in my hand.

"Err, thanks?" I didn't know the name of the small blade before now, but it did look pretty lethal. I tapped the base of the dagger to the tattoo that Marlow had instructed me to, and it sucked into my arm, sending a thrill through my system.

"Tatum! You need a light sword. Heads up," Drea called, and I looked up just in time to reach out and catch the long Excalibur-type sword she'd just thrown my way. It was heavy in my grip, strong steel with gold inlay. The blade looked sharp enough to cut glass.

"What makes it a light weap—" I started to ask, then the blade glowed at my touch.

Drea just grinned.

Okay, I might have been a newbie, but I was totally getting the hang of this demon hunter thing. Tapping the sword to my elbow tattoo, it sucked into my arm like the karambit, and I was ready.

My first demon call. It was a big deal. I just hoped I didn't do or say anything stupid.

As we left the armory, more hunters filed in. Even Aurelia was there with her husband, Theo. I'd gathered that like Arthur was in charge of Shade Academy, Aurelia was the leader of Lumen Academy. I had yet to hear anyone call her a principal or headmistress, but she certainly called the shots here.

Her mouth was pulled into a frown as her phone beeped incessantly on her hip. Walking over to Drea and me, she lowered her voice. "Be careful out there. All of these calls so close together remind me of the relic heist."

Drea's eyes went wide, and she nodded before stepping away.

Relic heist?

"Tatum, I'm clearing you to hunt. You up for that?" Aurelia's gaze pierced into mine and I nodded. Hunt meant *kill*, and boy was I ready to kill some baddies.

I turned and left the armory with the rest of my team.

It wasn't until we were on the subway heading for

Central Park that I had time to ask Drea what the relic heist was.

Drea shared a look with Jacob. "Last spring we got demon call after demon call. We quickly realized the Shades had emptied out the entire compound of hunters to go after demons that were either really low levels and less harmful to humans, or in much smaller numbers than we'd been led to believe. It was bad. We lost three Lumens that night."

Marlow growled. "Yeah, all so that the Shades could bring down the wards of Lumen Academy and steal one of our Avalon relics."

"Relics?" I asked.

Jacob leaned forward, lowering his voice. "In the lower level of the academy we have some pretty powerful magical objects. Some we stole from the Shades to keep humanity safe, and some were given to us by the archangels of Avalon. Either way, none of them should be in Shade hands."

"Who makes these calls? Obviously, humans can't see the demons." I looked at Marlow, sensing she would have the answer since she was our team demon scanner.

She held up her handheld scanner. "Every streetlight in town has one of these, and we get an alert at the academy when a demon is scanned in a public space."

Drea nodded. "We also monitor 911 calls for anything that sounds suspicious as the scanner technology can be easy to fool."

I frowned. "If this might be another relic heist, why aren't some of us staying back to protect the school?"

Skye tossed her glossy highlighted brown hair over one shoulder. "Because what if it's not and humans get hurt? We have to answer the call. Always."

Geez. This was already sounding pretty dangerous for my first official hunting mission, but I wasn't going to back out now. If those shadow snakes and creepy bat things were flying around Central Park, then I was going to slice and dice.

A dry twig snapped under my foot, and I winced. Marlow's head twisted in my direction, and she shot me a warning look. I glanced to my right at Jacob, but he just shrugged like it was okay I had made a noise.

The demon outbreak we got called in on was at the south end of Central Park, and the others were fanned out around the zone we thought the demons were in. It was a thickly wooded area, and I couldn't see Drea, Dash, or Skye, but I knew they were just on the other side of these trees. The plan was to close in on the group of demons from multiple angles to keep them contained to one area.

I mouthed "sorry" to Marlow and we continued forward. I made an effort to look where I stepped as we picked our way through the trees. The group of demons we stalked were in a wooded area of the park set away from some of the busier pathways, which was a small blessing. Since it was spring, the park was blooming with life, which meant

New Yorkers had already started to emerge from hibernation to celebrate the death of winter with a stroll through Central Park. The last thing we needed right now were spectators.

Marlow stopped suddenly as the needle on her scanner went wild. The screen that usually identified what level demons were near us kept displaying different numbers as if it were confused. Lights that previously had been blinking green turned red. She pointed the device ahead of her a little to our left and it really went berserk. The red light intensified and flashed rapidly as one of the dials started to spin.

I didn't need to be an expert hunter to know that her scanner was telling us there were demons close by. The reeking stench of sulfur and oil was evidence enough for me. I put a hand in front of my face, scrunching my nose at the putrid smells. Jacob's wings popped out and I knew it was because he sensed the impending doom as well.

Marlow shoved the scanner in the holster that was attached to her utility belt and pulled out her phone, quickly typing a text to the rest of our team spread out of sight within the woods around us. While she updated the others, I looked in the direction she'd pointed the scanner that had made it go crazy. Shadows flickered through the trees. If I didn't know better I'd probably explain it away as light filtering through the leaves as they swayed in the breeze, but I *did* know better. There was no doubt in my mind that those shadows were our targets.

I strained my eyes, trying to pick out what type of demons they were exactly. Maybe bird or bat-like? Without taking my eyes off the darting shadows up ahead, I put my fingers to the tattoo of the light sword on my bicep. It was the strangest thing to feel the handle of the sword materialize in my hand right before the blade elongated and peeled itself off my arm.

Marlow leaned over. "We're waiting for the signal, and then we're to attack," she whispered in my ear.

I nodded, keeping my gaze fixed on our targets. Just because the demons were a lower level didn't mean they were benign. Besides the fact that they could cause temporary paralysis or blindness to Watchers—among other things—when level one through three demons swarmed humans, they caused unbelievable amounts of emotional distress. Sometimes severely enough that they caused madness in their victims. And the most disgusting of all was that these smaller demons liked to target children because their innocence made them most susceptible to demonic influence. Just thinking about that made my stomach churn with revulsion.

These demons were truly the things that went bump in the night. I was looking forward to killing a bunch of them.

I held my body tense as we waited for Drea's signal. Jacob rocked on his heels and Marlow stood rigid with her sword in her hand. It was several minutes before our leader's loud piercing whistle broke the relative silence.

Pumping my legs, I shot forward through the thick trees

like a bullet. Jacob shot up into the air. Marlow and I raced and reached a small clearing where large stones jutted from the earth. We both skidded to a halt, our eyes widening as we took in the swarm of demons in front of us.

Shadow demons the size of small dogs but shaped like insects from my worst nightmares scurried over the gray rocks. Above them, a whirlwind of what I thought looked like rat demons with bat wings flew in circles, creating a mini tornado of demons so thick I couldn't see through it.

Whoa. That was *a lot* of super creepy demons.

My stomach dropped. Just beyond the trees I could hear childlike laughter. Past the cluster of demons and through the thick foliage, I saw a park full of small children playing.

Not today, hellspawn.

Skye and Dash suddenly appeared and leapt into action, taking point as the battle warriors of the group. They charged into the tornado of demons and started to slash left and right, carving a path for the rest of us.

Marlow shook herself, and then tugged on my arm. "Come on, let's do our thing," she said, right before releasing a battle cry and slicing into the demon nearest her, which looked like a tarantula but with more legs.

One of the shadow demons scampering around the rocks changed its trajectory and headed right toward me. Its multiple legs helped it shoot across the uneven terrain faster than I would have thought possible. I swiped at it with my light sword when it was close, but the hell-beast jumped at the last second, landing directly on my face.

When it's wiry legs dug into my hair, all logical thought left me and I dropped my sword, screaming and swatting at it, but my hands moved right through it. It might only look like a shadow, but I could feel the spindly legs of the demon on my neck and cheek and scalp, yet I couldn't rip it off.

Suddenly, the blade of a light dagger came at my face, stopping only inches from my eye. The demon let out a high-pitch squeal and then evaporated like mist.

Drea stood before me, light weapon in hand.

"Thanks," I muttered.

She bent down and picked up my dropped sword, handing me the hilt. "Don't lose this again," she said. "Remember, only light weapons kill these guys."

I nodded and grabbed it from her, equal parts embarrassed over how I'd just performed, and traumatized by almost getting my face sucked off by a giant spider demon. I mean, I didn't know if that was possible, but I'd seen all the *Alien* movies and that shadow demon looked a little too close to the facehugger creature in the movie for my comfort.

Drea tapped her hand against her wrist and pulled a short sword off her skin. The blade shone with a faint bluish-white glow like the rest of the light weapons. "Use this one for the demons that get too close."

After slapping the extra blade into my free hand, she jumped back into the fray, slicing and stabbing anything that got within her reach.

Okay, Tatum. It's go time. Don't make Drea regret bringing your newbie butt along.

Kicking off of the rocks where I was crouched, I burst into the melee with my light weapons held aloft. Just as a demon neared me, I felt a tingle along my arm, and then the blade's blueish-white light intensified, causing the insect demons in the vicinity to scurry away in fear.

Score.

It didn't scare all the demons though. A bat-chicken chimera creature flew at my head, and I slashed my large glowing light sword upward into its shadowy chest, making it poof and disintegrate in seconds. Another and another flew at me, the barrage of creatures swarming us in an attack so thick I couldn't see two feet in front of me.

"Ow!" Marlow yelled and I side stepped to where I'd heard her voice, cutting through half a dozen shadow demons on the way. There must have been over a hundred of them. Marlow was slumped at the base of a tree, a cockroach demon with wings was attached to her neck.

Without hesitation, I brought my smaller sword down and lashed through the back of the roach demon, but not before Marlow let loose with another wail of pain.

Crap. She'd been bit.

"Jacob! Get Marlow out!" Drea called to my left. With a swoosh of golden wings, Jacob landed beside me and scooped Marlow into his arms. She was shaking, teeth chattering, and I wondered if she was going to be okay. Jasmine was okay after her bite from a level two, but—

"Tatum, look out!" Skye screamed and I spun just as the ugliest creature I'd ever seen scampered into the air from its place on the rocks and flew at my face.

Not again.

Using both the swords in my grip, I made a protective X in front of me and pulled it apart just as the creature reached me, cutting it right in half.

"Help!" Dash cried out, and I had no time to even revel in the fact that I'd totally just kicked demon butt or thank Skye for warning me. It was absolute pandemonium. I spun and searched for Dash to find that he was pinned at the base of the large tree trunk, where demons had just dropped down on him from above. Skye was already coming to his aid, which was a relief as I was farther away.

Knowing that Dash had help, I focused my attention on the demon swarm. It had thinned, and now I could see there was someone in the center of their little shadowy tornado. Someone who had remained hidden up until now.

Another demon? Were they protecting them? I could only see the outline, but their form looked humanoid. Chills broke out on my arms.

"Guys, I think there's a level eight inside—" The words had barely left my lips when the flying demons parted, as if they shared a hive mind and were suddenly told to make a path.

The breath caught in my throat when my gaze fell on the woman in the crisp black cocktail dress. She had glossy black hair that was gelled back, falling in loose waves to her waist, and skin so pale it looked like she'd never seen the sun. She looked completely human, but I knew she couldn't be.

"Is that a…?" I couldn't even speak it.

"A level ten. Run!" Drea called out the command, but my legs locked in fear.

"Hello, Tatum, I have a message from your father," she purred in a silky voice that made my stomach roil.

Drea scrambled to get Dash up from where he'd fallen at the trunk of the tree, and Skye stood protectively in front of both of her friends, but I just couldn't move.

What if this message was about my mom?

My transparent white wings snapped from my back instinctively and I prepared to fly, but not until my friends were clear of this place.

"What's the message?" I asked, determined to keep her talking as Drea dragged an injured Dash backward and away from the level ten. Skye looked from Drea to me, sword pulled out as if she was deciding to go with them or stay and protect me.

Go, I wanted to shout at her. I had wings and she didn't.

"The message is this…" She grinned but the smile didn't reach her eyes. "If you do not return to your rightful home in the Netherworld, I will kill someone you care about."

My eyes narrowed. "Tell my *father* that my home is here."

"Wrong answer," she purred.

My mouth dropped open, but before I could even

process a response, she flicked her hand outward, and Skye was blown twenty feet across the clearing until she slammed into a tree. She dropped, landing upside down at an awkward angle on her neck. I could hear bones break from where I stood, and a scream of terror ripped from my lips.

"Skye!" I fumbled forward, complete shock ripping through me as the level ten moved with the speed of a leopard and zoomed in front of me to block my way.

"Come with me and no one else gets hurt." She snapped her fingers and a portal opened beside her, the familiar red and black swirls spinning in the air. I could barely see Skye behind her. Skye's head looked bent unnaturally and she wasn't moving, but I wasn't ready to accept what my eyes were seeing.

Skye's just unconscious. She's not dead. She's not dead. This isn't happening.

I hardened my resolve as I shifted my gaze and peered into the portal, seeing the outline of Shadow City beyond the layer of spinning colors.

I remembered my mom's message: I had free will, and I was a Lumen now, so neither Apollyon nor his demons could take me by force. He needed me to come to the Netherworld willingly for whatever his plan was.

Someone's sobs ripped through the clearing, and it felt like time stopped.

I peered behind the demon and spotted Drea hunched over Skye's limp form, shaking her wildly. Skye's head bobbed as if it were only held onto her body by skin alone, and I felt the blood drain from my face.

Was Skye dead? Did that monster seriously just kill my friend with a flick of her wrist?

I was going to pass out.

No. No. No.

"Come with me or I take another," she growled impatiently, and glanced at Drea.

"Please don't hurt my friends," I begged, unsure what to do now.

Maybe I should just go with her? She was a level ten for crying out loud. I wasn't a match for her and the power she'd just displayed.

"Step away from the portal, Tatum," Dash called out, and I looked over to see he was holding a light sword, white and gray-streaked wings snapped out behind him as he glared at the powerful demon. Blood dripped from a gash on his arm, but he seemed otherwise unharmed.

I swallowed hard.

"I'm not scared of you, *witch*," Dash sneered at the demon.

Okay, now that was stupid.

The demon grinned. This time it did reach her eyes lighting up her entire face. "You are such a disappointment, Dash Slate. Your power could have been unmatched had you chosen Shade."

Wait, what? This demon *knew* Dash?

The level ten cocked her wrist backward as if she were about to inflict pain on Dash, and I snapped.

No one else was getting hurt today. Not on my account. *Not* while I was still breathing.

With a scream, power shot from my skin like a bomb. Purple embers burst from my body and slammed into the demon, knocking her through the open portal and snapping it shut.

"Get Drea!" I yelled to Dash, who stared at the spot the portal had been with his jaw open. I didn't have time to process my shock, so I just ran toward Skye.

A moment later, footsteps pounded beside me, and then together Dash and I reached our friends. Drea was sobbing and still shaking Skye by the shoulders. Skye's eyes were open and glassy, devoid of life.

No. My stomach turned instantly sour.

"That level ten could come back any second and finish us off," Dash muttered.

I looked at Drea, who was completely broken by the sight of her dead friend, and then turned to Dash and pleaded with my eyes for him to do something. I couldn't hear Drea emit one more sob or I too would crack. I was barely holding it together.

"Jacob already took Marlow. Bring her to Lumen Academy," Dash said, nodding toward Skye right before he gripped Drea by the armpits and shot into the air with her kicking and screaming Skye's name.

Whatever shred of control I had left failed me. My eyes

blurred with tears as I slipped my arms under Skye's lifeless form. The angelic marks on my arms lit up, giving me the strength to lift her. With a kick and a flap of my wings I was airborne, only taking a quick second to peer down at Skye's lifeless body in my arms, hoping for the twitch of an eyelid or the rise and fall of her chest… but there was nothing.

This isn't happening.

The emotional impact of what just went down hit me so hard that I struggled to fly. I wobbled as I pumped my wings and ascended higher and higher into the sky, knowing that the silver bracelets around my ankles masked us from public view.

Healing center, just get her to the healing center, I told myself.

The healers who saved Gran were amazing. Surely they could fix Skye? I wouldn't believe it was final until a healer looked me in the eyes and told me she was gone. I wasn't a doctor. Maybe Skye was just paralyzed or something from a broken neck.

That sounds plausible.

Dash was a blur in the sky in front of me as I followed him across town. In less than ten minutes we were at the Lumen Compound. Dash bypassed some of the Lumen buildings, flying Drea to the academy, but I zeroed in on the healing center, dropping into the alleyway next to the building. Barely slowing to land, I ran to the entrance and sucked my wings into my back as I kicked one of the doors open with my boot.

When I stumbled in with Skye's body in my arms, the color drained from the nurse's face who was manning the front desk.

"Help her!" I screamed, rushing forward. "Call the healers! It was a level ten." I hurried to hand Skye to Rose, the nurse who'd helped me with Gran, when she reached up to feel the pulse at Skye's neck.

I started shaking my head, my hair whipping me in my face, before Rose even uttered a word.

Don't do that. Don't tell me—

"She's gone," Rose said, compassion and sadness reflecting in her gaze.

I couldn't stand anymore. My knees buckled and I fell forward, Skye still in my arms. A giant sob racked my body. "No! Get the healers… save her," I wailed.

My freak-out must have been heard by half the healing center, because one of the healers who'd removed the curse from Gran stepped into the waiting room and peered down at me. Her gaze went from my face and then to my arms loosely holding on to Skye.

Her face fell. "Oh dear."

"You have to try!" I stood, almost pitching forward with the weight of Skye's limp body still in my arms. "Try for me? Anything's possible, right?"

The healer shared a look with Rose and chewed her lip. "I can take a look."

Hope burst inside my chest and I all but threw Skye into

her arms. The next thing I knew we were running into the operating room.

"I'll take it from here. You can sit up in the viewing area," she said, and I nodded, tears tracking down my cheeks. I couldn't get them to stop. I could barely breathe.

I took the stairs two at a time into the upper viewing area of the operating room and pressed my nose against the glass as the healer laid Skye's form on the table and started to scan her with an open palm. Light burst from her fingertips and spiraled around Skye's body as my heart pounded in my chest. The light hit Skye's body and then fell to the side as if recoiling.

When the healer looked up at me and shook her head, it felt like something died inside of me.

"No!" I pounded the glass.

The healer reached out and closed Skye's eyelids, before raising a sheet over her face, and I fell into the chair behind me. Mind-numbing grief seized me then as a pit opened in my stomach.

First Gage.

Now Skye.

It was too much loss, too soon.

I grabbed my face, rocking back and forth weeping as I tried to get a handle on my breathing.

"I'm so sorry, Skye," I told the room, sniffling. It was my fault, it felt like my fault.

Skye's singsong voice filled the room: "It's okay, I don't blame you. It was that evil level ten." I froze, and one by one

I peeled my fingers away from my face and peered in the direction of the voice, and there was Skye.

Nope.

Not real.

I pinched my eyes shut, took a deep, calming breath, and reopened them.

"You should really look into waterproof mascara," Skye said, scrunching her nose in disgust as she stared at my cheeks.

My mouth popped open as I gazed at her spectral form sitting next to me. She was wearing the same outfit she'd died in; not a honey colored piece of hair was out of place. It was still tied up in its high ponytail.

"Sk-Skye… I… how—?" This was the point when I needed to finally call a therapist, right? Seeing ghosts was rock bottom. Maybe I was hallucinating.

Skye leaned forward and smiled. "Cael says hi."

I froze. "What?"

"I died, went to Avalon, and Cael gave me a mission here on Earth and said to say hi." Skye looked at her nails as if she was bored having to explain this to me.

I grasped my chest to make sure I was in fact still breathing and conscious. I only felt a little better when I detected the thump-thump of my heartbeat. "Skye, you died. Shouldn't you be upset?"

Skye nodded. "I'm a little pissed, not gonna lie. I was really looking forward to going on a second date with that senior hunter—he had the best biceps—but Avalon is amazing, and I get to live there forever now. After I help you of course."

Okay. Process words. Breathe. This is real.

Demons were real, why not spirits too? Or was she technically a ghost? Was there a difference?

"How can I see you?" I asked her.

She snort-laughed. "You're the daughter of the ruler of the Netherworld, a realm full of dead people. Come on, Tatum."

Were there ghosts in the Netherworld? I hadn't even noticed when I'd been kidnapped and dragged there against my will. I must have been too sidetracked by the god-awful ugly demons. Or maybe the dead didn't live in Shadow City?

But Skye was right, I was Apollyon's daughter.

Okay. I see dead people. No big deal.

Breathe in, breathe out.

"You okay?" Skye leaned forward and placed a hand on my knee, but it passed right through, sending a chill through the spot she touched. I stood and backed up a few paces.

I peered at her see-through hands and tried not to freak out. "I'm going to need a beat to get used to you being this way. I just don't know how long the adjustment period will be, but maybe no touching of the ghosty fingers for now?"

Skye grinned and stood. "Wooooooo." She walked toward me as if she were a zombie, and I rolled my eyes.

Was this seriously happening?

The door behind her burst open and Drea stepped in with Dash.

"Tatum!" Drea ran straight for me, passing right through Skye, which made Skye giggle, and then Drea crashed into me with a hug.

"I'm so glad you're okay," Drea said.

When she pulled back, she looked down at Skye's body covered in the sheet, and tears filled her eyes.

"Tell her I'm right here," Skye instructed me.

Umm, no. She'll think I'm crazy.

"I'm so sorry about Skye," I told Drea, who nodded, tears filling her bloodshot eyes.

"Tell her I'm here or I'll touch your legs all night long with my ghosty fingers while you sleep," Skye warned.

I squeaked. "Skye is dead but she's a ghost and I can see her. She's standing right behind you," I blurted and then covered my mouth.

Drea froze, slowly turning to look over her shoulder and only seeing a shocked Dash.

"Tell her you know about her dream of opening a nail salon and the crush she had on Dash all last year," Skye said.

I looked at Dash but stayed silent. If that was true, I didn't want to call Drea out in front of him.

"Tell her!" Skye pressed, stepping closer to me. "I need all my besties to know I'm still here. If I have to follow you for the next who-knows-how long, I want everyone to know I'm around."

I bit my lip and looked at Drea: "Skye says to tell you I

know about your dream to open a nail salon and…" My gaze flicked to Dash, and I winced. "And that you had a crush on Dash all last year."

A grin swept across Dash's face as Drea's cheeks pinked. "That hag! She told you to say that?"

I grimaced, and then Drea started to laugh. "Only Skye… she's the only one I told those things to. But how—?"

"I'm Apollyon's daughter, so I think I can see dead people." Hopefully only select dead people, because this was not a new gift I wanted to embrace.

Drea spun, looking in the wrong direction of where Skye was. "I love you," she whimpered. "I'm so sorry I couldn't protect you."

Skye went very still, nodding slowly. "Tell her the angels in Avalon are super hot and I'll be fine."

I relayed the message and Drea chuckled. "I miss you already," Drea said, and I could see relief wash over her. The tears dried up and she seemed okay with the situation. She was definitely handling it better than me.

"Let's back up to the part where you had a crush on me." Dash grinned and eyed Drea.

Our team leader rolled her eyes. "Last year. *So* over it now. You're like a brother to me."

That comment did little to wipe the grin from Dash's face. Drea's cheeks got redder by the second.

Skye suddenly cocked her head to the side and looked at me. "I gotta run an errand. Oh, by the way, Gage isn't dead."

She poofed out of existence then, leaving me reeling.

Gage isn't dead.

I swayed on my feet as the realization of her words settled over me.

She went to Avalon. She saw Gage.

Gage isn't dead.

G *age isn't dead. Gage isn't dead. Gage isn't dead.*

It was my mantra all through dinner with Gran, and all night as I once again slept next to the cracked wall in the sanctuary. I told myself I wasn't going to camp out in the sanctuary anymore, but in a heartbeat Skye's words changed everything and I couldn't help myself.

The entire school was in mourning for Skye. The flag was flown at half-mast, and her parents had been notified and were coming in for the funeral. Aurelia, Drea, and the rest of our crew all secretly knew that Skye wasn't exactly gone, so it was hard to really feel fully sad. In fact, I felt a prickle of annoyance that I hadn't gotten to properly question Skye about her mission to help me when she'd "run an errand."

What ghost runs errands?

Cael was vague with his missions, that much I knew from experience, so she probably wouldn't even answer me if I asked. Still, I wanted to interrogate the crap out of her when I saw her again. Especially about the Gage isn't dead part!

"Skye!" I whisper-screamed into the empty sanctuary when I awoke the next morning. No response. She was probably already on a date with some hottie Avalon angel.

Typical.

I sat up, rubbing my fingers through my hair, and walked over to where I kept my toothbrush, toothpaste, and a bottle of water.

If Gage was still alive, then what the heck was he doing still chilling in Avalon?

It hit me then: maybe when I'd broken the portal, Cael couldn't fix it and Gage was trapped there?

No. Cael was an archangel. If anyone could fix a portal, it would be him. Right?

Unless by "Gage isn't dead," Skye meant he was barely alive. What if he was getting angel surgery or something?

The anxiety over this entire situation was tying me into knots. I opened the front door of the sanctuary, stepped out into the oversized stone staircase, and spat my toothpaste onto the grass. The sun was up but it was still early. A sleeping bag on the floor for over two weeks didn't lend to sleeping in. The two guards who normally protected the portal were off duty since there was currently no portal to protect.

"Our dorm room is lonely without you." Drea's voice startled me, and I swiveled to see her approaching with a plate full of food. Cinnamon rolls, eggs, and bacon were piled high. My mouth salivated as she handed me the food.

"Thanks," I told her and started to dig in, shoving a piece of bacon in my mouth.

"Is Skye here?" Drea looked around the empty landing in anticipation and I shook my head.

"No sign of Gage either?" she asked.

I swallowed a chunk of cinnamon roll. "Nope."

"That's so like Skye to just drop the bomb on you that Gage is still alive and then go," Drea chuckled.

"I know. She's even annoying in death," I admitted jokingly.

We both had a snicker at that.

My mind went back to how quickly the level ten had snapped Skye's neck and I gulped. "Drea, what if she comes back… the level ten? I don't want anyone else—"

Drea nodded, a serious look pulling at her features. "I told my mom. We're not going to let anyone else get hurt." She tipped her head up to the roof and I followed her line of sight.

Hunters crouched at the edge of the roofline, wings extended as they stared out into the courtyard and beyond. They were so still they looked like statues.

Angel sniper statues.

Guilt wormed through my gut. "But maybe I should just go."

Drea reached out and smacked my arm. "Go to the Netherworld and do Apollyon's bidding? Are you crazy?"

I shrugged. Probably.

"Well, if that chick comes back and threatens to kill someone else, I'm going. I can't have anyone else go ghosty on me."

If I hadn't gone nuclear and blown her back into a portal, she would have killed Dash. I wished I could control my powers better and feel confident that I could do that every single time.

"My mom set up some new wards with the healers. They are anchored with angel stones. As long as we stay on campus, we are totally safe," Drea assured me.

Angel stones? Sounded fancy.

I nodded. Stay on campus. Easy peasy.

Drea stood. "Come on. Class in thirty. We can get some studying in before if we head to the library now. I can't have a novice hunter on my team."

I grinned. "You want me on your team?"

Drea gave me a look that said duh. "Even before Skye… I had plans to add you, but now we'll definitely need another warrior."

A thrill ran through me. "I'd love to be your warrior angel."

"Gotta make junior hunter first." Drea winked.

Oh, junior hunter was *mine*. My exam was later today, and I was going to crush it.

Nerves ate away at my gut as Aurelia stood before me in one of the training rooms. Drea, Dash, Marlow, and Jacob all shoved their faces into the small window peephole watching as I took my Junior Hunter Skills Test.

I'd just finished the written portion, and now Aurelia was pointing to various weapons on the floor. Daggers, broadswords, even a mace.

"What's that?" she asked, gesturing to a longsword. I could tell by the slight rainbow sheen on the blade that it was a light weapon.

"Longsword, but also a light blade," I said with confidence.

Aurelia marked something in her notebook and betrayed a hint of a smile. "And what would you need a light blade for?"

"A light blade will inflict the most damage because it burns through a higher level demon's skin, so they are the preferred weapons to kill any of the levels but are specially required to vanquish level one through threes because normal weapons will pass right through them."

Aurelia nodded, set her clipboard down, and then walked over to a box with a blanket over it that sat in the corner of the room.

Then she looked at me. "Be ready."

What? Ready for—?

She ripped the blanket away and revealed an animal cage. I barely had time to process what was happening when she kicked a latch on the door and a level one shadow snake slithered out of the cage and gunned for me.

Crap!

This must be the practical part of the exam. *Way to make it really authentic, Aurelia!*

My heart hammered in my throat as I fell into an army roll and grabbed the light blade Aurelia had just pointed to. By now the snake had reached me and lifted up on its belly, ready to strike.

Instead of waiting for it to lunge for me, I went on the offense and threw my weight forward, dragging the blade across its body and slicing it in half.

With a poof of smoke, it was gone.

My gaze flicked to the cage, wondering if any other creatures were waiting to jump out at me, but it was empty.

The Angel Gang cheered outside the door, and I grinned, looking at Aurelia hesitantly. "Did I pass?"

The master Lumen consulted her clipboard and then broke out into a full-toothed smile. "Welcome to Team Drea, Junior Hunter."

I whooped, throwing a fist into the air as the whole crew rushed into the room to congratulate me.

After a moment, Aurelia cleared her throat. "Mrs. Taylor will be expecting you, Tatum."

Right. My baby Lumen class.

I groaned. "I still have to go to that?"

Aurelia bobbed her head up and down. "Just for the semester."

I looked at my friends. "Catch up with you guys later?"

They nodded, and I grabbed my bag and headed out the door.

I was officially a junior hunter.

"Our core mission here on Earth is to protect the humans," Mrs. Taylor said as she walked past my desk and gave me a pitiful smile before tending to the thirteen-year-olds in her class. "We do that by keeping the demon population down and—"

Her desk phone rang, and she stopped talking. "Excuse me a moment." She walked over and picked it up, holding it to her ear.

One of the young teen girls sitting in front of me spun when the teacher was occupied and stared me down. "Is it true you fought a level ten yesterday?" She eyed me like a hawk sizing up its prey. Multiple heads swiveled in my direction, and I gulped.

Nothing was scarier than a bunch of middle school girls.

"Kind of." I mean we didn't fight her, so much as she killed one of my friends and said some very creepy things to me.

"What did it look like?" a young boy with reddish hair asked.

"Did smoke come out of its mouth?" a girl blurted.

"Did it really kill Skye?"

Holy overwhelming questions.

I swallowed hard, unsure what to tell them, then the teacher pulled the phone from her ear: "Uh, Tatum, you're needed at the healing center."

The healing center? Oh man. What if someone else was hurt? I *knew* this would happen. The level ten demon probably came back and hurt Dash for his nasty comment to her.

I shoved my things into my bag and threw the strap over my shoulder. I was halfway out of my seat when Skye popped into existence before me, and I jumped.

"Don't do that!" I hissed as everyone looked at me with frowns and furrowed brows.

Right. I was talking to myself.

"Spoiler alert: no one actually needs you in the healing center. Drea and the others staged a prison break," Skye told me, and then poof, she was gone.

She'd only been a spirit for a day and her popping in and out of existence was already getting old. I'm sure she knew that which is why she kept doing it.

Even though Skye had said nothing was wrong, I bolted out of the classroom anyway, nearly colliding with a teacher in the hall. Muttering my apologies, I rushed past her and jogged down the stairs rather than wait for the ancient elevator to come.

Reaching out, I pushed through the back doors of the academy which let out into the courtyard to find Drea, Marlow, Dash, and Jacob bunched near the wall, waiting for me.

Drea spotted me first. "Freedom," she shouted with her hands in the air.

I chuckled at her antics as the others joined us.

"What's the deal?" I asked.

"We felt bad for you having to sit in a class with the younglings," Jacob said.

"We thought we could celebrate your junior hunter advancement and ditch class," Drea added with a grin.

I shot Drea a look. "I'm sure this isn't something your mom would approve of."

"Which is why we should all keep this to ourselves," she said with a wink.

I couldn't argue with that. I was glad to be out of that class.

"Tatum," Marlow said, stepping forward. There was a vulnerability in her voice I wasn't used to from her. "Drea and Dash said you can see Skye. Is it true?"

Poor Marlow. She and Skye were super close.

"Yeah, I can," I said, offering her an encouraging smile.

That was the exact moment Skye decided to reappear. I jerked a little when she did, and the movement wasn't missed.

"She's here right now, isn't she?" Marlow asked, hope shining from her eyes.

"Hells yeah I am," Skye said, and I nodded.

Marlow clapped her hands together excitedly. "Tell her that I love her and that I miss her already and that I'm so sorry I wasn't there to save her." Marlow's hand went to the bandage on her neck where the demon had bit her during the fight yesterday. Because of that injury she hadn't even been there when the level ten killed her friend. "And tell her that she's missing a massive sale at Macy's this weekend, and I plan to buy a pair of shoes in her honor."

"So, she's standing right next to you and can hear everything you're saying. You can't hear or see her, but it doesn't work the other way around," I explained.

"Tell her if she's buying a pair of shoes in my honor, it should be those cute pink pumps we found together last month," Skye said.

Seriously? I was glad that Skye was happy and still around—kinda—but it was going to suck if I was stuck being a ghost interpreter for the rest of my life.

I opened my mouth to relay Skye's response when a crack of lightning split the cloudless sky above, followed by the loud boom of thunder.

Skye grinned. "You're going to like what comes next, Tatum," she said with a wiggle of her perfectly-tweezed eyebrows.

Huh?

"What's that supposed—?"

She popped out of existence just as a second bolt cut through the air, zigzagging down to Earth and striking the roof of the sanctuary. The impact shook the ground beneath our feet. We all looked at each other for a beat, and then took off for the stone structure.

My heart pounded against my rib cage as I reached the

wood doors and shoved them open. I'd camped out in that sanctuary for one reason, and one reason only: Gage.

My heart was telling me it had to be him.

I ran through the doors and my gaze brushed over the restored portal on the back wall and landed on Gage.

Holy naked man.

Gage was sprawled on his back in the middle of the room. He was still as a statue and didn't have a stitch of clothing on.

So. Much. Skin.

A zing of awareness ran through my body like a jolt of electricity, but I diverted my gaze to his face before I got an eyeful of anything I shouldn't.

Okay, that's a lie. I peeked a little. Naked Gage was a thing of beauty.

Running to where he lay, I dropped to my knees next to him. His eyes were closed but his chest moved up and down slowly, proving that he was alive and breathing.

A warm mix of relief and joy spread over me.

He was here. He was back. He was alive.

Coming up behind me, Dash ripped off his hoodie and threw it over Gage's middle, covering all his fun bits. The next moment, Jacob and the girls joined us and loomed over his body as well. All of us wore the same slack-jawed expression.

I took Gage's face in my hands and stroked his jaw with my thumbs. He had color in his cheeks and his skin was warm. I couldn't stop cataloging details that proved he was alive.

"Gage," I whispered, brushing the hair that had fallen over his brow, off his forehead.

Gage groaned, and then blinked open his eyes, focusing on me. "Tate." His nickname for me made butterflies take flight in my stomach.

"You're alive." I pressed my forehead to his, relishing in the touch of his skin on mine.

He inhaled. "Damn, woman, I missed the way you smell."

We were so close I could feel his breath on my lips, and it made me shiver. Tilting his chin up, he brushed his lower lip over mine—a slow back and forth, a gentle nudge. A sharp tingle of anticipation shot throughout my body, and I parted my mouth on an exhale, not wanting to wait a moment longer to taste him on my tongue.

Someone cleared their throat, and I jerked back, forgetting we had an audience. My cheeks heated.

Gage shot an annoyed look over my shoulder, and then glanced down at himself. He furrowed his brow. "Why the bloody hell am I lying naked on a stone floor?"

His reaction was so true to Gage that it broke the ball of tension in my chest. I burst out laughing.

Gage flicked his gaze to me with an *Are-you-high?* look on his face. A quick glance around said no one else was amused, so my laughter died off.

"We're about the same size," Dash said. "I'm going to go grab you some pants." He took off immediately. Even though he was wearing a t-shirt, Dash probably felt as naked as Gage without his hoodie and was anxious to throw on another to cover his face scar.

Jacob shook his head, the look on his face full of disbelief. "Man, you must have nine lives or something."

Keeping a hand against his waist to keep the hoodie covering him, Gage shot Jacob a side-eye as he struggled to sit up, wincing as he did.

Marlow gasped and I turned to her. Her eyes were wide and filled with horror as she stared at Gage's back.

I snuck a peek and had to swallow my own yelp of surprise. Two giant slashes ran parallel to his spine that hadn't been there before. Angry and raised, they were both at least an inch thick and a foot long, right where his wings used to be. I reached my fingers toward the marks and then pulled my hand back. It looked like the wounds were still healing.

"Gage, what happened?" I asked, and then glanced at the swirling portal against the far wall. I'd been so entranced by Gage's sudden appearance that I'd hardly given it a moment's notice, but it was back in all its blue and white glowing glory.

Gage peered over his shoulder and then scrubbed a hand down his face, a haunted look passing over him. "I've been stripped of my powers."

The room took in a collective gasp, but Gage just shrugged. "Whatever, it's fine," he said, but his jaw hardened, and his eyes took on their normal half-slitted scowl.

It wasn't fine. I could see by the distraught look on his face that it was far from fine, but I also noticed the walls come up around him as he closed the issue off to discussion. I was just grateful he was alive, so I wasn't going to push the subject.

Dash returned with a stack of clothes and wearing a new hoodie almost identical to the one he'd used to cover Gage.

"Thanks, bro," Gage said, and grabbed the clothes. He went to stand and swayed a little.

"Do you need help?" I reached to assist, and he gently shrugged me off.

"I'm fine," he mumbled.

I swallowed hard and nodded, trying not to take offense at his brushoff as I turned to give him my back so he could change.

"We'll wait outside," Drea said, and yanked everyone out with her.

I stood awkwardly, facing the door my friends had just pulled shut as Gage finished dressing.

Gage was back. He was alive and almost-kissing me, but also stripped of power and super moody.

Crap. Not ideal. I would prefer if he were reciting love poems and confessing his undying love or something equally mushy, but he did say he missed how I smelled and I was taking that as a win.

Eat your heart out, Claire.

I cleared my throat, not because I needed to, but because the silence was getting to me. It was awfully quiet behind me. I couldn't even hear the rustle of clothes anymore. What was he doing back there?

A hand rested on my shoulder, startling me, and I spun to face Gage, who was now dressed in one of Dash's hoodies and a pair of dark wash jeans.

Gage might have lost his Shade powers, but his ninja skills were still intact.

Now that he was clothed, I took a moment to take him in, to *really* look at him. Dash's clothes fit him near perfectly and were only slightly bigger, but the truth was that Gage could wear a potato sack and make it look sexy. That much about him hadn't changed—but it felt like something else had. His eyes were the same shade of wintergreen that I remembered, but the spark of life was gone, leaving a hollowness behind I wasn't used to.

Was that because of what Arthur had done to him, or had something happened to him in Avalon? I mean, nearly being killed by your father had to mess with your head, but so would being stripped of your powers.

"How long was I gone?" Gage asked, his accented syllables echoing off the thick walls of the chamber.

"Fifteen days," I answered, as Gage shook his head and blew out a breath of air.

Only a few feet of space separated us, but it felt like a chasm. I took a small step forward, eating up some of the distance between us. "I waited for you. Right here, almost the entire time." I pointed to my sleeping bag on the floor in the corner. "I didn't know what had become of you, but I hoped..."

"That had to be hard for you." His eyes softened imperceptibly, but I was so attuned to him now that I didn't miss it.

A lump formed in my throat, so I nodded rather than respond. He had no idea what that time had been like. Not knowing if he'd been alive or dead, or if he'd ever come back to me, had been torture.

"How did Arthur find out that you'd helped steal his talisman and let me go?" I asked, trying to focus on something else.

Gage ran an agitated hand through his hair. "My magic," he bit out. "He brought in a specialist who was able to pull traces of it off the safe we broke into. Once that lie fell apart, he was able to deduce most of the truth. He obviously didn't take it well that I'd betrayed him."

"Gage..." I took another step forward, bringing us almost toe to toe. His own father had attacked and injured him so brutally he would have died if not for the angels in Avalon. And it was my fault. If I hadn't blackmailed him into helping me, he wouldn't have been hurt. I didn't know what baggage this new Gage carried, but I had to wonder if he even wanted me in his life.

"You still have his talisman?" Gage asked.

I nodded. Aurelia had it under lock and key. A look of relief spread over Gage's face. "Good. His anger makes him unpredictable, and unpredictability is dangerous, but at least he's not as powerful as he would be with his talisman."

I took a deep breath to steady myself, sucking in a lungful of air that was tinged with Gage's unique spicy and sweet scent.

There were so many things I wanted to talk about. My feelings for him. His for me. Our last real interaction before he showed up in front of Lumen Academy on the brink of death had been explosive. We'd both said hurtful things, but that kiss…

My lips tingled from just the memory of it. There had been an attraction between Gage and me since the moment we met. We'd both tried to ignore it, but we were like magnets pulled to each other by an invisible force. Now that he was literally back from the dead, I wasn't interested in ignoring it any longer, but I didn't know how to break down these walls between us.

I couldn't help it when my gaze slipped down his face to rest on his perfectly sinful lips.

A low growl emanated from Gage's chest. It was only when I felt the rumble underneath my palm that I realized I'd raised my hand to touch him.

"You know I don't really hate you, right?" I said, referencing the harsh words I'd spat at him in the dark alleyway after our kiss.

The corner of his mouth pulled into a half-cocked smirk. "I know. But I still think you're my weakness."

I looked into his eyes so that I could read his expression. Being someone's weakness wasn't good, right?

"If I have to have a weakness, I'm glad it's you," he said, lifting a hand and running the pad of his thumb over my bottom lip. "So soft," he mumbled, and then his lips were on mine.

A whimper of relief ripped from my mouth, and he inhaled the sound, our tongues reaching out to meet each other. His hands gripped both sides of my face as I deepened the kiss, pressing my body fully against his. Gage growled and the butterflies in my stomach increased tenfold.

Kissing Gage was an out-of-this-world event. I'd never been so consumed by someone in my entire life as I was when our bodies were this close. His lips, the soft stroke of his tongue, the warmth of his breath, and the tender way he caressed my jaw with his thumbs, it was overwhelming in the best way and melted all the worries from only moments before into a puddle that leaked through the cracks and then disappeared.

Gage moved from my lips to my collarbone, peppering small kisses along the exposed skin there before moving up to my nose and planting one peck before dipping back down to my throat.

"Tate, you have no idea how long I've wanted to do that," he muttered against my neck.

I just nodded, not trusting myself to speak. I was drunk

on Gage and in disbelief that he was really here in front of me, holding me.

For weeks I'd slept on this cold hard floor in the hopes that one day Gage would walk back out of that portal alive, and now that he was here, I was in shock.

I finally collected myself and leaned back, meeting his stormy green eyes.

"Does it… hurt?" I asked, lightly skimming my hand over his back where the raised scars were.

Gage immediately stiffened and pulled away. "It's fine. Should we go out and see the others now?" was all he said, but I saw something shutter in his gaze before he turned away from me. He was blocking me out, hiding some part of himself, and that didn't feel good.

I took a deep breath, telling myself I needed to cut Gage a break. He'd been through a lot, of course it was going to take him some time to process before he wanted to talk about what happened in Avalon. Maybe we weren't on the exact same page, but we were definitely reading the same book. It was okay that we weren't perfectly in sync, because now that he was back we had time to get there.

We started to leave, but right before we shoved through the doors, Gage stopped and glanced over his shoulder at the portal to Avalon.

"Give me a second?" he asked.

"You're not planning on hopping back in, are you?" I asked with a nervous chuckle.

His gaze swung back to me, and he shook his head. "No, but can I borrow your phone? I need to check on Indigo."

Indigo! I had completely forgotten my Shade friend. I hadn't even checked to see how she was handling Gage's death-disappearance. I'd been a real self-centered jerk. Never again.

I scrambled to hand him my cracked screen cell phone. He took it with a nod.

Giving him a wobbly smile, I cleared my throat and then left the sanctuary, jogging down the stairs to join the rest of the Angel Gang on the lawn.

"Is he coming?" Drea asked.

"Yeah. He just needs a minute. He's talking to Indigo."

She nodded and hugged her arms to her chest.

"So is he… a Lumen?" Marlow asked.

"I don't know," I replied.

Frankly, at this particular moment I wouldn't care if he was a giraffe. The only thing I cared about was that he was back and alive. The rest could be sorted later.

"He's still a Watcher, and definitely not a Shade," Jacob offered.

I chewed my lip, preparing to announce that if he wasn't allowed to stay here I was gone, when Drea said: "Either way, he can stay. I'll talk to my mom. He's been through enough, so let's not mention the whole 'What is he?' thing in front of him."

Good idea. Put it in Pandora's box and pretend everything was okay. I loved it. Solid plan.

The door creaked open behind us, and we all spun with overenthusiastic smiles on our faces as Gage descended the steps and joined us.

"You can bunk with me," Dash offered as Gage handed me back my cell phone.

I caught Jacob's frown. I didn't think he wanted Gage dead, but I wondered how he felt about him being back and at the Lumen Compound. I hoped he wasn't going to cause any issues. The two of them weren't exactly buddy-buddy.

"Yeah, totally cool, you can stay here at Lumen Academy from now on," Drea added with an overeager thumbs-up.

Gage just scowled, clearly seeing through the façade.

"Skye died," I blurted, feeling a change of subject was in order.

That made Gage's eyebrows shoot up. "Damn… I'm sorry. I thought I saw her in Avalon when I was healing."

"Well, technically she's dead, but I can still see her because I can talk to ghosts now. Welcome back." I grinned.

That made Gage chuckle, and a bubble of warmth bloomed in my chest.

I did that. I made him smile.

A commotion drew my gaze to the doors of the community center and the academy. Hunters were filtering out onto the lawn; they must have seen the lightning. When their gazes fell on Gage, they glared. One even reached for a weapon.

"Crap." Drea rushed toward the armed hunter and waved her arms, yelling something I couldn't decipher.

Two senior hunters dropped from the sky where they must have been scouting the buildings above and landed on the grass. Their wings were outstretched, and swords drawn as they pointed at Gage, who stiffened next to me.

A growl sounded in Gage's chest and he stepped one foot forward, crouching as if to take flight, when he realized he was defenseless. I could see the moment he thought his wings would snap out but didn't, and it broke my heart in two.

I jumped in front of Gage, making it clear to any Lumens in the area that I was protecting him. "He's with us! He's a Lumen!" I yelled, but then wondered if that were true.

Well, he wasn't a Shade, and that was all that mattered.

The senior hunters looked at me, and then glanced at Gage standing behind me and frowned. "I know who that is, and Alstons are definitely *not* Lumens."

Grabbing my arm, Gage gently set me to the side so I wasn't his human shield anymore. His hands turned to fists and I saw the muscles tic in his jaw. "How about you come say that to my face," Gage retorted.

"He's with us," I growled. I called up my angel marks in case I needed to use force. The angelic script on my arms started to glow and swirl.

"That's enough," Aurelia's voice boomed behind me, and I spun to see the master Lumen coming out of the armory. "Go back to whatever you were doing!" she snapped at the assembled crowd and clapped her hands.

They all hesitated for a moment, but eventually started to walk away. The two armed Watchers who stood before Gage and me sucked their wings into their backs and sauntered off, but not before sneaking a glare at Gage over their shoulder.

No. He just got back. I don't want his homecoming to be like this!

"Gage, I'm so glad to see you are alive." Aurelia approached him with a genuine smile and my spirits lifted. If anyone could fix this rotten mood, it was her.

"You might be the only one," Gage ground out, and my heart sank. He swept his gaze over the retreating forms of the dispersing crowd. "I'm sure there's more than one Lumen here who thinks it would have been better if I'd died."

I saw the darkness swirling in the depths of his green eyes. Something really bad had happened to him in Avalon, or maybe he felt the Lumens had already rejected him. Either way, the old Gage was back, the one who counted on nothing and no one.

"I need some time alone, Tate. I'm going for a walk."

"But, Gage…" He just got back—literally back from the dead—and he wanted to leave me again? Why?

I frowned. It was impossible to not be hurt by that. "Skye's funeral is later. I thought…"

Reaching out, he brushed a finger across my lower lip. "I'm sorry I'm being so shitty. I just… I can't be looked at like that every day, okay? Like *I'm* a demon."

My heart broke at those words. He turned, grasped the gate's handle, and then left, mixing in with the crowd on the busy street.

There was movement at my back, and I turned, prepared to see Aurelia or Drea, but instead it was Dash.

"I'll keep an eye on him," was all Dash said before he slipped out into the crowd and disappeared as well.

The happiest half hour of my life had just turned into the saddest. Gage was back but he was still broken, and this time I wasn't sure I could fix him.

I wish I had an angel mark to fix my broken heart.

The rest of the afternoon passed with no sign of Gage. The evening came, and then Skye's funeral was upon us. Dash and Gage were still MIA.

I checked my phone for the millionth time, hoping to get another text from Dash that was more than the "we're good" he sent three hours ago.

"I'm sure he's fine. It's a lot to take in," Drea assured me.

Yeah it was, and I was trying to be sensitive to that, but I'd also slept on the hard ground for two weeks for that man and I'd only gotten one stinking kiss. I needed at least a dozen more—one for every night on that stone floor.

"Did you guys know that the angels in Avalon work out like six hours a day?" Skye piped in from her place on the edge of Drea's bed. "And they have weapons you wouldn't even dream of. I could blink and your head would probably fall off."

I rolled my eyes. "I highly doubt that."

"Want me to prove it?" Skye got right up in my face with her eyes wide open and stared at the tip of my nose.

I squirmed. "No. I'm good. I like my head where it is. You're intense. Dead Skye isn't my fav."

Drea and Marlow both perked up. "Skye's here?"

"What's she saying?" Drea asked.

I sighed, relaying the convo, and then spent the next ten minutes playing Telephone.

Although Skye was with us in ghost form, she'd said Cael had sent her here on some mission and then she would go back to Avalon for eternity, so I had to remind myself that I didn't know how long she would actually be with us. Even so, it was hard to have sympathy and feel sad about Skye's death when she was right in front of me telling me I needed to pluck my eyebrows.

"I'll meet you guys in the courtyard," I told them and slipped off the bed, straightening my black dress. I needed some alone time, and they seemed to get that. Even Skye poofed out of existence.

Making my way out of the dorms, I wandered through the rose garden in the courtyard aimlessly, watching them set up rows of chairs for the funeral. In the distance, I noticed the senior hunter Skye had gone on a few dates with hunched over the casket—Skye standing behind him in her ghostly form.

Please don't make me talk to him, I thought, and beelined it for the academy. I was so not in the mood to tell Skye's last conquest that she was a ghost. I was in such a rush to disappear that when I slipped into the elevator I just mashed a random button, focused on getting away. It wasn't until the doors opened at the basement level that I realized I was in that special section Dash had mentioned, the one where they kept the relics. I was officially on the mysterious SB floor.

I should have closed the elevator doors and gone back up. I was pretty sure I wasn't allowed down here. The button must be broken, because I'd pushed it before out of curiosity and it never took me down here. Something caught my eye in the room, and when I saw glass case upon glass case of shiny, pretty, magical things, I couldn't stop myself and stepped out of the elevator.

Holy relic heaven.

The place was lit up like a museum. Overhead lamps shone on display cases, illuminating the contents. Crystals, rings, daggers, books, chicken bones? There was so much to look at, I didn't know where to start. To the left of the large wide open space were the glass display boxes, but the right was stacked high with shipping crates. I moved to get a closer look at a book made of black leather that looked to have a real eyeball sewn into it, then the elevator dinged behind me.

Without thinking I leapt behind the shipping crates and hid, peeking through a gap in two crates as the elevator doors opened.

Aurelia stepped out with Theo and an older female hunter with long gray hair that I recognized as one of the librarians. I think her name was Mrs. Knapp. The trio moved to one of the cases, where Mrs. Knapp set a box down on the top of the glass. A small blue glow emanated from a crack in the lid.

"This should keep the demons or anyone using dark magic from being able to create portals here anymore," Mrs. Knapp muttered. "I've been working on it nonstop with the healers. At the very least, it should repel the energy long enough for us to call you, Aurelia."

Aurelia looked tired; her lips turned down into a frown. "Thank you, Michelle. This is extremely helpful and will surely strengthen the wards." Sighing, she brought her hands up to rub her temples. "I just wish we understood why the wards are failing us now. It doesn't make any sense."

"Do you think it could be the girl?" Mrs. Knapp asked.

The girl?

Aurelia dropped her arms and gave Mrs. Knapp a funny look. "Tatum?"

A small gasp escaped my mouth, and Theo snapped his head in my direction. His watchful eyes scanned the space. I covered my lips and held my breath, and the group continued talking a moment later.

"I think it's possible," Mrs. Knapp continued. "For centuries, the wards have kept portals from opening within our compound. Then this girl shows up, we learn she's the daughter of our greatest enemy, and suddenly portals are popping up everywhere on our grounds. The timing alone is suspicious."

Suspicious? What did that mean?

Aurelia was quiet for a moment. I wanted to shout that it wasn't true, but what did I really know about portals and protective wards? At the very least we *did* know the demons that emerged from the portals both times were looking for me, so in that sense it *was* my fault.

Aurelia shook her head. "No, we can't assume this has anything to do with Tatum, nor can we afford to have that suspicion grow within our ranks. She may be Apollyon's daughter, but she's a good kid. I don't believe for a second she'd do anything to purposefully harm anyone. If she does have something to do with the failing wards, it's not anything she can help, so it doesn't change our course of action. She's a Lumen, one of us. We protect each other. Fortifying the defenses around our community will be enough. It will have to be."

A warm ball of emotion formed in my chest at the motherly way she'd just laid down the law and said that I was one of them and to be protected.

Mrs. Knapp looked a bit affronted. "Of course, I didn't mean to imply that Tatum would do anything maliciously. Only that her presence seems to have triggered something."

Aurelia nodded, reaching up again to massage her temples. "I can't let anything happen to these students. After losing Arthur's talisman, the last thing we need is another attack."

We lost Arthur's talisman? I just told Gage we had it.

I probably should've stepped out and let them know I was there, but it would've been awkward. And if I was being completely honest, I wanted to hear more, so instead of revealing myself, I leaned forward.

Theo reached out and rubbed his wife's shoulders. "That wasn't your fault. They overwhelmed us, tricked us."

Aurelia shook her head. "No… we knew better. It's not like they hadn't done the same thing before. We should have done a better job keeping that vile object away from Arthur. We should have tried to destroy it. There's no excuse."

Theo frowned, concern for his wife clear on his face, but he didn't push the point.

Aurelia sighed. "Let's try to keep the information about Arthur's talisman from leaving this room. The last thing I want is for Tatum to worry that he could curse Joelle again."

My blood instantly ran cold. Arthur could curse Gran again?

Mrs. Knapp touched a spinning angel mark on the top of the box and the lid popped open, flooding the space with blue light.

Aurelia winced at the glow, but the corners of her mouth lifted in a grin. "Great job, Michelle. This will fix the problem, I know it."

They continued chatting about wards and protecting the school, but my name wasn't brought up again so it went in one ear and out the other. All I could think about was Gran and Gage. Could Arthur come after them again now that he had his talisman?

No way. I couldn't let that happen.

A spike of fear pierced my heart remembering how Arthur had almost succeeded in killing Gage once before, and that was when Gage had his Shade powers and Arthur *didn't* have his talisman. Arthur was a greater threat to Gage now than he'd ever been. And where was Gage? Out roaming the city like a walking target.

The sound of retreating footsteps and a closing elevator door brought me some sense of relief until Skye popped into view next to me. "I need you to tell my parents I'm still here."

My mind was spinning. I needed to find Gage. Arthur could have found out he was still alive and already be hunting him.

Skye got in my face, eyes wide and unblinking. "Hello? I need your help."

I shook myself. "Sorry. I'm all out of sorts."

"I'm sorry *my funeral* is bad timing for you, but suck it up, buttercup. I don't want my parents needlessly grieving."

I groaned. She was right.

I chewed on my lip, a sinking feeling growing in my gut as I realized I was only one person and could only do so much. I needed to do what I could to protect Gage, but of course Skye's parents should know what happened to her.

"Yeah, okay. Lead the way. I just need to make a quick phone call."

I tried calling Dash when I emerged from the basement, but he didn't pick up. I left a hurried message about keeping an eye out for Arthur or any other Shades and then followed Skye to her parents.

After explaining to her parents that their daughter was in fact an angelic ghost sent on some mission from Avalon, I was permitted to take my seat for the funeral. Her parents had actually taken it surprisingly well after I'd told them some horribly embarrassing things Skye relayed to me in order to prove her existence. I didn't want the entire school to know about my powers, so I kept my mouth shut as Skye walked through each row, commenting on what each person had really thought about her. She seemed keen on going through with the funeral and milking the drama.

I'd insisted on keeping the seat next to me empty in the hopes Gage would return. I didn't want to believe that he would leave me alone at a funeral for a ghost I was the sole interpreter for.

With a tissue in one hand, Marlow stepped up to the podium that stood in the garden tucked into the corner of the courtyard.

She grabbed the mic. "Skye was special," she sniffled, and my heart became heavy. I regretted not doing more to stop that level ten demon from hurting her.

"If she were still here, I'd want her to know that she was a bigger inspiration to me than she'll ever know." Marlow choked up and Drea stepped forward, taking over as she put her arm around her friend.

"Skye was one of the best warriors on my team," Drea announced to a few cheers from the crowd.

"Damn right!" Skye called back, and I couldn't help but smirk. There was movement to my right as some dude tried to take the seat I was saving for—

"Gage," I whispered as he slipped in the seat beside me. Reaching out, he grasped my hand and pulled it on his lap. My heart did somersaults in my chest.

He came back.

I melted into his side, resting my head on his shoulder as we listened to the rest of the service.

Gage and I didn't say a word to each other. We didn't need to. The soft strokes of his thumb over my palm said everything. He was here for me no matter what, no matter how dark his own journey was right now. We were in this together and that meant the world to me.

I could handle anything with him by my side.

The sweet moment was shattered by the sound of half a dozen cell phones going off. Mine included.

I looked down at it and frowned.

Lumen Academy Dispatch: Team Drea. Level four demon at Wild Ones.

I flicked my gaze to Drea, who was still giving her speech while simultaneously glancing at her cell phone. "And that's why I love Skye so much and will miss her," she ended quickly and stepped off the stage.

"Come on, we got a call," I told Gage, and a spark of interest lit up his face. Gage was a warrior through and through. If there was something that was familiar to him, something that would bring him some semblance of normalcy and maybe even a little joy right now, it was fighting.

We slipped into the aisle as Skye's parents got up to speak, and slowly made our way to the armory with Dash. Marlow and Drea followed behind us.

Jacob was already there when we stepped inside the building, talking to the armory master. "I need to check out five fake IDs for Drea Alcott's team," Jacob told her.

Whoa. I'm getting a fake ID?

Wicked.

"Can you make that six?" I pointed to Gage, who was admiring a set of battle knives on the wall. Grinning, he pulled one of the blades into his palm.

The armory master tucked a lock of brown hair behind her ear and shook her head. "I'm sorry, I don't have clearance for that."

The doors opened behind us, and Aurelia walked in. When she noticed Gage examining the weapon in his hand, she cleared her throat lightly. "Gage, until I can assess the extent of the powers Avalon has bestowed on you, I can't allow you out on missions. It's for your own safety, of course."

Staring at Gage's face as he realized that he was unable to go on missions with us was like watching a train wreck. Any last shred of light that had filled his eyes since he got back died in that moment. He set the knife down on the counter. "I understand."

He then gave her a curt nod and left the armory.

Crap.

"Gage!" Grabbing two random light weapons, I touched them to my weapons storage angel mark and ran out after him.

He spun as I reached him. There was so much hurt in his eyes, my heart shattered.

"It's not forever. Just until she tests your power," I told him.

His Adam's apple bobbed. "I don't have any power, Tate." His voice was dead, devoid of all emotion. It made the hairs on the back of my neck stand up.

"What?"

"Avalon stripped my power, okay? I'm basically human." He gazed at the floor. He couldn't even look at me.

Another hunter team left the funeral and jogged toward the armory to go out on a call. I had to sidestep to allow them to pass.

They stripped his power and took his wings and then gave him nothing in return? I just couldn't believe that. Or maybe I could. He was a Shade after all, the son of Arthur.

"Gage, that doesn't matter, okay—"

"Of course it matters." His throat sounded raw as anger crept into his voice. "They took everything that made me powerful and destroyed it. I'm weak, a liability, *nothing*."

I chewed the inside of my lip to keep from crying. "You

can still fight. We can brush up on your sword training and—"

"You should go," he interrupted, and stepped forward, hastily planting a kiss on my cheek. "Be safe."

Then he spun and headed across the courtyard to the main academy building.

No. This was all wrong, this wasn't how it was supposed to be. Why couldn't Cael have given him wings, or a few angel marks? Even *one* angel mark would have been enough, but he got nothing?

"Tatum, we've got to go." Drea's voice pulled my thoughts away from Gage, who was halfway across the lawn now. I had to focus on my team and not letting them down. We had some demon ass to kick, but after that I'd help Gage. My Pandora's box was getting full, but even so I stuffed my Gage-related emotions inside of it and took off after Drea and the Angel Gang. I was going to harness all of my anger and unleash it on some demons.

The entire subway ride to the club was a blur. I couldn't get Gage's voice out of my head.

They took everything that made me powerful and destroyed it. I'm weak, a liability, nothing.

So much for Pandora's box. There was clearly a crack in the lid.

"Remember to use a light weapon on any lower levels that might show up," Drea murmured to me as we hit the ground level.

I nodded, rolling out my neck and trying to mentally get in the game.

"You'll take Jacob's spot as flyer until I can fully train you to take Skye's spot as lead warrior. Cool?" Drea asked me as we power walked to Wild Ones Club.

I stopped right in front of the club and looked at her in surprise. "You want me to eventually be lead warrior?"

Drea cocked a grin and lowered her voice. "You can open and close portals, Tatum. Heck yeah I do."

Marlow pointed to the door, looking at the device in her hands. "We should get in there. The dark energy is amplifying."

Yikes.

Without waiting another second, Drea passed the rest of the people in line and stepped up to the bouncer, handing him her ID with a couple folded hundred dollar bills. "You wouldn't make a pretty girl like me and my friends wait in this long line, would you?"

The bouncer's gaze went right to her cleavage, and for a split second I saw a coiled dark snake around his neck. It reminded me of the snakes around the necks of the Shades I'd met at Shade Academy, and that made me shiver. I was starting to see a pattern with these. Although it seemed I was the only Watcher who could see them, they only appeared to be on people who weren't the most morally outstanding citizens

He grinned. "Come on in, dollface."

After barely glancing at our IDs, we were inside.

The stench of alcohol, sweat, and sulfur assaulted my nose the second we stepped into the place. The deep heavy beat of drum and bass rattled my chest as the music blasted through the speakers. The club was dark and lit only by black lights that made people's eyes, teeth, and colored clothing glow, but little else.

I flicked my gaze to the stage, where a DJ stood under a flashing neon sign that read *Blackout Night.*

Great. It was going to be impossible to see shadow demons here.

I glanced at Drea. The slightest bit of fear flickered across her face, but then it was replaced with determination. "Jacob," she called the male Lumen over. "Find a way to get the lights on."

Jacob nodded and then disappeared into the crowd as Drea turned to Marlow. "Marlow, start scanning people. Give us a signal if you find the demon."

Marlow inclined her head to the dance floor and then she was gone.

Drea chewed on her lip as she looked at Dash.

"What's wrong?" I asked her. I couldn't help but feel like there was something more going on than just finding this level four.

Drea looked at me, the whites of her eyes glowing in the black light. "If a level four goes unchecked feeding off the wrong human, it can cause big problems."

I swallowed hard thinking of the demon who'd fed from Stella back when the diner I worked at was attacked. My life as a waitress seemed like years ago, but in reality that was only last month.

"What kind of problems?" I yelled over the music.

Dash leaned forward, pressing closer to me. "Shootings, gang fights, crimes of passion, everything you hear about on the news."

Terror rushed through me. Were they saying that most of the awful stuff humans did was influenced by demons?

Spurred on by that revelation, I scanned the club until an idea hit me. I jerked my chin toward the back of the room. "I'm going to flirt with the DJ. If stuff starts to go down, I'll have a good vantage point from the stage and access to the microphone."

"Brilliant," Drea said, even as Dash frowned. Drea's blessing was enough for me, so I quickly blended into the crowd before Dash could stop me.

Bodies pressed against me, and I was jostled back and forth as I tried to reach the packed stage. I didn't have time to change from my funeral attire, but even so the black dress I wore wasn't too bad looking. My braided hair hung over my shoulder, and I wore light makeup. Hopefully, it was enough to entice this tool behind the turn tables to allow me into the booth.

Work it, Tatum.

I wasn't proud of using my looks to get my way, but in emergencies a girl has to do what a girl has to do.

When I reached the DJ booth, my eyes fell on the black snakelike shadow around the dude's throat. Two bouncers stood at each end of the stage, blocking people from going up.

Not ideal.

My gaze flicked back to the snake around the DJ's neck, and I suppressed a shudder.

Well, Drea and the team were counting on me, so I

pushed my theories about the neck snakes from my mind. Spinning to the large beefcake to my right, who was dancing with some blond chick, I leaned into him and whispered in his ear. "Boost me up on stage?"

After giving me a once-over, he nodded. Turning, I gripped the lip of the stage, which came to my chest. Two seconds later, I felt strong hands latch onto my waist and then I was flying. The dude basically lifted me like I was made of air, and I had to quickly tuck my legs under me or I was going to face-plant on the elevated platform. My feet hit the stage directly in front of the DJ booth and I popped up into a standing position right before the DJ.

His glowing red eyes met mine, then he flicked his gaze to where the bouncer moved in my peripheral.

"Can I come in the booth? It's my birthday!" I screamed as I leaned over the table. I sucked my bottom lip between my teeth and nibbled on it in what I hoped was a seductive manner.

Shame tried to rise up inside of me for acting this way, but I shoved it down.

Take one for the team, Tatum. If things get too uncomfortable, you can just fly away.

"Sure!" he grinned, looking back to the bouncer and waving him off.

I squealed in mock excitement and then went around the table to the side, where he opened a little half door for me. Stepping into the booth, I did get a bit entranced with all the dials and glowing knobs.

"What's your name, beautiful?" The DJ's hair was dark, and his breath washed over me, bringing with it the stench of liquor.

"Kallie," I lied.

A sly grin pulled at his mouth as he stepped up behind me and pressed his body against my back. Reaching around me, he started to fidget with the knobs. "Want to help me spin the next track?" he breathed against my neck.

Okay, I was totally going to throat punch him soon if—

The fire alarm blared, and the lights automatically kicked on, illuminating the entire club.

Bless you, Jacob.

With a hard shove, I pushed the DJ backward and yanked the mic from his table before scrambling out of the booth and to the edge of the stage.

I scanned the dance floor as people stared up at me, seemingly waiting for instruction.

That's when I saw it. The level four had the head of a bear but the body of a human… if said human had paws for feet and hairy hands. *Gross.*

"Drea, there!" I shouted into the mic, pointing in the direction of the demon.

Drea and Dash darted in the direction of the level four as I gripped the mic firmly in my fingers. "There's a fire in the back. Everyone needs to get outside," I yelled.

The crowd exploded into chaos then, trampling outward in every direction in search of the exit. I didn't see or sense a portal nearby, assuming I had that ability, so the level four must have walked here or something.

That thought was horrifying. How many demons were just aimlessly stalking the streets of New York looking to get into trouble? Clearly those scanners Drea had pointed out on the streetlights *could* be easily fooled. At least by one or two creatures. It probably took a demon mob to set them off.

"Tatum, behind you!" I barely heard Drea's scream over the blaring fire alarm. I had only just begun to turn and check over my shoulder when a force slammed into my back and then I was falling off the stage.

By the time I recalled I had wings and that using them in front of humans would be okay because they couldn't see them, I'd already slammed to the dance floor below. The fall wasn't a long distance, but I'd landed at an awkward angle. My left knee and right wrist took the brunt of the impact.

Ow.

After the zing of pain that ran through my body dissipated, I rolled onto my back and activated my weapons storage tattoo. Pulling a light blade from my arm, I looked up at the stage to see who had pushed me.

Holy mother of all things hideous...

An even larger demon stood over me, looming from his place on the stage. Goat head, three eyes, and *four* furry arms. The horns protruding from his head looked razor sharp.

I swallowed hard. *Great, there's two of them.*

With a well-executed kick up, I was on my feet and ready to slice and dice.

Okay, party time.

"I got your back," Jacob's voice came from beside me just as the alarms stopped their screaming.

"Thanks," I huffed, and no sooner had the words left my mouth than the ugly goat monster leapt from the stage with inhuman speed and grace.

Crap.

I raised my sword and it flared to life with a white glow that was ever so faintly blue. Jacob and I shared one look and then went ballistic on the creature. We took turns stabbing and slashing until he was a heap of shadows at our feet. With one final effort, the beast reached for my ankle, but I stumbled backward and ran into someone.

"I hate that we keep meeting like this," a familiar female voice spoke behind me, and chills ran the length of my entire body.

I turned slowly, coming face to face with Skye's killer.

"Run!" Drea shouted.

Level ten. Oh, this was so a trap.

Her glossy black hair fell to her waist in waves as she peered at me with a pursed lip look of annoyance. She might have looked like a human—granted, she was the most seductive and beautiful woman I'd ever seen—but her energy felt heavy, like a blanket made of lead that was smothering me. I could *feel* the evil within her. She felt like death, hate, wrath, and every other vile emotion I could think of.

My wings snapped from my back as I prepared to flee with my friends, and she grinned.

"Do I get to take another one?" She raised her wrist, pointed at Jacob behind me, and it felt like my soul left my body. I didn't know if it was triggered by anger or terror or what, but I had an out-of-body experience; time seemed to stand still, and all my power flooded to the surface of my skin and then released like a dam breaking.

Planting two hands on her chest, I shoved her. A shockwave of unseen force left me and blasted the she-devil across the room. She sailed over Drea and Marlow's heads, snarling, and crash landed at the far end of the room.

"You will *pay* for that!" she shrieked, and the walls of the club shook.

Oh, crap.

I stared at my hands, wondering what kind of power that was, when I noticed one of my angel marks was active and spinning. Arcs of glowing white swirls danced along the underside of my wrist.

Sweet.

"Get behind me," I called to my friends, who were scattered throughout the now miraculously empty club. The fire alarm had worked wonders, and the bear-headed demon was dead on the ground and disintegrating into shadows. The goat demon Jacob and I had killed had already disappeared.

Marlow, Drea, and Dash started to run to me when I saw the anger wash over the level ten's face, turning her pale skin ruddy. She was hell-bent on murder. She wanted to take another one of my friends, I could feel it in my bones.

"Don't," I shouted, and ran out to intercept her, passing Drea and the others as they fled to safety behind me.

Her hand flicked, and I reacted.

With a battle cry, I threw both arms out, and this time consciously pulled for my magic, thinking of protection. I envisioned a shield between my palms, similar to how I envisioned a portal, with no idea if that was even one of my abilities but letting instincts I didn't know I had guide me.

A purple translucent bomb of power exploded from my hands and collided with whatever dark magic she'd sent our way. Sparks of purple and orange showered the room, and the floor shook.

"You little pain in the ass!" the level ten demon screamed. The shaft of a glowing orange spear appeared in her fist.

What the heck was that? Now she was creating weapons out of magic?

I glanced over my shoulder to see my friends standing behind me with swords drawn. They hadn't left.

"Go," I hissed.

"You come too," Drea snapped back.

I wanted to, I so totally wanted to run home and watch *SpongeBob* with Gran and never see this evil demon again, but I feared if I let my guard down I'd be burying another friend, and this one might not come back as a super-annoying ghost.

Marlow gasped at something. I turned back just in time to see the spear sailing through the air, headed right for Drea's heart. I leapt to the side with every intention of intercepting the projectile when the space between the glowing spear and me opened up and some large creature flew out of it.

Is that a glowing lion with wings?

I blinked rapidly, barely having time to process what I was seeing, when the weapon crashed into the lion and broke apart into thousands of glittering pieces, falling to the floor, leaving the animal unharmed. The lion creature turned and looked up at me, and I went stiff with shock. He was the most majestic being I'd ever seen. Angel marks glowed on his light cream fur, and a pair of white feathered wings rested along his sides.

I tore my gaze away from the magnificent creature and looked at the level ten, surprised to see a flicker of fear in her eyes.

Lifting her fingers, she snapped, but nothing happened, and the fear that was once a flicker was now fully covering her face.

"You're not getting away that easily," the lion creature bellowed, his deep voice rumbling in my chest.

He spoke. The lion talked!

I squinted and saw waves of energy coming off of his body, wrapping around the level ten. The energy was translucent and hard to see, but it reminded me of high heat coming off of the concrete in summer.

The demon crouched on her heels and hissed at him, and I readied myself for another fight.

"Tatum, to me!" the lion commanded, and my spine straightened.

He knew my name! His voice was a mixture of human and animal, deep and rough, but oddly soothing.

He was clearly on our side, so I ran forward, blade drawn, and stood at his side.

"You have to behead a level ten to kill them," he coached me.

Awesome, behead someone. No big deal.

I knew she wasn't human, but she looked like one, or at least she had a few moments ago. Right now she looked straight out of a horror movie, head cocked to one side, rocking on her heels as black smoke rose up off of her skin.

If I could suck my thumb and rock in a corner I would, but there was no time; she was running.

Fast.

The lion creature had somehow managed to subdue her power and prevent her from escaping, but from the way his furry legs shook and he bared his teeth, I could tell the effort had cost him, so we needed to kill her quickly.

I wasn't sure what I was expecting his power to be, but when legit blue laser beams shot from his eyes and seared into the demon's legs, I realized it was definitely not that.

"Now!" he screamed.

The level ten fell forward, her legs burnt from the lion's blue lasers. I gripped my sword and swung it like a bat, aiming for a home run across her evil little neck. The edge of my blade sliced into it before hitting bone and severing that too. Her head flew from her body and landed at my feet.

Bile rose in my throat. I stood there in shock, holding the sword and looking at her head, which was now withering into a green, scaly, lizard-looking thing.

What the heck?

Don't vomit... don't vomit.

Breathing slowly through my nose, I managed to keep my food down.

I looked back to make sure Drea and the rest were seeing this and saw them on a knee, heads bowed in respect.

Oh.

Whipping my head back to the creature, I dropped to one knee also.

"Well done, Tatum. I'm Aurum, your guardian," he said, and chills broke out over my arms.

Guardian, like *guardian angel*? I had a freaking eye laser-shooting lion with wings as a guardian? I didn't know what to say, but that… was… awesome!

"Hi," I squeaked.

His voice became serious. "It's time for you to start preparing for your mission."

"Okay," I piped.

He definitely looked like he came from Avalon, but I wasn't sure of anything except that my friends seemed to know what he was, and that Cael must have sent him if he knew about my mission.

When I stepped closer, I experienced an eerie peace and stillness that I'd only ever felt in Cael's presence.

"And what's my mission?" Maybe he wouldn't be as cryptic as Cael. Maybe speaking angel-lions could be blunt. Fingers crossed.

His nose twitched and he bowed his head. "To destroy the Netherworld and free the souls Apollyon has trapped there."

"Uh…" I barely had time to process his bombshell when I was blinded by a glowing white light and then he was gone.

What. In. The. Flying. Laser beam Shooting. Lion. Was that?

"Drea!" Aurelia's voice snapped me from my trance and drew my gaze to the direction of the nightclub entrance. A group of master hunters filed in and then stared at all of us down on one knee in confusion.

"What happened? You texted 'level ten.'" Theo looked at his daughter, mystified, and then to the lizard head on the ground that was starting to ash and smoke.

Drea stood, cleared her throat, and looked at me.

"Tatum jumped in front of a demon harpoon to save my life and conjured a guardian of Avalon! Then she killed the level ten. We're fine now."

The master hunters all gasped at the mention of *guardian*.

Aurelia cleared her throat, looking around the space. "What was his name?"

I chewed my lip. "Aurum?"

Her eyes went wide. "Guardian Aurum was *here?*" Awe was evident in her voice, but I couldn't focus on that. I was still looping his words in my head.

Destroy the Netherworld? Free the souls Apollyon trapped? Who did they think I was and why were souls trapped there?

But then the answer came to me.

I was Apollyon's daughter, and like Cael had said, this mission was something only I could do.

A pit formed in my stomach at the thought.

With the curse lifted from Gran, and Gage healed and safe from Arthur back at the Lumen Compound, all I really wanted was to rescue my mom from Apollyon and call it a day. Freeing souls and destroying a Hell-like realm had not been on my life "to-do" list.

I gazed off into nothing, trying to process the last several minutes. Marlow slid in next to me. She nodded toward a semi-hysterical couple in the corner I was faced toward. "Their memories from the last thirty minutes will be altered," she said, obviously thinking I was worried about them when I hadn't even noticed they were there.

With a shake of my head, I focused on the pair. A master Lumen was trying to talk to them, but the guy was openly sobbing, and the woman talking animatedly as she moved her arms in flapping motions. I guess the club wasn't completely emptied before things got really weird. *Oops.*

"We only use memory alteration as a last resort," Marlow went on, "but sometimes it needs to be done."

I remembered when Gage told me that Stella's memories of the demon attack at the diner had been wiped and replaced to make her believe there'd been a power outage and attempted robbery. Messing with people's memories didn't sit well with me, but the couple across the room were clearly traumatized. Maybe it *was* best they went on with their lives without the memory of this supernatural event.

"How does it work?" I asked. "Is there a special gadget or something?"

"It's an ability only a few Watchers possess. Healers and master Lumens are the only ones permitted to use it."

The master Lumen laid his hand on the woman's shoulder and leaned in to speak with her. I couldn't hear what he said, but after a few seconds the woman seemed to relax. He moved on to the crying man next, and within a few moments he calmed as well.

"All right, let's head out," Drea said as she joined Marlow and me, Jacob and Dash in her wake. "The masters are going to take it from here. We've been instructed to go right back to the compound."

I nodded and we all filed out of the club. Drea fell into step next to me as we headed to the subway station.

She lowered her voice. "Mom wants to talk to you later about everything that went down tonight."

"That's not a surprise," I said with a dry chuckle.

"Tatum, what happened tonight was actually huge."

"Sure," I agreed. "Level ten demon attacks are no joke."

And they seem to love stalking me. Hashtag not blessed.

She shook her head, her eyes wide. "That's not what I mean. Guardian Aurum is the leader of the guardians of Avalon. He's basically a myth to most Lumens. Guardians are the only celestial beings that can still travel from Avalon to Earth, but it's not like they just pop down here on the regular. Aurum showing up with a message for a specific Watcher is unheard of."

I sucked in a lungful of chilly New York spring air and let it out slowly, digesting Drea's words. What I just heard her say was that there was something else that made me even more of a freak amongst Watchers.

Fantastic.

Being special sounded cool in theory, but the reality wasn't awesome. The pressure was starting to weigh on me, and I wasn't sure how well I was going to hold up under it.

"How many guardians are there?" I asked.

Drea shrugged. "Maybe a dozen. They are super rare."

The gravity of that hit me hard. "Okay, yeah, I can meet with your mom."

Would love to shower first and hopefully check on Gage.

"Mom said she doesn't need to see you tonight," Drea said, and I almost sagged in relief. "She wants you to get a good night's sleep first. It's been a long day, but definitely tomorrow."

"Thanks for the heads up," I said, and then both Drea and I fell silent.

It had certainly been a day: Gage's return, Skye's funeral, another level ten demon attack, and a visit from a guardian. After all that, sleep sounded good, but I wanted to check in on Gage first. Maybe a kiss from him would make this hot mess of a day seem not as bad.

Mmm, Gage kisses.

I'd only had a couple, but I was already hooked. Just thinking about it brought color to my cheeks and lifted my spirits. Maybe this day wouldn't be a complete dumpster fire after all.

CHAPTER
SIX

I assumed Gage would be waiting in the dorms for us to return, but when we got back to the Lumen Compound, I couldn't find him anywhere.

"Do you know where Gage is?" I asked Drea as I entered our shared dorm room. "I checked the courtyard, the cafeteria, and Dash's room. He's not any of those places."

Drea looked back at me with a frown from where she stood over my bed. Her phone was clutched in her hand. "I was just about to message you. I think he's gone."

What?

My heart immediately started to hammer in my chest. I must have misunderstood her. She couldn't have meant, *gone* gone.

"Like, he went to grab a late-night gelato?" I knew that was something he did from time to time. It was a plausible explanation. Or maybe he decided to go for another one of his long walks.

Drea shook her head, her frown deepening. "No, I mean I think he left the compound... for good."

She pointed at my bed, where there was a torn piece of notebook paper. Rushing forward, I snatched the paper up, my eyes flying over the short note.

Tate,

You mean more to me than anything in this world, I need you to know that. You were the only one in my life who ever saw goodness in me. But without my powers, I'm not sure who I am anymore, what my purpose is, or how I fit in this world. How can I protect you if I'm as weak as a human? I need to figure things out on my own and it's not fair for me to ask you to wait for me. I'll come back when I'm worthy of you and if you've moved on, I'll accept that.

Please, just be happy.

Gage

My hand shook as I read the letter three more times. I wanted to convince myself I was missing something or interpreting the note incorrectly, but it was clear as day: Gage had left me.

I lifted my gaze to Drea, her features blurry through the veil of unshed tears.

"He's... gone..."

She nodded, her lips pulling into a frown. "I'm so sorry, Tatum."

The first tear slipped from my eye and Drea quickly folded me into her arms.

"Why would he do this?" I asked as Drea hugged me and tears slid freely down my cheeks. "Why am I not enough?"

"You can't think like that," Drea said. She pulled back to look me in the eyes. "Gage is a totally different person around you. It's undeniable. Even Jacob has admitted it, and considering his feelings for Gage, that's a big deal."

I plopped down on my bed, and Drea sat next to me. "Tatum, it's clear from the letter that he didn't leave because of you."

I sniffed and looked over at Drea. "But he didn't stay because of me either."

Drea frowned. "Can you imagine being so powerful your entire life and then nothing? He could suck the light from an entire city block, and fly across town, and do magic, and now..."

"He's basically human," I finished for her.

Drea nodded, "I don't like that he left you in this way, but he's right that he needs to figure things out. No one is perfect, we all have baggage, but Gage needs to unload some of his before he's *the* guy for you."

"But... he can't be out there unprotected right now without his powers because Arthur has his talisman back and if he finds out that Gage is alive, I know he'll go after him."

Drea straightened, her brow instantly furrowing. "What do you mean Arthur has his talisman?"

Oops. I forgot she didn't know that I'd eavesdropped on her parents in the subbasement.

I quickly confessed what happened, how I'd overheard the adults talking about Arthur stealing his talisman back the day Skye died. I didn't bother telling her about how it could have been my fault that the demons were able to portal right into the Lumen Compound. Truthfully, with all that had happened, I'd mostly forgotten about that part myself, and it was hardly the most important thing to happen today.

"Talisman or not," Drea said when I finished, "Gage is aware how dangerous his father is. Probably more aware than any of us. He's not stupid and is going to do whatever he can to stay off of Arthur's radar."

All I could do was hope she was right. I tried to put myself in Gage's shoes then. If my dad almost killed me and I woke up in Avalon stripped of powers and then had my wings ripped off, would I come back and just jump into a relationship?

No. No I wouldn't.

I sighed as the gravity of the situation hit me. My happily-ever-after with Gage seemed impossible right now.

"Try to get some rest, okay?" She squeezed my shoulder.

I nodded, the shock of Gage leaving me after he just got back fully sank in about two minutes after I showered and crawled into bed. Everything Drea said about Gage was probably right, but that didn't make the heartbreak any less.

If you've moved on, I'll accept that.

How long was he planning on being gone? His words played out in my head as I sobbed into my pillow, and Drea pretended she couldn't hear me. It was a long time before I slept.

When I opened my puffy eyes the next morning, I told myself I wasn't going to shed another tear over Gage Alston. He was damaged. Fine. I got that, and I'd accepted him anyway. What I couldn't accept, *wouldn't* accept, was that he kept pushing me away.

Part of me wanted to run after him just to smack some sense into him. The other part of me wanted to shut down emotionally and never speak of him again.

"Yo, Tatum. Wait up!"

I glanced over my shoulder to see Dash jogging to catch up with me. I'd just left the Lumen Compound and was only half a block from the dorms, but I'd hoped to slip away unseen. I knew Aurelia wanted to see me this morning, but there was something I had to do first.

"I'm sorry about Gage," Dash said when he reached me, matching my steps so we walked side by side.

"Yeah, thanks," I said, and then shut my mouth. I wasn't interested in talking about Gage right now. I'd slipped past denial and gone straight into the anger stage of my grief.

"Where are you headed off to?"

"I need to make a stop at the bank," I said curtly without slowing my stride.

"The bank?" Dash looked over at me with a question in his gray eyes.

I nodded. "My gran gave me a key to a safety-deposit box that my mom left me. I'm going to check it out."

Mission "save my mom" was back on. If there was even one piece of information in that safety-deposit box that could help me bring her home, I needed to know it.

"Would you mind some company?"

"Depends." I lifted an eyebrow and shot Dash a side-eye. "Are you coming to support or guard me?"

Dash wasn't the type to just want to hang out. This was probably the most he'd spoken to me since we met. Something was definitely up, and I knew after that level ten attacked us a second time that Aurelia might want to put some restrictions on me. Even though Aurum and I had killed her, Apollyon could easily send another demon. I wondered if Aurelia sent Dash to babysit me.

He smiled. "Can't it be both?"

I barked out a short laugh. "Honesty, I like it. Sure, you can tag along."

Dash and I were mostly quiet the rest of the way to Lower Manhattan. Dash was a man of few words, and I was lost in my thoughts, so we paired well together today.

After we climbed the stairs that led to the bank's front door, I waited in line to speak with a teller. I fiddled with the key in my pocket while we waited, rubbing my fingers over the notches. Dash was like a silent sentinel next to me the whole time, and I found it oddly comforting.

I showed the key to the teller when we reached the counter, and gave her the number Gran had given me, as well as my ID. She waved over one of her associates, a young redheaded man, who could escort me to the vault where they kept the safety-deposit boxes. With a kind smile he asked that I follow him. I took a couple of steps after the bank employee before I noticed Dash wasn't following.

"I'll wait here," Dash said when I glanced over my shoulder at him. "Seems like something you should do alone."

He was probably right, but suddenly I didn't want to be alone. I nodded anyway and jogged to catch up to the employee, who hadn't noticed I lagged behind.

Within five minutes I was standing in the vault staring at a metal box roughly the size of a shoebox that sat on the small felt-lined table in front of me. After pulling the correct box, the redheaded employee had told me to take as much time as I needed. He showed me a button to push when I was finished that would call for his assistance, and then left.

I sat there for a full minute just staring at the box while I processed the fact that there was going to probably be something life changing inside. You didn't put something in a safety-deposit box for nearly eighteen years if it wasn't important. My hands shook as I finally inserted the key in the lock and turned it. Slowly pulling the lid back, I stared inside, surprised to see that the only thing inside was an envelope with my name on it. In it was a single sheet of paper.

Great, another letter. After Gage's note from last night, it was hard not to feel triggered. I don't know what I had expected. A family heirloom like a ring or some precious jewel… but a letter? I unfolded the page and fingered the pretty handwriting that was similar to Gran's with its curly script.

Taking a deep breath, I started reading.

Tatum,

If you're reading this, it means I'm probably dead.

My throat tightened at the severity of the first line, but I forced myself to keep reading.

I hate that I have to write this letter. Part of me wants to bundle you up and run, but I know that won't solve anything. He would find us, kill me, and take you. I've placed a hidden protection spell on you, but when you come of age, he'll be able to find you anywhere, so I need to stop him first.

My mom was talking about Apollyon, she had to be. This entire time I'd had a hidden protection spell on me?

I hope you will never have need to read this, but if I fail, there are things you need to know. Most importantly, I want you to know that I love you more than anything in this world. I made a lot of mistakes the last few years, but I can't regret them because if I'd taken a different path, I wouldn't have had you. The moment you opened your beautiful blue eyes and looked up at me, I realized what true love was and I knew I'd do whatever it took to keep you safe. If I don't make it back to you, I know your gran will raise you in a loving environment.

I paused, reflecting on the fact that, yes, Gran had raised me in a loving environment, but with the curse placed on her it had been anything but an easy childhood. My mother couldn't have known what Arthur would do though.

By now your gran has told you who your father is, Apollyon. I hope you don't judge me too harshly. I didn't know who he was when we first met. I thought he was a powerful Shade. I was young and naïve, and I thought I was in love. He is the reason I became a Shade. I followed my heart and betrayed my family in the process. What I didn't know was that he was using me. He needed an heir, but not just any heir, he needed a child who would inherit both light and darkness.

Chills broke out on my arms as I read that last line. I truly was a child of both. I knew my mother wouldn't have chosen to become a Shade for no reason. Could I fault her for falling for a Shade? Hadn't I done the same? It was obvious by the way my mom thought Gran had told me that my father was Apollyon that she didn't know Gran was cursed by Arthur all these years. I took in a deep breath and kept reading.

We come from one of the oldest lines of Lumen Watchers in existence, a chain I broke when I became a Shade. Apollyon targeted me because of my Lumen pedigree. I had always intended to choose Lumen, but when I met Apollyon, it was like a love spell had been cast over me. He was charming and handsome, and convinced me I should become a Shade. Only after we were married—

The breath caught in my throat. *Married!*

—and I got pregnant, did I learn that he needed to produce an heir with a first generation Shade from a long Lumen bloodline. The mix of his fallen angel blood, with my Lumen and Shade magic would produce a child of great power, a Shadowling.

A chill skated down my spine. That word, Shadowling. It's what the demons Apollyon sent after me called me. Now I finally knew what it was.

Apollyon is very powerful, but his reach is limited because he's chained to the Netherworld. He can only visit Earth for short periods of time and to do even that he must consume the soul of a lost one.

I stopped reading, my breath coming out in ragged gasps as I processed what my mother had written.

Consume the soul of a lost one. Apollyon consumed souls? Bile rose in my throat as I was reminded of what Aurum had said when he'd told me what my mission was. To free the lost souls and collapse the Netherworld. Maybe this was why… maybe Apollyon was… I shivered, unable to even fathom the possibility that he was a soul eater. I didn't want to read another word. I'd reached my max level of stress and trauma that I could take. But I also couldn't bear not to finish.

With a Shadowling heir, he can free himself from the Nether-world prison and rule Earth as he does the Netherworld. In order to do that, he needs to consume your soul, Tatum. When I learned of that, I fled with you. You won't ever truly be safe until he's destroyed. I'm going to try to kill Apollyon, but if I don't make it back, I've instructed your gran to hide you. A childhood in hiding isn't what I hoped for you, but I do want you to have a life. I am keeping this letter from your gran. The less she knows, the more protected she is. When you come of age, your powers will be greater than any Watcher before you. Train, learn to protect yourself, and someday I pray you finish what I may not be able to end today.

Be strong, my dear precious girl, and know that I love you— now and forever.

Above all, choose Lumen.

Mom.

I set the letter down on the felt table, stunned by all I'd just learned. My hands shook, my body felt numb, and a deep depression settled over me like a heavy blanket. In the past twenty-four hours I'd learned that my father was trying to consume my soul, and my sort-of almost-boyfriend ditched me.

I'd officially reached rock bottom.

The trip back to Lumen Academy was completely silent. Dash seemed to have picked up on the fact that I needed some time to myself. He just walked by my side, scanning the crowds for threats. Aurelia probably told him to follow me everywhere, which reminded me that I needed to speak with her.

When we reached the academy entrance, I waved him off. "I need to find Aurelia. I'll catch up with you later."

He nodded and turned to go when I called his name.

"Can you... let me know if you hear from Gage? I just want to know if he's okay." I was still kinda pissed he left, but I didn't want his dad to kill him.

He paused before answering. "Sure."

I spun, heading toward the academy, then Dash's hand snaked out and caught my wrist, gently.

I glanced up at Dash surprised to see a haunted look

cross his face. "I grew up in a Shade family in Los Angeles. When I chose Lumen, my father tried to kill me. It's where I got the scar." He indicated his face.

I gasped, caught off guard by his random admission.

"I had to flee Los Angeles, and I came here to hide out from my family. They're powerful Shade leaders and never would have let me live. I haven't been back since and don't plan on ever returning."

I had wondered why the level ten demon had seemed to know Dash. I didn't know how high up his family was, but to be recognized by a level ten, it must have been high. Maybe even higher than Arthur, which was a terrifying thought.

"Nobody else knows about this, but the reason I'm telling you is that I know how Gage feels, okay? I'm not trying to condone why he left, but you have to know what he went through wasn't easy. Whatever loving childhood you had, Gage and I didn't have that. We're fighters, and our sense of safety comes from the strength we carry with our powers, not from the people around us. Now Gage is powerless."

Dash's words hit me in a deep place. Fresh anger and sadness ripped through my heart in equal measure. Even with Gran's illness, my childhood was full of love, and I'd always felt safe. It might have been unstable at times when she got sick, but I never feared she would hurt me. I was grateful Dash had shared such an intimate and private part of his history all in an effort to help me to better understand Gage.

"Thanks for trusting me with your story." I pulled him into a hug and felt him stiffen, like he wasn't used to getting hugged, before his arms came around me. He patted my back awkwardly, and then we broke apart.

I grinned. "Not a hugger?"

He pulled his hood farther over his face. "Nah. More a fist bump kinda guy."

That caused laughter to peal out of me. Reaching out, I raised my hand and we smashed fists.

"See ya." He tipped his head, and I headed inside the academy to face my fate and a no doubt uncomfortable talk with Aurelia.

I found the Portal Master in one of the training gyms. There was a small rectangle window in the door that let me peer into the concrete room. When I spotted Aurelia, there was so much bright blue magic swirling around her I gasped. Sensing me, she spun and smiled. The magic dissipated to nothing as she waved me inside.

"Whoa, what was that?" I asked, forgetting all about the awkward talk we were going to have and instead focusing on the badass amount of magic I'd just seen swirling around her like a tornado.

She smiled sheepishly. "I admit I've always wanted wings. I'm experimenting with levitation by manipulating energy."

"That's amazing."

She grinned, but then the smile fell from her face. "Thanks for coming to see me. I wanted to talk to you about last night."

A stone sank in my stomach, and I cleared my throat.

"Tatum, the fact that the leader of the Avalon guardians threw himself in front of a level ten demon to save you is… well, you should be very honored," she started off saying.

Heat crept up my cheeks as embarrassment consumed me. I hadn't really thought of it as an honor. I also didn't thank him for saving me from that spear. I'd been too in shock of seeing a giant flying cat to act normal.

Facepalm, Tatum.

Aurelia placed one hand on each of my shoulders. "Drea told me what he said to you. What your mission is."

Aurum's words came back to me then. *Destroy the Netherworld and free the lost souls Apollyon has trapped there.*

"I had no idea souls were trapped in the Netherworld, and I have even less of an idea how to destroy an entire realm," I shared honestly.

"It's a herculean task, but the angels of Avalon wouldn't give you a purpose you aren't equipped to handle," Aurelia said solemnly.

I frowned. "I don't even know what it means. How do I free them? Where do I free them to?"

Aurelia squeezed my shoulders. "That's for you to figure out, and I have no doubt Aurum will guide you on that path. That is his job as a guardian after all."

The heaviness of my mission was too much for me, and I realized that I didn't want to keep secrets anymore, they just weighed me down even more. Pulling the note my mother had left me from my pocket, I handed it to her. "I want you to read this."

I needed another person to know that Apollyon was out to consume my soul in an effort to free himself and take over Earth. It was too heavy for me to carry alone, and I trusted Aurelia.

She frowned as she opened the letter, and when she glanced down at it, she gasped. "It's your mother's handwriting."

Wow. How close were they?

I nodded.

She scanned the pages, and I watched as all manner of emotions crossed her face. Her eyes widened in shock, her lips turned into a frown, and her free hand reached up to clutch her necklace. It felt oddly comforting to see another person be as surprised as I'd been when this information was dropped on me. When she finally finished reading, she lowered the letter and pulled me into a hug.

"Oh, Tatum." Her voice was thick with emotion.

Aurelia's motherly instinct level was an eleven, and I imagined that this was what my own mother would have been like had she been here to raise me. My throat constricted with emotion as I held on to her and just soaked in the comfort.

I'm not alone. I don't have to go through this alone.

When we finally pulled apart, I gave her a small smile.

"This explains a lot." Aurelia handed the letter back to me. "And reinforces what I was going to tell you, which is that I would like for you to have another hunter with you at all times whether on or off the campus."

"A bodyguard?" I thought of Dash and how he'd followed me to the bank.

Aurelia shrugged. "Yeah, I take the safety of my students very seriously, and now that I know Apollyon will do anything to get you to go to the Netherworld, I'm not taking any chances."

"Okay," I told her. I wasn't interested in putting up a fight, and if my Lumen babysitter was Drea, Dash, or any of the others from our team, it wouldn't be so bad.

Aurelia visibly relaxed at my acceptance. "I know you want to go and save your mom, and I promised I would help, but—"

"I'm going no matter what," I said quickly, cutting her off. If she was about to tell me I couldn't go looking for her because of what was written in that note, I was outta here. Rescuing my mom was non-negotiable for me.

"Absolutely," Aurelia said. "What I was going to say is that now that I know Apollyon is after *your* soul, I don't think sending in a small group of hunters with you is going to be enough. I think we need to amass a Lumen army, and you'll need to train every free second of every day to be ready."

Amass an army?

That sounded serious, but she wasn't wrong. What if I went down to the Netherworld and got my soul gobbled up by my psycho dad and freed him? That would be beyond bad. I was all for having extra help, but there was one problem...

"That sounds like it might take a while and I can't bear to think of my mom there alone, hurt, and wondering what's going on here," I confessed. Just talking about my mom caused the lid of Pandora's box to crack, allowing my emotions to leak out and overwhelm good sense. Now that I'd read the letter and knew that Apollyon had essentially tricked her into becoming a Shade, I wanted her back more than ever.

"What if we could send a quick word to her, tell her to hold on?" Aurelia offered. "I can contact the other academies and ask for volunteers to go to the Netherworld in a month's time for a rescue mission."

My heart hammered in my chest. "Send word to my mother in the Netherworld? That's possible? Why haven't we done this before?" A month wasn't ideal, but it wasn't too bad if we could be sure we'd get her back here safely.

A flicker of fear passed over Aurelia's face. "It's not without its difficulties, but if it was possible, would you be willing to hold off going there until I can rally a proper attack?"

I nodded. I could wait a little longer if my mom received word that she hadn't been abandoned and that I was coming.

Aurelia looked more relaxed now that I wasn't going to go rushing into the Netherworld alone. "We'll send word to her tonight. In the meantime, you need to practice your portal power control with me."

I groaned. I was really hoping for a nap and a trip to a local shrink, but I guessed duty called.

"Stand over there." She pointed to a spot across the room.

With a sigh, I tucked the note into my pocket and walked to the far wall. She pulled an apple out of a bag that lay on the floor and set it on her open palm. "Open a portal and take it."

Okay, clearly she knew I was food motivated, but it would have to be a candy bar to really get me excited.

"A portal in the same world? What's the point?"

She raised one eyebrow. "The point is that if you can collapse space and cross a distance in the same world, you can escape any danger. We will start with a distance of fifteen feet but imagine if you could portal from New York to Connecticut."

My eyes widened. "Is that possible?"

Aurelia chuckled. "Of course. It will take a toll on your energy, and there are dangers involved, so it's something you should only do in an emergency, but if you master this skill, there's no telling what you would be capable of."

Holy portal power!

"Can you portal to LA?" I asked. Now I just wanted to see the extent of her power.

A sly grin pulled at the corners of her mouth. "I once portaled to Paris for my twenty-first birthday. I slept for two days afterward because it sapped so much of my power. Do not recommend."

I smiled at that and remembered how I had passed out after I'd made a portal from the Netherworld back to my apartment building in New York City. It definitely took a lot out of me. And made me super hungry.

"I thought the whole compound was warded against portals being opened within the boundaries," I said, thinking not only about the relic in the subbasement that was supposed to strengthen the wards—which I wasn't supposed to know about—but also how big of a deal it was the two times demons had opened portals from the Netherworld into Lumen Compound the month before. It wasn't something they'd thought could be done.

Aurelia shook her head. "Our wards just keep demons and Shades from portaling into Lumen Compound. We can still use our light magic to portal in, out, and within our compound. So we won't have any issues training."

I nodded, thinking that sounded reasonable, and then tucked into my lesson.

An hour later, I'd cracked the concrete floor and nearly cut Aurelia's hand off when trying to get the apple by closing the portal around her wrist too quickly. She didn't seem too bothered though. In fact, I think she was a little impressed.

"Not bad, Tatum," she told me when we were finally done.

I snorted. "I almost took your hand off!"

She shrugged. "On my first day of in-world portal practice, I burned my eyebrows off. It's a long story not worth repeating," she added when she saw the excitement in my face.

"Oh please, repeat!" I begged.

"Repeat what?" Drea popped her head in the room.

"Nothing," Aurelia said quickly.

"When she burned her eyebrows off," I told Drea as she joined us.

Drea smiled wickedly. "I found pictures last year."

"You will not show those to anyone," Aurelia said sternly, but I could sense she was on the verge of laughter. "That was a very embarrassing time in my life that I wish to never live again."

Drea and I burst into snickers, and an unwelcome image of Gage suddenly flashed into my mind. Agony sliced through my heart and the laughter died in my throat. It was like I was trying to get back to normal, but my heart wouldn't allow it. I still couldn't believe he'd just left like that.

Aurelia noticed the change and placed a hand on my shoulder. "I'll make the arrangements for tonight. Be ready after dinner."

"Yeah. Of course," I said, with a small and unconvincing smile.

She swept her gaze over my face again. "I was sorry to hear about Gage leaving. He's welcome back anytime."

Was my heartbreak that apparent?

I just nodded, and with an encouraging smile of her own, Aurelia left, leaving Drea and me alone.

"What's tonight? What arrangements?" Drea asked.

That helped shake me out of my funk. "Your mom has a way to send a message to my mom in the Netherworld. We're going to contact her this evening."

Drea's smile faded, and her dark skin paled to a lighter brown. "She… she said that *she* was going to send a message for you?"

"Yeah. Why?"

Drea exhaled, a mixture of alarm and anxiety flashing across her features. "There is a relic she can use to link with someone's mind across the worlds, but last time she tried to get an urgent message to Cael in Avalon, she was badly hurt."

I frowned. "What? Hurt how? Why didn't she just use the portal to go to Avalon and speak to Cael?"

Drea shook her head. "The portal only works once. You ascend and that's it. It's not an open free-for-all. If she wants to contact another realm it gets really complicated and dangerous."

Oh man, now I felt awful. I didn't want her mom to get hurt trying to save mine.

I fumbled for the right words. "Well, she doesn't have to."

Drea shook herself. "No, I'm sure it will be fine. My mom wouldn't have mentioned it if she couldn't handle it."

But I wasn't so sure of that. Now I wondered if that's why I'd seen a flicker of fear across Aurelia's face when she spoke about getting word to my mom.

Don't let me lose them both, I prayed to the angels of Avalon. I wasn't sure I could handle that.

What I thought was going to be some small ritual where Aurelia sat in an empty classroom and closed her eyes to try to contact my mom, turned out to be a much bigger deal. When Drea and I met her in the lobby of the academy, there were nearly half a dozen Lumens, including Theo, dressed in battle gear. The gold-winged insignia pin on their breastplates identified them *all* as masters.

"We're going to an off-campus building so this relic doesn't disturb the wards around the compound," Aurelia explained. "But don't worry, we picked a location that's easily defensible in case our efforts draw demons."

Oh great.

We were doing something that was possibly going to attract demons. Good thing Drea and I were always armed. I glanced at the long sword tattoo on her arm and the two small daggers on my own. We could fight if need be, but I doubted the need would arise with this many master hunters present.

Mrs. Knapp suddenly stepped out of the elevator doors with a small box in her hands, and Skye was right behind her.

"All set," Mrs. Knapp said as she gave Aurelia a curt nod and handed the wooden box to Theo. This box wasn't like the one I'd seen in the subbasement before. This one was highly decorative with swirls and burned etchings on the side. Angelic script.

Aurelia looked over our group as Skye stepped up next to me.

"Let's move," the Portal Master barked, and then spun and led us outside. I went to follow, then Skye stepped in front of me. I tried to sidestep her, not wanting to ghost through her, but she moved with me, blocking me.

"Skye, move," I whisper-hissed. "You can come, but we gotta go."

"Don't go. This ends badly," she said, and I stood stock still as I stared at her face. She looked terrified, eyes wide, mouth set into a grim line, and wringing her hands. I wasn't used to serious Skye. It kind of freaked me out.

"What? Can you see the future now too?" I laughed nervously.

She ran a hand through her long brunette hair and rolled her eyes. "No. But I feel..." She paused, struggling to find the right words to explain. "...timelines, possibilities, choices not taken. And none of them are good. Don't go. Call this off."

Why was she doing this right before we were going to contact my mom? This was the single most important thing to me right now.

"Skye, my mom's stuck in the Netherworld, and she needs to know I'm coming for her. We're just sending her a message to hold on," I said, and tried to sidestep her again.

When her cold hands rested on my shoulders and then phased through my torso, I yelped and lurched backward.

"Tatum Powers, I'm assigned to look after you, and I'm telling you: this ends badly for someone no matter how I see it," she growled.

I frowned. "Can you be more specific? What did you *see* exactly?" I pressed her.

She looked unsure. "It wasn't a vision or anything, more of a feeling, I can sense—"

"Skye!" I snarled. "If you don't want me to go, and you can just zip up and down to Avalon, then why don't you fly down to the Netherworld and give a message to my mom? Then I won't need to do this at all."

She put one hand on her hip and glared at me. "I can't get to the Netherworld, genius. If I tried, I'd get stuck there for eternity, or worse, become Apollyon's next meal."

I gasped. So it was true, he *ate* souls.

A shiver ran through my body. I guess Skye knew everything now that she was dead and conversing with the angels of Avalon on a daily basis.

"Look, Skye, if you can't help me, I need to go. I can't leave my mom in a Hell realm for another month without any hope. We've got half a dozen master Lumens. We'll be fine," I told her just as the front door to the academy opened and Drea stuck her head in. "What are you doing? Everyone is waiting."

I looked at Skye one more time and then walked to Drea, doing my best to ignore the icy chill that swept over me when I passed through Skye. I had to know my mom was all right. If Skye was just going to blab about random feelings rather than give me a concrete vision, then I would ignore her.

But an unwanted part of my mind whispered, *If ignoring Skye is such a solid plan, then why is there a pit in the bottom of my stomach?*

We all stood in the center of an abandoned industrial loft in the Meatpacking District. With drywall and tools strewn around the room, it looked like it was under construction. We were on the second floor. Aurelia stood in the center of the space with Drea, her father, and me. The master Lumen she'd brought stood like sentinels in a corner of the room with weapons drawn.

"I have a confession," I squeaked just as Aurelia was about to lift the lid on the box and reveal whatever was in there.

"What is it, dear?" Aurelia asked.

I blew air through my teeth. "Skye showed up as we were leaving and said this was a bad idea. That she had a feeling it would end badly."

There. I said it. My conscience was clear.

Aurelia raised one eyebrow. "A feeling?"

"That's what I said! But I would never forgive myself if something bad happened on account of me and my desire to contact my mom," I told her honestly. "Maybe we shouldn't be doing this?"

She smiled and reached out to grasp my hand. "You're not the only one who wants to contact your mother, honey. I'm excited to speak with Emery as well. I've taken every precaution for this little venture. I promise you." Her gaze flicked around the room at the master Lumens.

I nodded, feeling marginally better about the whole thing. If Aurelia thought it was safe, then it probably was. "Okay."

Drea's hand slipped into mine and squeezed as Aurelia popped the lid off the box.

Holy tiara from Avalon!

A supernatural blue glow swirled and arced around a tiara made of solid gold. It was otherworldly, with circles and rings that resembled planets, and filigree so delicate it looked like spun sugar. Small stones were sprinkled throughout the design like stardust. The piece was so beautiful it took my breath away.

"The Diadem of Avalon has been entrusted to the

Lumens for millennia. It allows the wearer to merge minds with anyone in the universe," Aurelia explained.

Mind merging? How about mind blown?

Theo looked at his wife with pride. "Aurelia has been practicing with it for a decade."

"It takes a lifetime." Aurelia blushed and reached in to grasp the edges of the tiara, handling the precious item with care.

My heart hammered in my chest as I remembered what Drea had said about her mom getting injured the last time she did this. Drea must have been thinking the same thing.

"Mom, be careful," she whispered next to me.

Aurelia smiled at her daughter. "Last time was an emergency, I was rushing and not in the right headspace. This is different. I have all the time I need." Her voice was smooth, hypnotic, like she'd been doing yoga for an hour before this.

"Yes, take your time. No rush," I urged her, nerves creeping in on me again. I half hoped Skye would pop back in and tell us to stop if she really felt something awful was going to happen. But Skye never came, and before I knew it Aurelia was lifting the diadem to her head.

"I'll tell her how much you miss and love her, and that we're coming for her," Aurelia said to me.

I bit the inside of my cheek and nodded. I wasn't even allowing myself to think of the possibility that my mom might not be alive, that Apollyon killed her for interfering in my Ascension Ceremony. Nope. Not going there.

Aurelia sat cross-legged in the middle of the room as

Theo, Drea, and I backed up. She took a deep breath and then placed the relic on her head.

Nothing happened.

I was expecting maybe a flash of color, or for her to gasp, or scrunch her face, but *nothing* happened. She sat with her hands folded in her lap, head slightly cocked, and mouth set into the slightest of smiles.

"Emery," she whispered faintly, and the hairs on my arms stood. The air charged around us then, and that's when something *did* happen.

Aurelia levitated off the ground, only a few inches, but her entire body lifted as the blue glow of the Diadem of Avalon trickled down her neck and shoulders, covering her entire body.

Aurelia gasped, then laughed as tears collected in her eyes.

What the what?

"She's talking to your mom," Theo said. "The conversation is just playing out in her mind."

Drea stiffened beside me. "That's how she got hurt last time. Instead of reaching Cael in Avalon, she mind merged with a demon who intercepted. It caused her a lot of pain."

I winced. That was possible? Mind melding with a demon? That sounded like my worst nightmare.

I looked down at Aurelia for any sign that a demon was mentally torturing her, but she was just grinning ear to ear with silent tears rolling down her cheeks.

Mom.

Aurelia once said that she and my mom were close, so I was glad my mom would hear from a familiar person and know that I hadn't abandoned her. It gave me a deep peace in my soul.

"I'm getting some demonic activity readings!" one of the master Lumens shouted from the corner, shattering the peace that had fallen over me.

Theo moved then like a lightning bolt. Rushing forward, he grabbed my shoulders and hauled me up and threw me over his shoulder in a fireman hold and then sprinted toward the door on the far side of the room.

"Hey, what the heck?" I yelled as Drea ran after us.

"Sorry, Tatum. This was Aurelia's plan if demons decided to crash the party," Theo said.

My gaze flicked up to see one of the masters shaking Aurelia from her trance just as four portals opened inside the room.

Not one. Not two. *Four.*

"No!" I screamed and kicked as Theo burst through the door and dragged me down the hall. "I can help! I can close them!" I screamed.

Theo's hold was strong, and Drea must have known the plan too, because she was following us without a word of disagreement. She pulled her sword and ran beside us quietly.

When we got outside to the street, Theo set me down and looked sharply at Drea. When his daughter nodded, he released my shoulders and ran back inside. Drea dropped to her knees, clicked on the anklets that would make me invisible if I flew, and then stood to face me.

"Fly us home. That's an order." Drea's words were no-nonsense, but there was a slight quaver in her voice. This was her freaking mom and dad we were leaving behind.

I shook my head. "Drea… four portals. I know your mom is the Portal Master and all, but *four*."

Drea chewed her lip in anxiety. "Fly us home." Her command was weak at best.

I wished Drea had wings and that I could push a button and force her to fly home without me. I didn't want her rushing back into the fray with me, but I was definitely going back in there.

I shook my head. "Take the subway. I'm going back in to help the—"

"Are you crazy? That's my parents. We're both going!" she snapped and pulled a second blade from her arm.

I grinned, reaching up to pull my daggers off my skin. I was kind of a bad influence, but in this case I was hoping it was in a good way.

We made it just inside the entrance when Skye popped back into view.

"I told you," she yelled at me as Drea and I sprinted toward the stairs, both our minds focused on getting back up to the second floor.

"Not the time, Skye," I snapped back.

Drea scanned the area next to me but didn't say anything as we ran through the building.

Skye vanished, immediately reappearing in front of the door to the stairwell. "Tatum Powers," she shouted, holding her hands out in front of her as if she had the authority to stop us when in reality we could just run right through her. "Do not let Drea into that fight. She won't make it out alive."

I skidded to a halt right before the door, grabbing Drea's arm as I did to stop her as well.

"What? How do you know that, Skye? You said you couldn't see futures."

Skye clenched her fists in frustration. "I know with certainty that if she enters that fight, every possible outcome leads to her death. And it's not her time."

"What's going on?" Drea demanded, her gaze jumping around the room as if she might be able to spot Skye any moment. Now that the course was set, Drea wouldn't back down or turn away. What could I possibly say to change her mind and let me go upstairs without her?

I opened my mouth to try to explain, when a terrible shriek came from above, followed by a tortured scream.

Was that Theo?

Determination washed over Drea's features and I knew there was no way she would listen to anything I had to say. I wasn't going to lose another person I cared about.

Drea spun toward the stairs, and before thinking too hard about what I was doing, I flipped the dagger in my hand and cracked the handle against the side of her skull. She dropped immediately, and I fumbled to catch her before she crumpled to the ground. A hundred percent dead weight, she sagged in my arms, out cold.

I winced. "Sorry."

Skye's eyes rounded as she took in Drea's unconscious form. "She is going to be *so* pissed at you when she wakes up."

"Yeah, well, she'll be alive, so it'll be worth it," I growled.

Blunt ghost Skye was not my fav.

I adjusted Drea so that I grabbed her under the armpits and then quickly hauled her over to a storage closet. Pulling her into it, I set her down on the floor and then slipped back out the tiny space, flipping the lock once I closed the door behind me. A sealed door wasn't going to hold my fierce friend, but if she woke before the battle was over, it would at least slow her down.

Taking the stairs two at a time, I raced back up to where Aurelia and the other master hunters were. As I neared the second floor, I heard swords clanging, demons screeching, and hunters grunting. I was reaching out to turn the knob when Skye poofed beside me.

When I looked at her, she wore a grim expression. I steeled myself for her to tell me someone else I cared about would die if I opened this door.

"Nothing you do now can keep someone you love from going through a life-altering change tonight." Her voice was ominous.

My brow furrowed. *Huh?*

"Someone else dies?" I asked, hand stilled on the knob, heart smashing against my breastbone.

"No one dies. Well, their old self dies metaphorically I guess, but—"

"Skye!" I hissed. "I open this door, I don't open this door, does it matter?"

She shook her head. "You can't stop what's coming now."

A chill broke out onto my arms and then she was gone.

No one dies. Focus on the no one dies part, Tatum!

Turning the knob, I yanked the door open and took in the scene before me.

It was absolute chaos, a war zone with so much going on my brain couldn't process it. The four portals at the corners of the room were still open. Aurelia hadn't closed any of them and now I could see why.

Shades.

A pair of Shades stood in front of each portal which allowed the demons to filter through unfettered while they fought off the master Lumens. All these demons were ugly looking level sevens and eights, not the lower levels I was used to. This was going to be a bloodbath.

I needed to help.

Charging into the room, I raised my two light daggers and made a crisscross motion, slicing one of the demon's backs, which caused him to hiss and spin toward me.

"Tatum, no! Run!" Aurelia growled.

"Not a chance!" I yelled back as the demon before me raised his serrated claws and prepared to slash my face.

Not today, pal.

I faked a move to draw his attention toward my right hand and then slammed the dagger in my left hand into his hairy throat, shoving it all the way in to the hilt. His hideous muzzle-like mouth popped open in surprise and then he dropped to his knees as I pulled out my weapon.

I didn't wait for the demon to disintegrate. I needed to close one of these portals.

Running to the one nearest me, I skidded to a stop before the floor-to-ceiling windows and stared past the pair of Shades guarding the red and black swirling circle. Sparks and black smoke spit from the portal's open mouth, and I crinkled my nose at the overwhelming stench of sulfur.

Will I ever get used to this sight?

Part of me hoped not.

Holstering my daggers, I lifted my hands, readying myself to hammer the wretched gateway with my magic, when I locked eyes with one of the Shades protecting it. My heart fell into my stomach.

Indigo.

"No," I whimpered, lowering my hands.

My Shade friend had just recognized me as well and stared back at me with a slack jaw. The Shade next to her, a male I didn't recognize, was locked in a battle with Theo, as a demon started to step out of the portal and into the room.

Indigo faltered, lowering her sword. I wanted to hug her, and apologize for going MIA after Gage disappeared, but now wasn't the time. A blur moved to my left and I didn't have time to warn her. One of the master Lumens came out of nowhere and cracked Indigo in the side of the head.

"No!" I screeched as she went down like a sack of rocks.

I spun to snarl at the Lumen and tell him she was with us, but he was already engaged in a fight with a vicious looking demon with three horns and a set of bat wings.

Okay, on my own, then.

The portal was now left unguarded, and I was grateful it was Lumen protocol to incapacitate Shades, only killing them as a last resort. I was quite confident no one would hurt Indigo as she lay helpless on the ground.

Spinning to face the portal, I lifted my hands again and pulled for my power. Since my adrenaline was pumping and because I'd been practicing with Aurelia earlier in the day, my magic came to me easily. It was as if it was just sitting underneath my skin, waiting to be called upon.

I tried to peer through the sulfuric smoke and swirling red magic to see Shadow City beyond, but I couldn't make anything out.

Mom.

My chest tightened, but I had to trust that Aurelia had contacted her and that my mom would hold on until we could amass an army to rescue her.

My power flared to life in my palms, and I pulled my purple magic into a ball between my hands. Reaching out, I spread my palms and covered the portal with my magic as if I were throwing a blanket over it. Remembering what Aurelia had taught me earlier in the day, I grasped the edges of the portal, feeling for the place that this realm became another, then started to fold the corners of the portal inward, making it smaller and smaller as if folding a towel.

Aurelia's technique was working beautifully. *Fold. Fold. Fold*, I chanted to myself until the portal was smaller than a dinner plate. When it was that size, I saturated it with my magic, feeling the burn throughout my limbs as I fed the now tiny, manageable sized portal my power.

A sizzling sound filled the air, and then with a pop the portal sucked shut and disappeared. I sighed in relief and turned around to search for the next portal just as Aurelia shouted, "Hellhound! Don't let it bite you!"

I froze in terror as my gaze fell upon the creature. A furry beast that looked like a cross between a werewolf and a dog stood before me with his lips bared in a snarl. Shadows and smoke moved across its skin; fire licked over its spine. My stomach dropped. Its teeth were razor-sharp points, eyes glowing red, and paws full of two inch talons.

Mommy. This thing was definitely going to creep into my nightmares.

"Shadowling," it snarled, its voice raking over me like a barbed whip. I pressed my hands against my ears. When it spoke, my brain throbbed.

I backed up slowly until I was flush against the window that led to the alley below. The hellhound crouched, curling its lips back to display every pointed tooth, and then before I knew what was happening, it pounced.

I didn't even have time to scream before it smashed into

me, claws digging into my shoulders as the impact of his body shattered the glass pane behind me.

No. And then I was falling.

"Tatum!" Aurelia's scream died off as I fell backward. I snapped my wings out, trying to flap them, but it was too late. My back hit the ground first, then my head cracked into the concrete, and everything went black.

I came to with blurry vision, and a fanged and furry beast hovering over me.

My head felt like it had been carved like a pumpkin, and my brain was mush. I couldn't think straight, couldn't see straight; nothing made sense. Nausea roiled in my belly as I fought to remember where I was and what happened and why this hideous creature was drooling over me, looking at me like I was his next meal.

"Master Apollyon has a message for you," the creature said, and I screamed as the pain in my head reached epic proportions. It was complete agony to listen to.

I waited for him to reveal the message and get off of me when he bared his teeth and lunged. I yelped, preparing for the bite and realizing *that* was the message, when a streak of darkness crashed into the creature and ripped him off me.

I struggled to my feet and dizziness washed over me. Blinking rapidly, I tried to focus on the fight as bits and pieces of the last few minutes returned to me. The hellhound… falling from a window… but the rest was still missing. And now the hellhound was locked in a battle with—

"Gage?" I questioned my sanity then, reaching up to probe the painful spot on my head only to come away with fingers full of sticky warm blood.

Everything blurred, and I was trying to track the two figures before me when I heard the crunch of bone.

The dizziness became too much, and I collapsed to the ground, sure I'd heard Gage scream out in pain before the darkness took me again.

I was still mentally foggy when I blinked awake sometime later. I squinted against the ray of light hitting me in the face, basically blinding me, but when I went to lift my right hand to shelter my eyes, I couldn't. Shifting out of the sunlight and into a more upright position, I looked down to see Gran sitting in a chair next to my bed. She clutched my hand tightly, even in sleep. A quick glance around the room confirmed I was in the healing center.

"Gran…" I said quietly, leaning forward to softly nudge her awake. Despite my gentle efforts, she jerked awake, eyes wide, until she caught sight of me.

"Oh, honey," Gran said as she rose and planted a kiss on my forehead. "I'm so glad you're awake." She squeezed my hand but didn't let go as she stared at me. A frown pulled the corners of her mouth down. "If what I went through over the last twelve hours was anything like what you had to endure when I was unconscious from that horrible curse, I'm so sorry."

The bags under Gran's eyes told the story of how worried she'd been, so I didn't bother mentioning that what I went through was probably worse because I thought she was going to die.

I smiled back at her, trying to reassure her that I was all right. "The important thing is that we're both here, alive and well," I said.

The events from the night before suddenly rushed at me, and I gasped: knocking Drea out and locking her in a closet, the four portals, demons had been everywhere, Shades fighting Lumens, and then I'd gotten shoved out of a window by a hellhound.

Wait... had Gage been there as well?

My memories were foggiest where that was concerned. I reached out to probe the back of my head and my fingers brushed over a thick, bumpy scab.

"They said it was lucky you have advanced healing powers, otherwise you'd have needed surgery and staples in your scalp," Gran muttered.

I exhaled in relief, but then my brain kickstarted. What if Drea was still in that closet? I might be alive and well, but what about everyone else?

Throwing the blankets off my legs, I was a half-second away from jumping out of the bed when I realized I was in a hospital gown and nothing else. There was definitely a chill running down the center of my back. With a frustrated growl, I flopped back on the bed as I squeezed my hands into fists. Not ideal.

"How is everyone else?" I quickly asked. "Are Aurelia and Theo okay? Where's Drea?"

My friend was probably so stinkin' mad at me right now, but that wasn't what was important. I needed to make sure she'd stayed in that storage closet the whole battle. Skye's warning about Drea dying rang in my head. I didn't even want to think about what might have happened if she'd woken and gotten out before the fighting was over.

"Drea's fine, but we lost a master Lumen," a tired voice announced from the doorway. I jerked my head up to see Aurelia standing there. The normally well put together Portal Master had dark circles under her eyes, her usual perfectly-styled head of tight curls flattened in some areas, and she wore the same clothes as the night before. "It was a bloodbath," she admitted, scrubbing a hand down her face as she entered the room.

I was relieved to hear that Drea was okay, but a person died and that was on me. We never would have been in that building if I hadn't insisted we contact my mom. I was warned it would be dangerous, but I never for a second believed it would result in a loss of life.

"I know what you're thinking," Aurelia said, easily reading the look on my face. "It's not your fault."

I shook my head. "It really is, though."

Gran covered my hand with her own. "You can't blame

yourself. Not a single one of us is guaranteed tomorrow. We're Lumens. It's the job we signed up for."

"Joelle is right," Aurelia said. "And Todd agreed to the mission, he volunteered for it. His sacrifice won't be in vain." Aurelia took a deep breath. "But I have news about your mother. The connection was a bit shaky, but I was able to let her know we're coming for her."

I looked over at Gran. There was a smile on her face. Her eyes were shiny with unshed tears. "Thank you for contacting my daughter," she said to Aurelia.

Aurelia nodded in acknowledgement. "It was the right thing to do. In fact, I wish I'd tried sooner, because what I learned from her in return is priceless. She told me that Apollyon has been diverting human souls to the Netherworld to consume them for power. He must be stopped."

Gran gasped, and I furrowed my brow in confusion.

Both Gran and Aurelia had read my mom's note. We all knew Apollyon had souls in the Netherworld and consumed them to get power. But... diverting souls? Was that a thing? From where? What did that even mean? I didn't know enough about where a soul went when it died to know how this was an issue. The only soul I knew was Skye, and she went straight to Avalon. But maybe that's because she was a Lumen?

"Diverting souls? My mom's note didn't mention that," I croaked, imagining my psychotic father leaning over Skye's ghostly form and slurping her up like a soup.

I shivered at the thought. No wonder Skye didn't want to go to the Netherworld to relay a message to my mom.

Aurelia nodded. "Emery's note revealed he's been consuming souls, which in and of itself is horrific, but she probably didn't know where he was getting them from when she wrote it. According to your mother, he's been stealing souls that are not bound for the Netherworld. That must be what Aurum meant when he charged you with freeing the trapped souls. I didn't realize they were souls that never should have been in the Netherworld to begin with."

The gravity of what she'd just said hit me like a ton of bricks.

"Where were they supposed to go?" I asked.

Aurelia and Gran exchanged a wary look. "For centuries, Lumens have been tasked to fight evil and protect humanity here on Earth, but eternity… that's another matter altogether. We're not privy to that mystery. But from what your mother said, Apollyon found a way to intercept souls that were intended for somewhere else and drag them to his domain."

That sounded awful. What if a soul was supposed to spend eternity in peace in Avalon but instead was taken to a Hell-like realm and eaten? Maybe Skye knew… I mean, she was technically dead.

"And that's not all," Aurelia went on, "your mother also knows *how* Apollyon is diverting the souls. We got cut off before she could tell me though. It was always a priority to rescue Emery from the Netherworld, but now it's even more so. She has information that could stop all of this, and if innocent souls are being taken to and trapped in the Netherworld, then we need to help Tatum release them. I've moved up the timeline. We're going for her in two weeks. You have a lot of catching up to do before then."

I was both excited and terrified by the change in plans. I wanted to rescue my mom... like, yesterday... but I'd just got my butt whipped by a hellhound. Was I really ready to face whatever the Netherworld could throw at me?

I caught my breath.

The hellhound. Gage!

How could I have forgotten about that? I leaned forward, ready to jump out of the bed, and then remembered I wasn't dressed. *Where the heck are my clothes?*

"Gage saved me last night. Did he manage to kill the hellhound, or did it get away?"

Hope started to blossom in my chest. He could be back safely within the Lumen Compound right now. I could see him in a few minutes and get that kiss I'd been craving, right after I chewed him out for leaving me, of course.

A crease formed between Aurelia's scrunched eyebrows. "Gage? He hasn't come back, honey. No one knows where he is."

The hope that had started to grow a moment before leaked out of me like helium from a balloon. "But... he fought the hellhound. Saved me from being bitten."

Aurelia was silent for a moment and then slowly shook

her head. "No. *You* fought the hellhound. Gage wasn't there." The tone of Aurelia's voice softened. "I know you miss him, but you hit your head pretty hard. Things must have been incredibly confusing."

They were, but I was more sure than ever Gage had been in the alleyway with me. I'd seen him battling the hellhound before everything went black. My imagination hadn't made that up. Right? Without Gage, I would have been a chew toy for that monster.

"No, he was there," I insisted.

Aurelia exchanged a look with Gran. I turned to Gran and then back to Aurelia. It was clear neither of them believed me.

"He. Was. There," I pressed them both.

Just because they didn't see him didn't mean that he hadn't been there. But did that mean he fought the hellhound and then left me lying in the alley unconscious and unprotected? That wasn't something Gage would do. He would have at least stuck around to make sure I was safe before taking off again.

Aurelia took a deep breath. "Let's just be glad you weren't bit by that hellhound. Then we'd have a real issue on our hands. Get some rest." She reached out and squeezed my shoulder.

I dropped the Gage subject and she turned to leave the room when I remembered Indigo.

"Aurelia?" I called out, and she turned to me. "My friend… a Shade I met named Indigo, was there and unconscious. She's a good person caught up in a bad crowd. Did she make it?"

I held my breath. I couldn't bear the thought of hearing she died.

Aurelia nodded. "All of the Shades got away," she said before she left the room, saying she had a few more team members she needed to check on.

I had a sinking feeling about all of this. I know Gage wanted his space, but where did he go? He must have stayed in town and was watching over me. He was there last night; I would swear it on my life. He'd pushed that hellhound off of me.

But was he hurt? Was he worse than hurt?

The hellhound had taken me down with ease and I had all my Lumen powers. Granted, Gage had years of training, but none of his abilities or former supernatural strength. He was, by his own admission, a weak human.

Fear pierced my heart. Gage might have said he needed time to figure his life out alone but forget that. I was going after him and nothing was going to stop me.

I hadn't wasted any time getting dressed and busting out of the healing center. I swore up and down to Gran that I was fine, and she let me go. I still had some aches and pains, but I'd also slept for half a day, and so I was ready to rock and roll. Even though Drea and I shared a room, I knocked on our door before entering.

"Come in," she called from within. Gran had said that she'd dropped off a fresh set of clothes for me at the healing center while I was unconscious, so she couldn't be too mad at me… right? Even so, I took a deep breath before pushing open the door.

Drea looked up from her bed and her face clouded with anger the moment she spotted me.

"Hey," I said.

"Hey," she said, and then diverted her attention back to the magazine she'd been flipping through.

Okay, message received. She was definitely still pissed at me. Better to dive into this conversation rather than put it off. I needed Drea's help if I was going to be ready to storm the Netherworld in two weeks and somehow find Gage before then. And also, Drea had quickly become one of the most important people in my life. I didn't like my friend being mad at me.

"Drea, listen, I'm really sorry about knocking you out, but Skye said that if you entered the fight you'd die."

Drea lowered her magazine, and still glared at me, but I think there might have been a hint of softening in her gaze.

Since she was letting me talk, I plowed on: "Skye was right about things going south if we tried to contact my mom, so there was a good chance she was right about your death as well. I wasn't willing to gamble with your life."

She rubbed the back of her head. "You didn't have to

knock me out," she grumbled. "Not all of us have super healing like you do."

I winced. I'll bet her head was still killing her. "Would you really have listened to me if I'd tried to reason with you?" I asked.

She pressed her lips together, and after a small eternity sighed and shook her head. I could see the fight leave her. "No. I would have gone anyway. I guess that means you saved my life."

Skye chose that moment to poof into the room.

"Actually, *I* saved her life. Make sure she knows it was me and not you. You're just the one that almost got her killed by not listening to me in the first place." Skye put one hand on her ghosty hip.

I rolled my eyes. "Skye's here and she wants you to know that it was actually *her* that saved your life."

A tiny smile hovered on the corners of Drea's mouth. "Thanks, Skye," she said.

Skye tried to poke me, but her finger just disappeared into my shoulder. "Don't forget the part about how you were wrong not to listen to me."

"Don't push it," I growled at her.

Drea's gaze bounced around the room, still looking for Skye even though we both knew she wouldn't be able to see her. I pointed to the space next to me where Skye stood to give Drea at least an idea where to look.

Drea's gaze moved back and forth between the spot where Skye stood and me, making it clear she was talking to both of us. "I want your word that if something like this ever happens again, you'll tell me and give me the freedom to make the choice on my own. Got it?"

Skye looked at me: "If I tell you she is going to die if you don't knock her out, then you knock her out again."

I chuckled.

"What did she say?" Drea pressed.

"We'll give you a choice next time," I told her. Hey, a little white lie wasn't going to hurt. I didn't want to deal with this right now when I had soul diversion and Gage on the mind.

I sat on the edge of Drea's bed. "So, I need your help."

"What's up?" she asked as she set her magazine on the nightstand.

I chewed on my lip in nervousness. I didn't want her to think I was crazy too. "I swear Gage was there last night and saved me from the hellhound."

Drea sat up straighter. "Gage? You saw him?"

I nodded, but then sort of shook my head. "I mean, in my defense, I fell out a window so it's a bit fuzzy, but yes I saw him. It had to be him. I was about to get bit, but Gage tackled the hellhound off me and fought it. I blacked out before I really saw what happened."

Drea frowned. "That hellhound was found in four different pieces and Gage doesn't have powers."

I blew out a breath, considering her words. "He's a trained swordsman," I said thoughtfully.

"Okay, let's say Gage saved you last night from the hell-hound, what do you need my help with? Clearly he left you there alone after he sliced and diced the beast, so I know you're not about to ask me to go looking for him with you."

I winced. "Go looking for him with me?"

Drea rolled her eyes, and I put my hands out. "Maybe Dash and Marlow or even Jacob could help too. Drea, he could be hurt, and he didn't really leave me alone, because that place was crawling with Lumens."

I looked to my left, hoping Skye would agree with me, maybe even tell me where he might be, only to realize she was gone.

Awesome. Most unreliable ghost ever.

"Dash can't help, he split town. Marlow is—"

"Dash split town? Where?" I sat up straighter.

Drea shrugged. "He left a weird note under my mom's door about needing to head back to the west coast to check on family."

Chills broke out onto my arms. "Drea, Dash's family is dangerous, he wouldn't go back there."

She must not know his story, at least not the part about how he got his scar, because she was suddenly wearing a very concerned look. I didn't want to share his personal info, but I had a feeling the "Dash going back to LA" thing was a total lie.

"He's with Gage," I growled.

"What?"

I just knew it. I felt it in my bones. "They've been all chummy, going on walks together. I'll bet Gage got hurt last night trying to save me and called Dash."

Drea gave me a pointed look. "They went on *one* walk together and it was more of Dash following behind Gage. I doubt they are besties."

I opened my mouth to speak when there was a knock at the door. "Come in!" Drea yelled.

The door opened and Aurelia stood there with one of the master Lumens from last night. His arm was bandaged, and he nodded when he saw us sitting on the bed.

Aurelia looked slightly worried. "Tatum, I've just been going over Master Hunter Hartland's debrief and he said something I thought you would want to know."

I looked at the master Lumen with confusion.

He cleared his throat. "I was the one that found you and took you to the healing center."

Oh.

I stood. "Oh my gosh, thank you."

He held out his good hand to stop me, as if rejecting my thanks. "I wouldn't have been able to do that if not for the Alston boy."

I froze, every single muscle in my body going rigid.

"Gage? You saw him there?" *I knew I wasn't crazy!*

The Lumen nodded. "He was covered in blood, screaming for help. When I tried to fly him to safety, he refused and said to take you. By the time I went back for him, he was gone."

I sagged into the bed as Drea gasped behind me.

"Sorry," he muttered.

"No." I shook my head. "Thank you for telling me."

Aurelia dismissed him and then looked at Drea and me. "I'll put out a call to all Lumens working tonight. If anyone sees him, they'll bring him to the healing center."

I just nodded, numb, as Aurelia said goodbye and closed the door when she left.

When the door clicked shut, Drea finally spoke: "All right, where do we start looking?"

Relief spread through my limbs, and the numbness fled. I knew she'd be with me, and there was no way I could sit by idly if he was hurt, which was possible since the master Lumen confirmed Gage had been covered in blood. His or the hellhound's? I'd been too terrified to ask.

"I was thinking Gage's safe house. The one on Long Island."

I thought back to our almost-kiss there and how he'd broken the chains from my feet with his talisman.

Looking determined, Drea shoved off of her bed and grabbed her cell phone.

"You're a good friend," I told her with a smile as we stepped out into the hallway.

She raised one eyebrow. "The best. You knock me out yesterday and today I'm helping you look for your boyfriend."

My belly warmed at the word "boyfriend." Technically, Gage had never asked me out, but I kept my mouth shut. Now wasn't the time to argue semantics.

The trip to Long Island took forever and wasn't exactly fruitful. Drea picked the lock on the small bungalow, and we rushed inside only to find out that there wasn't a scrap of furniture left in the place. The marks on the carpet where the couch and bed used to be were still there though, as were two full trash bags on the kitchen floor. We ripped open the bags looking for clues. The only thing the trash revealed was food that hadn't rotted yet, giving us confirmation that he'd recently moved out. Probably even within the last day.

Did he know I'd come here? He knew that *I* knew where his safe house was, and so was that why he moved? Or maybe he'd had a run-in with his dad and was trying to avoid him.

"I don't see anything here. Maybe check some other places he might be?" I called to Drea, who was investigating a different part of the house.

"Hang on. Come look at this." Drea's voice held a note of fear that spiked my heart rate.

I hurried down the long hallway to the bathroom where Drea was, and gasped when my gaze fell on the blood-stained tub.

Streaks of blood and thin black strands lined the tub, and there were gashes and broken tiles along the shower wall.

"Is that *hair?*" I stepped closer, my heart in my throat.

Please don't be Gage's hair and blood.

Drea crossed the room, sidestepping me because I'd frozen in horror. She ran her hand over the white surface of the tub, scooping up some of the strands. Bringing them to her nose, she inhaled and then rubbed them between her fingers.

Okay, slightly weird, but I was down for it if it led us to Gage.

Please don't lick it.

"It's fur." She sounded as confused as I felt.

Fur? I glanced at the gashes on the side of the shower wall, realizing they could easily be claw marks. I could think of several demonic creatures that had fur and claws.

"Looks like a demon attack went down here," I said, trying not to fully lose my mind. "The master Lumen who saw Gage said he was covered in blood. What if Gage's blood somehow attracted a demon, or his dad sent one here after him?"

She cocked her head to the side, her gaze thoughtful. "It's

plausible. If he killed another demon, the body would have just disappeared."

I wasn't sure of anything at the moment. "Maybe this is just leftover blood and fur from the hellhound attack?" I didn't have an explanation for the broken tiles, but maybe they weren't even related.

"But then where is Gage now?" Drea asked.

I shrugged. This was all I had—the only place I could think of to look.

I ran my tongue over my teeth as I tried to reason the rest out and think of who else might have an idea of where he went. Would Gage contact Indigo for help? Probably not. He wouldn't want to involve her in his mess.

I paused as something occurred to me. Could Indigo have told Arthur about Gage being alive, and *that's* how his dad knew to send demons after him?

Indigo was the one Shade that I knew for sure knew about Gage being alive. She might have even known about this house.

What if… *no!*

I shook my head, immediately dismissing the suspicion before it even had a chance to fully form and grow in my mind. I wasn't going to think that of Indigo. I'd spent time with her; she was good, even if she was a Shade. She'd risked her life to bring Gage to Lumen Academy when he was dying, and I'd seen the indecision in her eyes when she was protecting that portal. I trusted her. End of story.

"I don't know where Gage is now," I said. "The only

thing that brought him out before was when I was in danger with the hellhound—" I stopped mid-sentence, and a grin pulled at my lips.

"No," Drea said, shaking her head hard enough that her tight curls slapped her cheeks. "I don't like that look."

It was a crazy idea, but if Gage *was* watching over me, it might draw him out.

"I'll do something dangerous in public and he'll try to save me again. It's too random that he was there when I was attacked by that hellhound. He must be watching over me."

Drea just laughed. "What are you going to do, go skydiving without a parachute and hope he catches you? Besides, he's clearly injured and can't just jump in front of another hellhound for you. Come on, Tatum. Plan B. What else you got?"

This *was* my plan B. Plan A was coming here, and I was running out of options.

"What if I went to Shade Academy and tried to walk inside and see his dad? Think that would bring him out?" I mused.

Drea face-palmed herself and pointed to the tub. "He's probably unconscious somewhere healing from wounds. That's a lot of blood."

Crap, she was right, but I still had to try. I glanced at all the red in the tub. I wanted to lie to myself and say that blood probably wasn't his, but if Gage was hurt, then all the more reason to try and find him. "I'll just get close to Shade Academy, but I won't go inside."

"Yeah, you can't go inside. You're a Lumen now remember? The wards would eat you alive," Drea added.

Right. Another element of danger. That was good. If Gage was watching over me and able, then surely he would intervene.

"It's worth a shot." I moved to go to the front door and Drea snaked her arm out and stopped me.

When I looked into her brown eyes, I saw compassion there. "Tatum, I care about Gage, I really do. And I want him safely back with us, but not at the expense of your life. If he doesn't show up, we'll drop this and let him come home when he's ready. Agreed?"

I swallowed hard. Drop looking for Gage? After knowing he was possibly hurt because he jumped in front of a hellhound for me? No way. I knew Drea was just trying to protect me, but I couldn't give up on Gage. No matter how stupid that note was and his decision to leave.

I flicked my gaze back to the bathtub and all the blood there.

"Okay," I lied to her for the second time today.

I couldn't stop looking for him. Just like if Drea were in this situation, I wouldn't stop looking for her. I was going to find him, even if only to smack him in his beautiful face and tell him he could never kiss me again as punishment for leaving me and basically breaking up with me on a piece of paper.

"This is crazy. *You* are crazy," Drea repeated for the tenth time as we rounded the corner to Shade Academy. I eyed each passerby, searching for Gage or anyone wearing a hat and hoodie and looking like they were trying to go incognito.

I stopped at the gelato cart that Gage and his buddies had once been at and absentmindedly ordered a scoop of chocolate.

Pulling out my phone, I texted Indigo.

Me: *You okay from last night?*

Her reply was immediate.

Indigo: *Yeah, but can't talk to you anymore. Delete my number. I'm blocking you. For your own good. Bye, friend.*

It was like a shot to the chest. First Gage and now Indigo.

Me: *Wait, have you heard from Gage?*

I shot a text back quickly, but no reply came. Tears welled in my eyes, but I sucked those little weak droplets back and then growled.

"Whoa. What's going on?" Drea asked, and I handed her my phone.

Indigo was a friend, something I'd never had a large supply of, and her abrupt cutoff hurt. Bad. Even though she'd said she was doing this for my own good, I still couldn't numb the sting of her blocking my number.

Drea frowned and handed me my phone. "I'm sorry. We should go now."

The gelato cart guy handed me my scoop and I paid him, scowling at the black skyscraper before me.

Stupid academy for glorified demon security guards!

This plan wasn't working. Gage hadn't appeared like I'd hoped, and now I didn't know what to do next.

Maybe he was fine. He was a badass with his sword and he'd cut that hellhound to pieces. The blood on his clothes was probably from the hellhound. After he'd gotten that master Lumen to fly me to safety, he probably went to his place in Long Island to clean up and then left town to go find himself, or whatever his early quarter-life crisis entailed. Maybe he wasn't following me like I thought. Maybe he'd happened on me falling out the window by chance as he was leaving town…

But the blood… the fur… *that* was real. Dash leaving town abruptly was real too and didn't make a lick of sense after he'd divulged he would never go back to LA. Or maybe the problem was just that I wasn't in enough danger? If Gage was looking after me like I'd hoped, maybe I needed to up the ante.

"How close can I get without getting zapped by the wards or whatever?" I asked Drea.

Her eyebrows shot up. "Technically, the doorway but—"

I waltzed across the street licking my gelato in full view of every person in Soho as Drea yelled my name.

Come on, Gage, I mentally taunted. *What we had was real, you wouldn't just leave. Would you?*

I made it to the other side of the sidewalk and a few students stared at me. One of them looked familiar.

My heart pounded in my chest as I walked another step closer to the front door of Shade Academy. Two steps. Three.

As I neared the door, a pressure settled over my skin.

The protection wards.

I lifted my leg to take the final step and an arm hooked under my armpit.

"Are you insane!" Dash's familiar voice growled into my ear as he dragged me away from the door and into a neighboring alley.

"Looks like you're not chillin' on the West Coast after all, huh?" I taunted. My eyes raked over his face and the bruises and scratches there. A small snake of anxiety started to slither in my belly. Why was he all banged up?

Guilt marred Dash's features.

"Yeah, Dash…" Drea's annoyed voice filtered down the alley as Dash cleared his throat, his cheeks pinking. "I thought you had to help family."

Dash sighed. "I had to get away for a bit and help a friend. I didn't want a lot of questions asked."

My heart leapt into my throat. "Which friend? And why do you look like you've been in a demon fight?"

A conflicted look crossed over his face and then he sighed. "Gage got injured, he called and I—"

I stepped closer. "Where is he? Is he okay?"

Dash sucked his bottom lip into his mouth and stayed silent.

Drea advanced on him. "Dash Slate, we are a team. Gage may not have powers, but as far as I'm concerned he's a Lumen and we take care of our own. If he's hurt, then let us help."

My heart swelled at the way Drea was standing up for Gage.

Dash scrubbed a hand down his face and then nodded. "Follow me."

Gage was staying only a few subway stops over, off Canal Street. Dash led us up to a seedy apartment that was directly over a pawn shop whose window was so frosted with grime from the outside you couldn't see in.

When we finally reached the apartment door, Dash stopped with his hand on the knob and looked at me. "He's in a dark place. Go easy on him, okay? I've been there."

His words shocked me, and the reaming that I was about to do on Gage for leaving me that stupid note suddenly diminished. My annoyance with him morphed into genuine concern.

When we stepped into the apartment, the coppery scent of blood immediately hit my nostrils and I rushed forward. Knocking Dash out of the way, I fumbled through the apartment in a blind panic until I spotted Gage.

He lay on the bed, covered in a mass of crusted gashes and barely healing wounds.

"Dash, he needs a healer!" Drea sucked in a breath behind me.

Dash rubbed the bridge of his nose, his shoulders hunched with fatigue. "Rose just left. He didn't want to be brought into the healing center."

Drea's eyes widened. "This is *after* the healer?"

I was flooded with so much emotion that the physical act of keeping from crying was painful.

"Yeah. She saved his life." Dash's words brought me to my knees before Gage.

I reached out and held one of his limp hands in mine. He appeared to be fast asleep, eyes closed and chest slowly rising and falling.

"You big idiot. Who takes on a hellhound when they have no powers?" My throat tightened as I took in the sight of him. The gashes were deep and a few inches apart, indicating they were claw marks.

One of Gage's eyes cracked open, and his gaze roamed over my face, making hope spread through my chest.

"Must have been to save a pretty girl." His voice was hoarse, but damn him, he was still charming, even on his death bed.

I grinned, but then the smile fell from my face. "Not pretty enough for you to stay."

Drea and Dash simultaneously cleared their throats and then left the room, closing the door behind them.

Gage opened both eyes and then started to sit up, wincing in pain when he did.

"No, lay down." I tried to gently push him back down, but he growled at me and sat up fully, causing some of his cuts to weep fresh blood.

Dash said to go easy, and I went right for the jugular. *Good one, Tatum.*

"Listen…" Gage started.

I shook my head. "No, *you* listen. We don't need to date, or kiss, or be whatever, okay? You're clearly not in the right mindset for a relationship, so it's no biggie. But you could have just told me that instead of running off." I folded my arms over my chest. "We can just be friends, but that doesn't mean you have to leave the safety of Lumen Academy."

Gage's eyes flared to life, looking greener than I'd ever seen them. "Is that what you want? No more kisses, no more *whatever*? Just to be friends?"

My heart ached at the thought of it. "I'm cool with whatever you want," I lied. Third lie of the day. I was on a freaking roll.

His gaze narrowed. "I want to kiss you and never stop."

His admission made the breath whoosh out of me, and I couldn't help the grin that graced my face. "I mean, I could be down for that too."

The corners of Gage's lips turned up and he leaned forward, wincing in pain as he did. Popping up on my knees, I came to him, letting him take my face in his hands. Instead of kissing me, he rested his forehead on mine and exhaled. "Tate, I never wanted to hurt you. I just want to be the kind of man you deserve. A strong man who can protect you, who is your equal."

"That kind of man stays no matter how hard it gets."

Tilting his head, he brushed his lips over mine. It was barely a kiss, and his injuries forced him to pull away after only one brief joining of our mouths, but even so, the pain he'd caused me over the last few days started to slowly leak out of me.

People weren't perfect, and Gage was far from it, but there was too much potential for me to walk away over one mistake.

"Tate," he breathed.

I swallowed hard, looking him in the eyes.

"I'm sorry I ran off. It's the only thing I know how to do when things get tough," he confessed. "The way Aurelia sidelined me like I was some newbie who'd never seen a demon... it was the straw that broke the camel's back."

I reached out to find a spot on his skin that wasn't injured, and stroked his arm. "It must have been tough losing your wings and whatever else happened up there," I said, referring to his time in Avalon, which he hadn't yet talked about.

A pained look swept across Gage's face. "You have no idea."

"I'm a good listener." I leaned forward. "I could try to understand."

Gage sighed. "It's... still a bit raw and hard to explain. Give me some time and I'll tell you."

I took a deep breath. It wasn't exactly what I wanted to hear, but promising to tell me later was a start. I wasn't going to beat him up for that.

"Let's go back to Lumen Academy. You can train with the sword, show Aurelia how powerful you can be, and she'll put you on our team. I know it."

He needed purpose, and I was trying to give that to him.

He nodded. "Too bad she didn't see me cut that hellhound to pieces. She might have cleared me for battle right there."

"I knew it the whole time! Even before one of her master Lumens said he saw you, I knew you'd saved me from that beast." I reached out to smack his arm and then thought better of it.

Gage gave me a halfcocked smile. "Turns out I can't really leave you. Only stalk you from a few blocks away."

"Slightly creepy, but in this case totally romantic." I grinned. He chuckled and then grabbed his stomach with a pinched expression.

"Okay, lay back and rest," I said, and this time he let me coax him to lie back on the bed. "We're going to the Netherworld to save my mom in two weeks, and I want you by my side."

Would Aurelia allow that? I had no idea, but we both needed something to look forward to, so I would figure out a way to make it happen.

The shockwave hit me right in the chest. My back slammed into the concrete wall before I'd even registered that I was thrown off my feet. I landed in a heap on the floor, coughing and sputtering as I struggled to suck air back into my lungs.

"Always be on guard," Marlow said as she reached down to help me up, the least she could do after laying me out with one of her shockwaves. "Demons pack a hard punch, and some of the higher level ones have some really scary powers. Same thing goes for Shades. They won't think twice about putting you down, and since it's now common knowledge you can close portals, they're going to be gunning for you twice as hard as anyone else in a fight."

Great.

Pain lanced my side as I got to my feet. I took a shallow breath and gingerly prodded the sore spot. "I think I might have cracked a rib," I complained.

Skye poofed into the training gym, her hair up in a sleek ponytail. "Then it's a good thing you heal fast," she quipped.

Yeah, beat up Tatum because she heals fast. Awesome.

Due to my super angelic healing, my friends were taking the train Tatum thing to epic levels. They didn't hold back.

I let out a humorless laugh. "Yeah, good thing. Hey, Skye."

"Skye's here?" Marlow's head snapped up and she did what everyone did when they heard Skye was in the room: search the space like they'd be able to see her. I pointed in Skye's direction so Marlow at least knew the general area to look. "Ask her about the archangel-Watcher dating rules. I want to know if I should be saving myself for one of those hunks or not."

Skye perked up. "Tell her that it's kinda frowned upon but not really off-limits. Definitely worth the wait, at least in my opinion. I mean, we've all seen some of the archangels. Day-um, right?" She fanned herself.

Oh no. I'd been in this situation before. If I didn't shut this down immediately I was going to get stuck translating a gossip session between these two.

"Skye, why are you dressed like that?" I asked, abruptly changing the subject. Usually Skye showed up runway ready. Today she was dressed in workout clothes similar to what Marlow and I wore.

Skye flipped her ponytail over her shoulder. "I'm here to take you to your training with Aurum, and I'll be assisting."

My stomach bottomed out. "Training where?"

I hadn't seen the winged lion since we'd killed that level ten together.

Skye chuckled. "We're obviously going to Avalon. You don't train with a guardian here on Earth."

Avalon? I straightened. I hadn't been back since I'd ascended, and Drea's lesson came back to me then about only being allowed to go once.

"I thought you could only go for your Ascension Ceremony and that was it?"

Skye stepped closer to me. "You're a special cupcake, you get special rules."

I rolled my eyes. "What kind of training?"

Skye planted her hands on her hips and shot me an *are-you-dumb?* look. "Destroying the Netherworld and freeing trapped souls is no small task. Did you think Avalon was just going to let you bumble around without proper training and preparation?"

I blinked back at her. *Well... yeah.* I'd assumed Avalon was responsible for doling out the missions and then left it up to us Watchers to fulfill them. I did have all the fancy swirly marks. Part of me assumed that was all the help I was going to get.

"I *am* getting training," I argued, and pointed to Marlow. To be fully honest, Aurum was hella powerful and that freaked me out a little. I could probably get killed if I trained with him.

Marlow's brows pinched in confusion as she listened to only one side of our conversation.

"And that would definitely be enough if you'd grown up at Lumen Academy and this was a regular mission. But lucky you, you're a super special one-of-a-kind gal and get all the extra attention. So, get your game face on, girl, because this is happening."

Just then the door to the gym swung open and Gage entered. The butterflies in my stomach instantly awoke and started to run amok.

He looked *good*. Real good.

I frowned.

Maybe a little *too* good for someone who'd been bedridden only yesterday. We brought Gage back to the Lumen Compound three days ago. He'd been in the healing center ever since. I'd visited him last night and he'd definitely looked better than the day I'd found him, but not *this* well. Dang, those healers were good at their job. What had once been deep gashes on his face, chest, and arms were now only very faint lines. And rather than sporting matching shiners, he had only the slightest tinge of bruising under his eyes. My frown deepened as he walked toward us without so much as a hitch in his gait.

"You look good," I said when he reached us, meaning how well he'd healed, but Gage took it in a different direction. He looked me up and down, slowly, and I swear the temperature in the room jumped at least ten degrees. In a black sports bra and high waisted yoga pants, I suddenly felt nearly naked.

"So do you," he replied huskily, his gaze stopping on my

mouth and holding. His tongue darted out to swipe across his bottom lip and I almost spontaneously combusted. Any concerns about the speed of his healing completely left my brain, along with any other thought that didn't include his lips pressed against mine.

I swayed toward him. I wanted a taste. Now.

"I think I need to get a hose to cool you two off," said Skye's voice, shaking me from my Gage-induced stupor, and I jerked back a step, remembering we weren't alone. Marlow and Skye were still there. Embarrassment instantly washed over me.

"That's some major eye fu—"

"Skye," I shrieked, batting a hand at her only to have it ghost through her shoulder and a chill to sweep up my arm. Yuck. I hated that feeling.

Something started to chirp from the other side of the room.

"Shoot, that's me," Marlow said. She jogged over to her gym bag and pulled out her phone, tapping the screen to turn off her alarm that sounded like a chirping bird.

"Gotta go," she said. "I have a class in five. But good job today, Tatum. You're really coming along." She turned to Gage. "It's nice to see you up and moving around. I hear Dash is looking forward to testing your sword skills when you're ready."

"Oh, I'm ready," he said confidently. "There's a thing or two I'm looking forward to teaching you Lumens. The first being how to fight dirty."

Marlow chuckled, and then sped out of the room with a wave.

Once she left, Skye started to circle Gage. "You know, I never paid too close attention to Gage since he was a Shade and all, but I can totally see why you're into him." She stopped directly behind him and openly ogled his butt. "Nice. I approve."

"Oh my gosh, Skye. Stop." I mean… she wasn't wrong, he had an amazing ass, but even so, I didn't like her talking about it. There was just something extra uncomfortable about spirit-Skye checking out my kinda-sorta-maybe boyfriend.

Gage's perceptive gaze didn't miss the slight flush of anger on my cheeks. "She's talking about us, isn't she?"

"Not exactly."

A grin spread on his face. "She's checking me out, then?"

"Ohh, smart too. I like that," Skye said as she snuck a peek at his package and then wiggled her brows. At that, a ball of possessiveness caught fire in my gut, and I shot Skye a death glare, but all it did was cause her to giggle.

"Skye, seriously, if you don't stop I'm going to make it my mission to find out how to stab a spirit," I growled.

"Too easy," she said in a singsong voice. "I'll give you a few minutes with lover boy, and then we're outta here. Aurum is waiting." She disappeared with a wink.

Right. Aurum. Winged lion who shot lasers from his eyes.

I swear, Gage had the ability to scramble my brain like no one else. It was one of his special skills, at least where I was concerned. The moment he walked through the gym door I'd completely forgotten Skye was here to take me to see the guardian angel.

"I think I like this look on you," Gage said as he prowled toward me.

"What look?" I asked as he tugged me into his arms.

Gage's grin turned downright scandalous. "The jealous one."

I started to protest, but he cut me off.

"It's hot."

My throat went dry when I caught the look in Gage's eyes. The green practically smoldered. In that moment I wanted nothing else than to explore this connection between us. We'd hardly had a minute alone since we'd reunited. My schedule was packed before Aurelia contacted my mom, but that was nothing compared to what it was like now. Practically every minute of my waking hours was filled with training, or classes, or even more training.

I ached to just have some time alone to be with Gage. To just be a girl hanging out with a guy she was into. To maybe do something utterly normal like to go on a date or watch a movie.

Gage angled his head down, smoothly lining his lips up with my own. Leaning forward, I brushed my lips across his, peppering him with a small kiss before pulling away. Skye could pop back at any moment and drag me away. I wasn't up for starting something I couldn't finish, so I kept our kiss brief. I was determined that the next big kiss between us wouldn't be rushed, or interrupted, or born out of a near-death experience.

Heaving a sigh, I pulled out of Gage's arms. "I've got to go train with my guardian, Aurum, now. That's why Skye was here."

"Aurum?" Gage asked, the seductive look slipping right off his face as concern flooded his gaze.

Right. Gage wasn't there at the club. I didn't even know if he knew who Aurum was.

I started to explain what happened the night he took off, but he stopped me again. "Oh yeah, at Wild Ones. Dash told me what happened. I didn't know you would be training with the guardian though."

A nervous laugh bubbled up my throat. "Neither did I."

Of course, that was the exact moment Skye decided to poof back into the room. She held her hand over her eyes. "Is it okay to look? Everyone is dressed, right?"

I rolled my eyes at her antics.

"How long will you be gone," Gage asked, unaware Skye had returned.

"A few hours. A few days. Who really knows," Skye answered for me.

"A few days?" I shouted, jarring Gage. "You can't mean that."

"Days?" Gage echoed, his voice filled with the same amount of alarm as mine.

"Gotcha again," Skye said with a laugh. "No, you won't be gone more than an hour or two. Aurum is the leader of the guardians of Avalon. He doesn't have days to waste with you."

That was an insulting way of saying it, but it was good. I didn't want to be gone for too long.

"Skye says an hour or two," I said to Gage. "She was messing with me."

He nodded, but his mouth was pressed into a straight line, clearly broadcasting his displeasure.

I knew why I was anxious about meeting with Aurum; the winged lion was intimidating. But I didn't really understand Gage's apprehension. Maybe he just didn't like the idea of me jumping to another realm, especially when it was one he wouldn't be able to reach? He was always so protective over me.

"Let's go, Tatum." Skye went to grab my arm and drag me out of the room, but her hand just went through my bicep. She smiled when I shivered from her ghosty touch. "If you don't hop to it, I'll do that again."

"Okay, okay," I said with my hands in the air as if that would ward her off.

Man, she was a bossy spirit.

"I gotta go," I said to Gage.

He shoved his hands in his pockets. "Sure. I'll go find Dash. We have a sword training session. See you when you get back?"

I nodded, my gaze lingering on him before I turned to follow Skye out of the gym. He offered me a smile of encouragement, but it didn't meet his eyes. Something told me my maybe-boyfriend didn't like it when I went off doing potentially dangerous things.

Skye talked to me for the whole short walk from the academy to the sanctuary in the middle of the Lumen Compound.

As we approached the sanctuary steps, I waved to the two guards in front of the large wooden doors, and they nodded as I passed. Aurelia had given the order that I could enter any time I pleased.

The blue and white swirling portal still made my breath catch every time I saw it. I was so glad it had been restored when Gage had come back. Just like the first time I entered the sanctuary on the day of my Ascension, I could smell flowers and sunshine and hear a faint melody drifting through the air.

The portal to Avalon called to me.

Whatever anxiety I had about seeing Aurum again melted away as I wandered toward the bright vortex.

"Hold on a minute, we're not going the same place you visited last time. I need to work some of my soul magic."

Soul magic?

I didn't know what Skye was talking about, but I stopped to let her do her thing.

A look of concentration overtook her face, and after about half a minute of silence she lifted an arm toward the portal. A tendril of white light leaked from her fingertips and leisurely floated through the air. When the light reached the vortex, the whole portal pulsed and then turned a beautiful lavender shade.

Wow.

"All right, now we're ready," she said.

"What did you just do?" I asked.

"I changed this portal's destination to a new location in Avalon. It's only temporary though, so we should get going." With that, she bounced forward and then jumped into the portal ahead of me. I only paused a moment before following after her.

There was a tug at my navel, a serene feeling spread over me as a golden light flashed, and then my feet hit the ground. I looked up and gasped. I was standing in the middle of the most beautiful meadow I'd ever seen. It was like I'd been transported to New Zealand or something. Tall grasses and lavender bushes blew in the wind as the flat meadow gave way to a hill. Off to the left was a giant mountain with a trickling waterfall. It was so peaceful I could lie down and take a nap right here.

"Hello, Tatum." Aurum's voice pulled my attention to my right. He stood before me fully covered in battle gear, and I gulped. Skye was at his side, hand on a weapon, and I was shocked to see that she was no longer semi-transparent but looked fully corporeal.

"Skye, you're…"

She grinned. "This is how I look here. How all Watchers look when we pass from the Earth realm and return home."

Whoa.

"Hey." I waved shyly at Aurum.

Aurum nodded to me and then stepped forward, lifting up his paw before slamming it to the ground. The grass shook, and suddenly metal walls grew up from the soil and started to stack sky-high.

What the...?

I ducked, crouching in case one of the panels fell on me. One by one, the pieces of steel stacked on top of each other, creating a dome around us and only stopping to leave the top open for natural light. We were now encased in a giant stadium of sorts, and I no longer felt like a peaceful nap was on the agenda. Armor suddenly appeared on my body as well, seemingly out of nowhere.

What kind of crazy Avalon magic is this?

"Welcome to the arena," Aurum bellowed. "Here you will go through simulations and training to prepare you for the task ahead."

I was already tired just thinking about it. Couldn't we have some coffee and just get to know each other first? He was jumping right into the hard stuff, and my muscles were still sore from my sparring session with Marlow.

"The task of freeing the trapped souls of the Netherworld?" I confirmed.

His upper lip quirked, baring a sharp fang. Was that a smile or did he want to eat me?

"And also destroy the Netherworld and defeat Apollyon," he said matter-of-factly.

"Yeah we can't forget that," I added dryly.

The guardian's wings snapped out, and I bristled. "I have made hardy warriors out of absolute buffoons. I take this job very seriously. I will not fail you."

Okay, that was kind of sweet... minus the buffoon part. He and Skye shared some personality traits.

"Thanks," I smiled.

Skye stepped away from the guardian and began to circle behind me as Aurum's eyes lit up with an eerie bluish glow.

Please don't eye laser beam me.

I tensed. "Okay, now it kinda seems like you guys are about to jump me or something."

"Attacks in the real world won't come with a warning," he said calmly as Skye let loose with a battle cry behind me.

What the hell?

I spun to see my friend wearing the look of a psychotic murderer. Her face was contorted into a determined grimace, her sword raised high over her head as she came at me.

"Skye!" I ripped my sword from my arm tattoo and yanked it up to defend myself. Just as she was bearing down on me, a cream colored paw batted the back of my knees and my legs crumpled, bringing me to the ground.

I growled as I fell at an awkward angle and my elbow jabbed into my side. Skye's sword came down blindingly fast and I barely had a moment to lift my metal-cuffed arm and intercept her attack.

"Geez, Skye, this is practice!" I yelled at her as I stared in horror at the dent she put in my armor.

"I agree," Aurum's voice came from behind me. "Skye, you're at a ten and I need you at a six."

That was rich coming from the dude who'd just side-swiped my legs.

Skye sulked but nodded. "Sorry, I got excited."

I got up and brushed off my pants, turning to glare at my guardian. "I thought you were on my side? What's with the leg swipe?"

I'd remember that.

He grinned, this time displaying all of his teeth. "Your father won't go easy on you, so neither will I."

I exhaled deeply, trying to get my emotions in check. "How often are we doing these little practices?" I crouched and readied myself for another attack.

Aurum crouched as well, mirroring my stance. "Daily, twice daily if needed."

My eyes felt like they might bug out of my head. Twice daily? I was going to die with that amount of training, but there was no time to complain, because I saw a barely visible shockwave burst from Aurum's forehead. I dropped to the floor, lying flat against the grass as the attack sailed over my head.

"Hah!" I started to celebrate and then a yelp ripped from Skye behind me as she got knocked over by the shockwave I'd dodged. I didn't even try to hide my smile as I shoved back to my feet.

It seemed like these little surprise attacks went on for hours, but in reality was probably only twenty minutes or so. I was shockwave slammed, attacked with fire, nearly stabbed, and knocked down at least a dozen times. My skin was littered with bruises and minor cuts. I was filthy and sweaty and panting for air when Aurum called a halt to this part of my training.

"Let's move to another, more important training." He gestured for Skye to step over to him.

I tensed, ready for them to both try to kill or maim me in some way or another.

"You can relax now," Aurum said.

"Hah! Nice try." I gripped my sword, feeling my blood pressure rise.

I was cagey. No one would get the drop on me.

Skye lowered her weapon and then set it on the grass. "No, seriously, this is soul magic practice now."

I relaxed, but only a little. "Soul magic?"

Aurum sat on his back legs, giving his wings a little shake as he settled, and peered at me. "Every living thing has an energy, and that energy is condensed into a unique signature called a soul."

I knew what a soul was. Or at least the concept of it.

"Except for like trees and plants and stuff," Skye added.

Aurum tipped his head in agreement. "Although there is a sort of group soul magic involved in those, but yes, Skye, good point."

The guardian lifted a paw, indicating Skye. "Skye's soul

is in Avalon where it belongs, which is why she is solid here. If you were to really concentrate right now, using the same magic you use to make portals, you could connect with Skye's soul energy."

Skye winced, as if preparing for me to reach out and spiritually grab her or something.

I raised one eyebrow. "You want me to *connect* with Skye's soul?"

Aurum nodded once and then said nothing. Tough crowd.

"Why exactly?"

Skye groaned. "Because you can't free the souls from the Netherworld if you don't even know what a soul feels like!"

Okay, fair point. Did I want to know what Skye's soul felt like?

Not really. But here goes nothing.

I pinched my eyes closed for a moment and then took a deep breath, feeling for the power I normally used to make a portal.

"That's it, now don't open or close anything. Just exist with the energy," Aurum coaxed me, and I held back my chuckle at the Yoda vibes he was giving off.

I called the energy up and then did nothing, just left it there to permeate my entire being. When I opened my eyes, I gasped. There was a thick silvery cord going from me to Skye and then also me to Aurum. It was like an umbilical cord waving through the air and disappearing into their chests.

I sensed Skye's nervousness that I would screw this up, and also Aurum's bravery and shock over something. I could *feel* their emotions.

"You connected with us both on the first try." He sounded pleased, and a warm feeling filtered through our new bond that I took to be encouragement.

I grinned, feeling like I'd gotten a gold star on my assignment. I was about to say something when suddenly the walls of the stadium shook and the cords between us snapped.

What the heck?

One by one, the panels dropped, folding in on each other, slamming into the ground. It wasn't until a flicker of fear washed over Aurum's face that I realized he wasn't the one collapsing the arena.

A voice boomed as if on a loudspeaker. "I'm coming for you, daughter. You will serve me and my kingdom and not the traitors of Avalon."

Chills ran the length of my entire body as a metal panel slammed to the ground in front of Aurum.

Aurum lifted his head and roared the most terrifying and commanding sound I'd ever heard, and the shaking stopped. The panels were half stacked, half fallen when the guardian met my no doubt frightened gaze.

"I think that's all for today, Tatum," Aurum said. He looked to Skye, who nodded.

I shook my head. "Whoa, wait a second, how was Apollyon able to do that? Is he *here*, in Avalon?" I turned in a circle, scanning the area but not seeing anyone else besides the three of us.

Aurum looked up into the bright sunlight and then back into my gaze. "No, he's not here. The four realms are all connected. He is the master of the fourth realm, and therefore has a small amount of power over the other three."

I frowned, processing his words. "Four realms? You mean two. Avalon and the Netherworld?" It hit me then. "Oh, and Earth. So three?"

Skye chewed her lip, looking nervously at the guardian.

"Cael and the others don't think you can handle too much information all at once, but I believe they underestimate you," he shared.

That wasn't cool. Did Skye also think I couldn't handle hearing stuff?

I glared at her, and shame colored her cheeks.

"Four realms?" I pressed him.

He nodded. "Earth, Avalon, the Netherworld, and Tartarus."

I swayed on my feet as anxiety gripped me. "Tartarus? What's that?"

"You might know it as Purgatory. It's a holding realm, a neutral place where all souls go to be judged," he said.

Purgatory? "But… so Apollyon's been…"

Aurum nodded. "He's been diverting each and every soul from Tartarus to the Netherworld, where they suffer forever and are robbed of their chance at eternal peace."

Anger flared up inside of me, but I tamped it down and

nodded. I already knew Apollyon had been diverting souls, my mother had told Aurelia that, but I had no idea where from until now.

"So, Tartarus is just empty?" I asked.

"Yes. And it will remain that way until you release the souls to go back there." He pawed the ground twice with his massive paw, showing his frustration with the current state of things. "The Netherworld didn't even exist until Apollyon created it," he continued. "It was only ever supposed to be Avalon and Tartarus. Most souls make it directly to Avalon from Tartarus, and the ones who don't stay where they are until they've earned their Ascension."

"Earned their Ascension? But they're already dead, so how would they even do that?"

"Hey," Skye said, looking offended as she crossed her arms over her chest.

I grimaced and then shot her an apologetic half-smile. I didn't mean to offend her; it was just hard to remember she was technically dead when the girl still had so much life in her.

"A soul can still change, even after death," Aurum said, drawing my attention back to him.

All this stuff was really deep and starting to make my head pound. This was information that Aurelia and the top Lumens didn't even know, but Aurum was telling *me*. It was too much to process on the spot, but I still wanted to know as much as he would tell me.

"Where is Tartarus? Can I go there?" If I was going to be sending souls back there, I should at least check it out.

Aurum looked sad. "It's lost. We haven't been able to find it since the Netherworld was created hundreds of years ago."

Lost! How did you lose an entire realm?

Oh, I was going to kill that man who called himself my father. I was going to kill him good.

After Skye and I portaled back to the academy, I sat in the sanctuary for a good ten minutes just staring at the wall and letting my mind chew on what I'd just learned. The Netherworld didn't exist until my evil father created it and then rerouted the souls to go there? How much more vile and wicked could someone get?

Skye had poofed out of existence minutes ago, and when I finally dragged my butt outside, I went in search of Gage. Maybe a date night was in order if we could find the time?

I checked the library first and then the gym, but he was nowhere to be found. It wasn't until I peeked into the third training room that I spotted him. He was sparring with Dash. Both guys were shirtless and had their swords drawn and were going at each other like maniacs.

Be careful! I wanted to shout as I slid into the room, worried Dash would cut an appendage off my nearly-human maybe-boyfriend, but the more I watched the more

I wondered just how powerless Gage really was. He was fast, and strong. At one point he landed a boot to Dash's chest and hurled him across the room with one kick.

What?

Maybe there was some residual Shade power left in him? But as if reminding me that he was stripped of his power in Avalon, Gage turned his back to me. My gaze landed on the two gashes between his shoulder blades where his wings had been taken. They were finally healed over, but the angry twin scars spoke of trauma from Avalon that he'd not yet shared with me.

From his spot on the ground, Dash arched his back and sprang to his feet. For once he was free of his regular hoodie, giving me a rare unimpeded view of his face and upper body. He shook his head, flinging his long hair off his face and revealing the jagged scar that ran down the side of his jawline.

"That all you got?" Gage taunted Dash.

Dash's muscular physique was similar to Gage's, so on the surface the pair appeared evenly matched, but as I watched, Dash engaged some of his angel marks—the elegant swirls glowing white over his biceps and upper chest—showcasing his advantage over Gage.

"Game on," Dash said right before he jolted into motion, moving so fast he blurred. I couldn't track him, but somehow Gage lifted his weapon in time to intercept Dash's blow. Sparks flew from where their swords connected.

I gasped. Dash had almost split Gage's head open. If

Gage hadn't blocked Dash's strike he'd have been eating steel. Surely this had gotten out of hand.

Gage must have heard my gasp, because even as he pushed back against Dash's sword with his own, his gaze flicked toward me. That was all the distraction Dash needed to drop low and swipe Gage's feet out from beneath him.

Gage landed with a thud, and before he could recover Dash stood over him with the tip of his sword pressed against Gage's throat.

"Do you yield?" Dash asked, chest huffing with the force of his breaths.

Looking equally winded, Gage's eyes narrowed on his opponent. "Only because you cheated."

Dash tilted his head, a chunk of his black hair falling over his face and hiding his scar, but then he broke into a grin. "Winning at all costs isn't cheating. Didn't you tell me that?"

Gage let out a deep chuckle. "I did."

Dash tapped his sword to his weapons storage mark on his rib cage and it suctioned to him, turning into a lined tattoo. He offered Gage a hand up, and Gage got to his feet and patted Dash on the back good-naturedly.

"Next time I won't go easy on you," Gage said.

Dash barked out a laugh as he bent over to swipe a sleeveless hoodie from the ground and slip it over his head. "Next time I'll fight you with my dominant hand."

I shook my head. *Guys.* I'd probably never truly understand them, but I was glad Gage and Dash seemed to be getting along so well. Gage needed to know there were people who had his back now.

"That was impressive," said a voice to my left, and I jerked my gaze to see Aurelia walk through the doorway on the far wall and toward the pair.

How long had she been watching?

Gage immediately tensed. A spark of panic flashed in his eyes before he wiped his face clear of emotions.

"Hey, Aurelia," Dash said as Gage walked to a gym bag and pulled out a towel. He wiped the sweat off his face and then grabbed the bag and jogged over to me. His chest still glistened when he reached me. I wouldn't lie and say it wasn't difficult to keep my eyes on his face.

His wounds were all nearly healed now, and I reminded myself to run a thank you gift to the Lumen healers. They were miracle workers.

"Hey, beautiful," Gage said as he leaned over and brushed his lips over my forehead.

Beautiful? Dang, I couldn't ignore that the term of endearment made me go a little melty inside.

I cleared my throat, catching Aurelia and Dash speaking in hushed tones behind Gage, but then refocused on him.

"So, are you going to get dressed, or just walk around Lumen Academy half naked?" I asked, using that as an excuse to sneak another peek at his muscled pecs.

"You want me to cover all this up?" Gage indicated his naked torso with a sweep of his hand.

No. Definitely not.

"Yes," I said with a straight face.

"Liar," he chuckled, but then ran a towel over his chest and threw on a black t-shirt, leaving me a little disappointed.

Aurelia finished her conversation with Dash and then turned toward us. "The healers have been looking for you, Gage. They said they didn't clear you for training yet, but that you disappeared from the healing center earlier today." Tilting her head, she quirked an eyebrow and waited for Gage's response.

Busted.

"Gage!" I smacked his arm.

Gage folded his arms over his chest and shrugged. "I cleared myself. I feel great, and as you saw, I'm perfectly fit to train."

Aurelia nodded slowly. "Yes, I can see that, but they wanted to run a few more tests on you. Apparently some of your labs came back abnormal."

My stomach dropped. *Abnormal how?*

"Probably because of something they did to me up in Avalon when they patched me up," Gage retorted. "You can discuss that with the archangels if you'd like, because I'm not interested in being a lab rat."

I blinked at Gage in surprise. I got that Aurelia unknowingly hit a nerve, but that was a little defensive. What was going on with him? Maybe he wasn't used to people caring about his welfare and so he was suspicious of Aurelia's intentions?

Dash cleared his throat loudly and I looked back and forth between Aurelia and Gage, trying to figure out how to help defuse the sudden tension in the air. I didn't want Gage running off again, but I also didn't want him skipping out on anything that would keep him healthy.

Surprisingly, it was Dash who stepped in. "I'll keep an eye on him," he said to Aurelia. "If he acts sickly in any way, I'll rush him right to the healers."

Aurelia shifted her gaze between Dash and Gage, and then heaved a sigh. Weariness shone from her eyes. "Gage, we just want to protect you. You're in a more vulnerable position right now than you're used to. We're not your enemies. You know that, right?"

Gage rolled his tongue in his cheek, his face remaining hard, and for a second I was sure he was going to quip something like, "Are you sure about that?" but instead he nodded and said, "Yeah, I get that. And I appreciate it. I just don't like all the tests and being cooped up in the healing center."

Aurelia nodded. "I won't force you to get any more testing done, but I do recommend it. The more we understand about the changes you've gone through, the better."

Gage tensed up next to me, but I don't think Aurelia noticed.

"I'm fine, really," he said. "Just anxious to see some action. I'm not used to being benched."

A small smile curled Aurelia's mouth. "I believe that. You certainly caused my people an awful lot of trouble when you were a Shade. I'm glad we're on the same side now."

Gage looked down at me. "Yeah, me too."

I felt another warm fuzzy feeling in my chest. I knew what he really meant was that he was glad the two of us were on the same side. I agreed.

"Gage, I'll talk to you in a few days about getting skills tested to join missions," Aurelia said, and Gage's entire face lit up.

"I… that would be awesome." He fumbled over his words and my heart filled with so much gratitude for Aurelia in that moment.

Aurelia nodded and opened her mouth to speak again when her cell phone rang. She pulled out her phone and then frowned at it before putting it away.

She looked to Dash. "Will you come with me? There's something that needs to be handled. It won't take long though."

I was instantly on alert. Something had clearly happened, and I wanted to know what.

"Sure." Dash tipped his chin toward Gage. "See you back in the room, man."

"Yeah," Gage said in return, and I watched Aurelia and Dash leave.

"You okay? You seemed a bit defensive about the tests at the healing center," I asked when the door closed behind them.

A dark look crossed his face before he nodded. "Didn't

sleep well. Just still getting used to stuff here. They don't make us do that stuff at Shade Academy. I'm not really used to being told what to do."

My heart melted at that. I couldn't imagine what it was like to be a Shade one day and then be stripped of power by the angels of Avalon the next. Being Arthur's son, he was seen as the prince of Shade Academy and given whatever he wanted, and here he had to follow all these rules.

"But Aurelia offering to test you so you can go out on missions is pretty cool," I changed topics and Gage grinned.

"That will be awesome," he agreed.

"What if we went on a date?" I pressed my body against his in an effort to distract him further. His eyes went half lidded, and before he could respond I decided to mess with him. "Oh, that's right. You don't date or do relationships." I stepped back with a playful grin, throwing his words back at him from Shade Academy and the days of our fake dating.

He reached out and grabbed my hips, yanking me toward him with a half-cocked smile. "Woman, get over here. There is no one I would rather date than you."

Tipping his mouth to mine, our lips met in a spine-tingling kiss.

Mmm... finally.

I opened my mouth to deepen the kiss when my phone buzzed in my pocket. I ignored it, immersed in the deliciousness that was Gage, but it buzzed again. And again.

No.

Gage pulled back and looked at me. "Blowin' up."

I sighed and pulled my phone out, looking down at the person who had interrupted that amazing kiss. When I saw Indigo's name, my heart sank. Gage stiffened when he caught sight of it too.

Indigo: *I could be killed for this, so delete these after you receive them.*

Indigo: *Go to the Trinity Church cemetery tonight at midnight.*

Indigo: *Arthur is meeting Apollyon and they are talking about your mom. That's all I know.*

Indigo: *Tell Gage I miss him and hope he's okay.*

Indigo. My throat suddenly felt bone dry.

"Your mom?" Gage asked.

I nodded, trying to wrap my mind around the whole thing. I reread the texts three more times before deleting them.

"Hey, Gage… wanna go on a date to the Trinity Church cemetery?"

Gage chuckled. "Sounds romantic."

If they were planning something about my mom, I needed to know what it was, consequences be damned.

"Stop pushing!" Marlow whisper-screamed as we huddled inside the surprisingly decent sized mausoleum and fought for window space.

Dash shot her a glare. "I'm six-feet-two inches tall, Marlow. I can't see. Move over."

"I'm six-three," Jacob added.

"I'm six-four," Gage said as if this was a competition.

Clutching his sword to his chest, Gage crouched on his heels next to me as I reached out and smacked all of the men on the arm one by one. "Play nice! No one is comfortable."

Drea chuckled as Gage, Jacob, and Dash all looked at me then and said nothing. We all stood inside of the twelve-foot-wide stone room that held four sarcophagi. The window of the mausoleum was tiny, maybe twelve inches by eighteen inches and we were all pushing for a visual on Apollyon and Arthur. The issue was that the window was a mere two feet off the ground so you had to crouch on your knees or heels to be able to see anything.

Marlow swung around so fast then that she nearly clipped Dash in the chin. "If you are not manning the audio equipment, or your father is not Apollyon, then *step back.*"

Ouch.

Drea, Dash, Jacob, and Gage stood and stepped back, and Marlow rolled out her neck, putting her tablet up on the tiny stone windowsill so she could look down at it. "There. Now I have room to work."

I rested on my knees and glanced down at the tablet. There were eight or ten audio tracks playing sounds of wind and other creepy cemetery noises, like a tree scratching against a gravestone. When I'd told Drea where Gage and I were going tonight, she'd insisted the entire team come to support me. Marlow had rigged up the cemetery with listening devices every forty feet so we could get a decent audio of what they said without being seen. The last thing I wanted was Gage to be spotted by his dad *or* for Apollyon to see me.

Skye suddenly appeared right in front of the tiny glass window, and I yelped, covering my mouth with my hand.

"They're coming." She grinned and then poofed out of existence.

"Skye!" I hissed, my heart pounding so loud in my chest I was sure the entire room could hear it.

"What did she say?" Drea tugged on my braid.

I sighed, trying to get my wits back. Seeing a ghost actually appear in a cemetery was the stuff of nightmares. Even if it was a somewhat friendly, slightly annoying, and unpredictable ghost.

"She said they are coming." I hadn't seen Skye since we returned from my training session in Avalon, so I hadn't told her we would be here. How she knew what we were even up to was beyond me. I just imagined her and Aurum watching me from Avalon and plotting different attacks to test my skills. All of a sudden, a tingle shot up my spine and my power surged inside of me. There was a reddish flash of light outside the window and then it was gone.

What the...?

"Master Apollyon," Arthur's voice crackled on the audio and the entire mausoleum went stock still.

Marlow turned the audio down so that they wouldn't hear themselves talking, and I scanned the cemetery for a visual. The second we'd stepped inside the cemetery I'd gotten a rush of energy, but nothing like the one I'd just felt. When I'd asked everyone else about it, they'd looked at me like I'd grown three heads—except for Gage. He'd just said cemeteries can be a source of power for Shades. Something cryptic that I was definitely going to ask him about later. Was the energy surge I'd just detected me sensing the portal and Apollyon?

"Over here!" Jacob hissed from the other end of the mausoleum, where he was crouched in front of another window.

I stood, scrambling over four stone caskets and all of my

friends. When I reached the second window, I fell on my knees next to Jacob.

"Did you find her talisman?" Apollyon's voice played out of the tablet Marlow held. Marlow was right behind me and bopped Jacob out of the way with her hip.

Talisman? Whose talisman?

Across the cemetery, I saw two tall figures bathed in moonlight, Apollyon being slightly taller than Arthur, his long feathered wings draping behind him like an inky black robe. I wasn't close enough that I was worried they would see or hear us, which was a relief. There was a spinning portal to the Netherworld right behind them.

"No, Master, I've looked everywhere. I've scanned the girl's storage unit myself. There is no trace of Emery's magic on any of the belongings."

My blood ran cold at Arthur's words.

Emery's magic? Storage unit? *My* storage unit? The room swam around me as I tried to process what this meant and not have a panic attack.

There was a crash as Apollyon pointed to a gravestone and it burst into a hundred pieces. "I can't kill her until I've broken her spell that ties our powers! In order to do that, I *need* her talisman."

Gage's father bowed his head. "I know, Master. I'm sorry, I have my best team on it, but—"

Apollyon was a blur of movement; one second he stood before Arthur and the next Arthur's back was against a tree with Apollyon's hand wrapped around his throat. "You've been loyal to me, but I will not hesitate to replace you. Find Emery's talisman or I'll find someone else to lead Shade Academy in New York City."

"Yes sir," Arthur croaked out.

Apollyon released Arthur, and Gage's dad fell to his knees gasping for air. The ruler of the Netherworld then scanned the cemetery, and I froze, shrinking away from the window.

"The hellhound I sent to bite my daughter and force her to return to the Netherworld was killed by *your* son," Apollyon said suddenly, and I looked over at Gage to see the blood drain from his face.

Goose bumps rose on my arms. How would biting me force me to the Netherworld?

Arthur looked shocked. "He's alive?" he growled, and my stomach turned sour. There was not an ounce of compassion in hearing that his son wasn't dead. If anything, he sounded mad about it.

Apollyon nodded. "Since your boy deprived me of my daughter, I'll also leave it up to you to get Tatum to the Netherworld. My demons can't drag her there, but maybe *you* can."

Arthur growled. "Now that I can do."

Gage moved then, standing protectively over me as if readying for an attack even though we were safely concealed from his father in the mausoleum.

Apollyon gestured to the open portal behind him. "I'll be back in three days' time, and when I come I want that talisman and my daughter, or I will spill your entrails all over this cemetery, are we understood?"

Three days! No. We needed more time than that to amass the army to save my mom.

Apollyon turned, not giving Arthur a chance to respond before striding toward the Netherworld portal. There was a crackling noise, then a flash of red lit the cemetery briefly.

Apollyon was gone.

I looked at Gage to see that guilt marred his features. If Arthur wasn't a threat before, he definitely was now.

"It will be okay," Gage breathed. "My father isn't nearly as powerful as he would be if he had his talisman."

I winced, reaching up to rub the back of my neck. "Yeah, about that…"

I was so screwed.

I exchanged a guilty look with Drea. She was the only one I'd told about Arthur's talisman having been stolen. She grimaced and then nodded, indicating I should inform the others. After taking a deep breath, I quickly told the group about Arthur getting his talisman back the night of Skye's death.

"Tate, this is bad." Gage started to pace the tiny space.

"Why would a hellhound bite force me to the Netherworld?" I asked, my brain on overload.

Gage and Dash shared a quick look I couldn't interpret.

"Dude, who cares?" Dash said. "Apollyon is after your mom's talisman. And from the sound of it, getting it means he'll be able to kill her and break some kind of spell she put over him."

Drea nodded. "Yeah, it seems like your mom must have cursed him to link their souls or something and he can't remove it without her talisman."

It sounded similar to how Gran's curse could only be taken off with Arthur's talisman. My mom was one smart cookie, but now we had to protect her.

I swallowed hard. "We need to find that talisman before Arthur does."

Gage cleared his throat. "I have an idea."

Everyone turned to stare at Gage, who bent over to look out the window. "My father's gone," he said when he straightened. "Let's get out of this cramped space."

We quickly filed out of the cold stone structure. I ran my hands up and down my arms, unable to rid myself of the goose bumps prickling my flesh. I was getting a weird vibe in this place, like invisible fingers were running over my body, but each little pinprick sent a jolt of energy into me.

Seeing the motion and mistaking it as me being cold, Gage wrapped an arm around my shoulders and pulled me against his side. The sensation didn't stop, but I appreciated the gesture anyway. Being in Gage's arms just felt right.

"So what's your idea?" Drea asked Gage.

"I know someone who might be able to help us locate Emery's talisman before my father does," Gage offered.

I perked up, waiting for him to go on.

"That's great," Drea said, and the rest of the group nodded as well.

Heaving a sigh, Gage ran a hand down his face. "Yeah, but you're not going to like this next part. The person I know that can track a magical signature to certain locations is in England… and she's a Shade."

My heart sank. Both of those things were going to be an issue. England was super far and working with Shades was super out of the question for the Angel Gang.

Drea crossed her arms over her chest and shook her head. "There's no way my mom is going to let us jump on a plane to the UK. Especially not to go and see a Shade."

"I wasn't planning on asking your mom's permission," Gage said flatly.

I loved Drea, but she did tend to involve her mom in a lot of things that might be best done solo. For better or worse, I kinda operated on the philosophy of "better to ask for forgiveness than permission," but Drea was a serious rule-follower.

"Everyone hold up," Marlow cut in. "There's someone else here." Her brows furrowed as she inspected the device in her hands. I couldn't tell what was happening, but Marlow looked concerned.

I was instantly on alert as we all glanced around the cemetery. It was dark and there were a lot of places a person could hide.

What if Arthur is still here? What if he attacks Gage?

Pulling away from Gage, I activated my weapons storage mark and pulled a twelve-inch gold dagger off my arm. Gage hefted his own sword at the ready, and the rest of the group armed themselves as well.

"Wait! It's just me," a female voice called to my left, and I spun in that direction.

Jacob's wings snapped from his back so powerfully that they made my hair fly into my face. Wasting no time, he shot in the direction of the voice. I jerked my head, flinging the loose strands from my eyes in time to see Jacob brandish his sword, angel marks glowing white on his arms and neck as he pressed the tip of his weapon against the underside of Indigo's chin.

Indigo stood still with her hands up in surrender and her eyes wide. "Whoa. I come in peace," she said.

"Jacob," I yelled as I re-stored the dagger and sprinted toward the pair. "Put down your weapon. That's Indigo!"

"She's a Shade," he grumbled under his breath, but let me tug his arm down when I reached him.

"She's my *friend*," I said, shooting Jacob a glare.

"Yeah, back down, bro." Gage's voice boomed behind me, and Jacob took a step back, glaring at him.

I got that Shades were technically the enemy, but that didn't mean every single one of them was evil. Probably only most of them were. Jacob had some serious biases he needed to work on. Not to mention he still hadn't fully worked out his issues with Gage, but now wasn't the time for that.

Indigo spotted Gage behind me and went to him, throwing her arms around him. "I'm so glad you're okay," she said.

He smiled down at her. "It's really nice to see you, Indigo. I owe you my life."

She returned his smile with a watery one of her own. "I don't intend to let you forget that."

He barked out a laugh. "Noted."

Turning away from Gage, Indigo looked back at me.

"Indigo, what are you doing here?" I asked as I threw my arms around her. She held herself stiff for a moment before returning the hug, but she wiggled out of my grasp after a few short moments.

"I wasn't sure if you were going to make it," she said. "So I came here to check out what was going on just in case. Ever since I saw what Arthur could do to his own son..." Indigo's eyes started to shine, but she sniffed and rubbed them, not allowing any tears to fall. "I never questioned my decision to become a Shade. Humans aren't perfect, and they can be downright evil, so what was the point of devoting my life to protecting them, right? I never thought we were really causing any harm, but now..." She shook her head. "Maybe I've been wrong all along, and now it's too late."

A single rebellious tear leaked from Indigo's eye and streaked down her face. I couldn't help but tug her back into my arms and hug her tight. "It's never too late."

"She's right," Drea said from behind me. I pulled away

from Indigo and we both looked at Gage and my Angel Gang. Marlow, Dash, and even Jacob were nodding their agreement. My heart swelled.

A small but hopeful smile started to lift the corners of Indigo's mouth, but then it flatlined as her face filled with concern. "Did you hear all that? Tatum, Apollyon wants to kill your mom. I'm so sorry."

"We heard it," I confirmed. A tight fist of trepidation squeezed my heart, but I tried not to let it show. "We were just talking about how to stop that from happening."

Jacob retracted his wings and his angel marks stopped glowing. "We just need to figure out how to get to England to visit a Shade and then back again without the head of the Lumens figuring it out," he said as he returned his sword to a tattoo that started on the back of his neck and ran down his spine.

Drea frowned but didn't immediately shut down the idea of going without notifying her mother.

Skye poofed into the group then, surprising *no one* except me. "I think I can help with that!"

"How?" I asked after getting my heart rate back down from her jump scare, and everyone looked at me.

"That's exactly the problem," Jacob said.

"No, sorry. Skye's back and says she can help us with getting to England," I said.

Understanding dawned on everyone's face except Indigo's, and I took a quick minute to explain the highlights of

Skye's death and current ghosty state. She looked kinda freaked out, but I didn't have time to deal with that now.

"Okay, Skye," I said turning toward my spirit friend, giving the rest of the group an idea of where to look. "What do you suggest?"

"Just open a portal and go there," she said.

I sighed, my shoulders and hope sinking. That wasn't a viable suggestion. I was still working with Aurelia on my portal making abilities, and I certainly wasn't at the place where I could make a portal to the UK and transfer seven people and one ghost across. What if I totally lost concentration and cut an arm off?

"What did she say?" Drea asked.

"She told me to open a portal to England. But I can't. I don't have that much control over my powers yet. It was a bad idea."

"Hey," Skye objected. "I don't have bad ideas. Every idea that comes from my beautiful head is utterly brilliant and foolproof."

I cocked a brow at her.

"Listen," she went on. "I get that you're still flexing your portal making powers or whatever, but there are three very important things you have now that you didn't before."

"And those are?" I asked while the rest of the group waited patiently for me to talk to her.

Lifting her hand, she ticked a finger in the air after listing each thing. "One, you are Apollyon's daughter so you have extra juice from being here in the cemetery. Two, there are a crap-ton of souls that are connecting with you right now, and three, you have a Shade."

Souls that are connecting with me?

"What souls?"

"Don't you feel them?" Skye asked. "You're in a cemetery with the remains of hundreds of people. Their souls are reaching out and touching you from the Netherworld."

I let out a yip and jumped back, swinging my head back and forth looking for all the invisible souls Skye was talking about. "Where are they?" I shouted.

"Tate, what's going on? What's wrong?" Gage asked.

"Skye said there were souls touching me!" I ran my hands over my body, brushing off anything that felt weird. It was like watching a spider crawl on TV and then suddenly feeling them all over.

"What?" Gage said.

Skye started laughing her head off. "Okay, I might not have explained that the best way possible. Sorry. It's not that there's a soul touching you like I can..." To prove her point, she ghosted her fingers through my face, and I reared away from her. "It's more like you're siphoning energy from them. The veil between the Netherworld and Earth is thinnest in cemeteries, and you and your father share the soul sucking gift."

I frowned. "Never say that last part again." I would never *suck* a soul.

Okay, I was going to put the soul siphoning thing to rest, as long as there weren't a horde of ghosts walking around, I didn't really need all the details, but I did want to get to the bottom of the Shade thing.

"So, why does it matter that Indigo's here?"

"Technically, you don't need a Shade to make the portal," she went on. "But since Shades' powers are rooted in the Netherworld, connecting with one of them will help you stabilize your portal, which is important because we don't want the portal collapsing and cutting anyone in half."

Horror clutched me in its icy hold. Aurelia once warned me that could happen and here I was just worrying about an arm getting cut off.

"Aurelia never mentioned that connecting with a Shade can stabilize a portal," I said.

Skye shrugged. "It's a bit of a cheater method. Aurelia probably didn't even bother teaching you about it because Shades and Lumens never work together, so what's the point? But the important thing here is that all you have to do is pull in enough power while connecting with Indigo and *bam*, you'll be able to make a portal to England." She snapped her fingers. "Easy peasy! And when you want to come back, go find a cemetery there and do the same thing."

Could Skye be right?

I translated her plan to the rest of the group and caught Gage and Indigo sharing a look.

"What do you think?" I asked them.

"We do get an extra burst of energy from places like graveyards. Or rather, I used to," Gage said. "It feels like small shocks. It's actually a little uncomfortable."

That's what I'd been feeling since I got here. Maybe if Indigo and I teamed up our power boost, we really could do this.

"I'll bet that's why Apollyon and Arthur wanted to meet here," Indigo cut in.

That was a disturbing thought. I also found it interesting that demons couldn't go to cemeteries but Apollyon could. Maybe it was because even though he was an evil douchebag he was still an angel of Avalon, albeit a fallen one.

I frowned. "Why can Apollyon go to cemeteries but demons can't?" Gage never told me exactly what would happen if a demon stepped foot in a cemetery, only that they couldn't.

Gage and Indigo shared a look, as if giving up these Shade secrets was wrong.

"It's not really that demons can't come here, but that if they do they get sucked back to the Netherworld," he said.

Ohhh. That made so much sense, especially if the veil was thinner between the two worlds there.

I glanced at Drea and the others, but they didn't look surprised by this new development. There was so much information about this world I still didn't know. Sometimes it was hard not to be bitter that they'd grown up with the truth while I was still playing catch-up, but Gran had given me a wonderful childhood, so I couldn't regret that.

Gage turned to look at me. "If Shades get extra power from here, I could see why you might too as Apollyon's daughter. I think what Skye is saying makes sense. Do you want to try making a portal to England?"

"I like him." Skye winked at me, but I ignored her.

I scanned the faces around me, stopping on Drea. She was our group leader. She picked at her fingernails and bopped her foot up and down in a nervous gesture. The entire group stared at her as she weighed the different options in her mind.

After what seemed like forever, she nodded. "Let's do it. We don't have time to waste if Arthur is also looking for Emery's talisman, and my mom would want me to do whatever I could to save Tatum's mom."

I reached out and squeezed Drea's hand in thanks.

"Just don't kill us with this portal," she shot back.

I dropped her hand and groaned. "Thanks for the vote of confidence."

Skye jumped up and down and rubbed her hands together. "We're going to England! I've always wanted to see the Wizarding World of Harry Potter. Oh, and Stonehenge, and of course Buckingham—"

"Skye! We aren't sightseeing. Help me do this," I hissed.

She stuck her tongue out at me and gestured to Indigo. "Grab her hands and connect with her like you did with me and Aurum in Avalon. Once you've connected, envision where you want to go and then pull on her power as you make the portal. You need to be the last to step through as it will close behind you."

I cracked my neck. *Yeah, no pressure, I've got this.*

"I've never even been to England. I've never even been out of the country. How am I going to visualize a place to go there?" I voiced my fear.

A sad look came over Gage's face. "I think I can help with that." Stowing his sword in a sheath on his back, he pulled out his phone and scrolled through some pictures. It took a while but finally he handed it to me, and my heart dropped into my stomach. There was a young Gage, I'd guess maybe ten or eleven, standing in front of an ancient looking mausoleum. It was covered in moss and vines, but there was something achingly beautiful about it. Behind him were a thicket of trees. Fog lay on the ground; shafts of sunlight pierced through the leaves. It was one of the most stunning photographs I'd ever seen. When I looked at his face, my throat tightened with emotion. Young Gage wore a haunted expression.

"My mother's grave. Family plot in Highgate Cemetery. It's in London, which isn't exactly where we need to get, but it's close enough." His voice was rough, and I nodded, handing him the phone back.

"Thank you." I cleared my throat.

Reaching for Indigo's hands, I took them in my own and she grasped them without question. Closing my eyes, I took in a deep breath and pulled up the image Gage had shown me in my mind. There weren't proper pathways, just leaves and dirt trails cut into the earth. It was as if the bodies of the dead and nature had become one.

When I had a firm visual in my mind, I tapped into my

power and then tried to reach for Indigo's energy signature and connect with her like I had with Skye during training. I'd only done something like this one time before, so I was still unsure of what I was feeling for, but now that I'd opened myself up, it was like I was connecting with *everything*. A breeze of power moved over me and through me. My friends spread out around me were like heat signatures in my mind's eye. It even felt like I could feel the beating heart of the Netherworld drumming beneath my feet.

Energy swirled around me, calling out to me, and I found that it was the most natural thing in the world to reach out and link with it, so I did.

"Help us," a voice whispered.

"Free us," another said.

"Save us," a third chimed in.

What the hell? I shook my head, trying to dislodge the random voices.

"Okay, rein it in, cowboy, you've connected with the souls of the Netherworld," Skye shot beside me.

Crap.

"I'm right here," Indigo said. "Focus on me."

I swallowed hard, following her voice with my power, as if that were possible. There was a pull on my energy as if the souls in the Netherworld didn't want to let go, but I fought against it.

Indigo, I thought. *Sweet, slightly misguided, good taste in shoes, Indigo.*

A surge of power rushed through me then, and I knew I'd connected with her.

"I feel it!" she shouted, slightly panicked.

"What now?" I yelled, hoping Skye hadn't left me. If she poofed out before we crossed over I was going to kill her again.

"I don't know. Make the portal," she shot back.

I don't know?

Great. It was like the blind leading the blind.

I started to panic, but then someone came up behind me, pressing their chest to my back.

Gage?

Their energy felt different from Indigo's and the souls I'd unknowingly linked to before. Different, but still powerful and equally alluring.

"You got this," Gage whispered in my ear. It *was* him. "Focus on the image, on where you want to portal to." Gage's lips brushed over the shell of my ear as he spoke to me in calm tones. The lack of alarm in his voice grounded me, helping to refocus me on my task.

The photo. The vines crawling up the stone, the mist and light pouring through the trees. I concentrated on the details in the photo and then tried to open a portal. A burst of power shot out of me, and my knees went weak with the sudden loss of magic.

"Something is happening," Drea squeaked.

Good. I wasn't going to open my eyes just yet and lose my concentration, so I just kept pushing my power into the space behind Indigo, while also pulling on her power. It was a nearly impossible dance but—

"It's working! That's the place." Gage's voice held awe, and I couldn't help but pop my eyelids open then.

I gasped. Looking over Indigo's shoulder, a three foot portal had opened. I could see the mausoleum where his mother was buried through the opening and it was just like the picture, albeit a bit more worn down and no sunlight brightened the area as it was early morning, before sunrise in London. The portal opened wider until it was finally big enough for us to walk through.

I inhaled, relaxing, and trying not to freak out or put more pressure on myself, and the portal grew wider as I pulled for more power.

"Go. I'm not sure how long I can hold it," I said, feeling Indigo's power suck into me and then out through my hands. She was like a battery that stabilized my power so that I didn't have to strain to keep it flowing full blast.

No one moved, they just cast unsure glances at each other.

"I'll go first." Skye zoomed through Indigo and my arms and then into the portal. "See, I'm perfectly fine." She waved from the other side.

Was she joking? It's not like she could die twice, but maybe it would rip a soul apart? I didn't know.

"Skye went through and is fine," I shared.

I felt Gage shrug behind me. "Good enough for me," he said, and then stepped toward the portal.

"I'm going next!" Drea yelled and ran through with her head dipped low.

Everything is fine. Keep your friends alive. Just stay cool.

Marlow was next, then Dash and finally Jacob went right after him. I felt some fatigue in my limbs, but as soon as it came it was replenished with a new source of power. Indigo? The souls? Was this what my father did? Because it was *super* creepy.

"Keep the connection with Indigo. Have her step back into the portal," Skye coaxed.

I relayed the information to Indigo, and she nodded, backing into the portal while holding my hands as I walked forward.

Going to London for a visit, nothing to see here. I scanned the New York cemetery one final time to make sure we were still alone. I didn't want anyone following us. We were. And so without another thought, I stepped through and halfway across the world.

The portal closed behind me once I stepped through and let go of Indigo's hands. I took a moment to get my bearings. The angel marks on my arms swirled, and the depleted energy I felt from making the portal was instantly replaced with vitality.

Glancing around the place, I did a quick headcount and noticed that Skye was already gone.

She's probably halfway through the Harry Potter experience by now, I chuckled to myself. The weird ghost had grown on me.

When my gaze rested on Gage, I froze. He stood motionless before his mother's mausoleum, and I looked at the others. "Give us a minute?"

They nodded, moving farther down a worn path to give us privacy.

I walked up and trailed my fingers down Gage's back.

"We could pick up some flowers and set them here before we leave," I offered.

He nodded, staring at the closed door to the structure.

"Do you want to go inside? We have time. We can—"

"Nah, I'm fine." He turned to face me, and his expression was unreadable. "Remember when I told you that people weren't born bad, they become it?"

My heart thumped in my chest at the memory of our fight in the alleyway after I'd learned Apollyon was my father, and how it led to our first kiss. The fight—and the kiss—had sprung from anger as much as passion. I nodded.

"My mom said that when I told her I wanted to be a Shade when I grew up. Now I wonder if she was subtly telling me to pick Lumen." Confusion crossed his features, and I reached up and cupped his face in my hands.

I didn't know his mom's situation and why she chose Shade, but I had a feeling if she was married to Arthur, she saw the worst of it and didn't want that for her son.

"I think she'd be proud of you now," I told him.

He smiled, leaning down to plant a soft kiss on my mouth. "She'd have liked you. She was also stubborn and persistent."

"Hey!" I smacked his arm and laughed, but the laughter died in my throat when a scream pierced the air.

Gage and I bolted out onto the main pathway to find Indigo and the Angel Gang surrounded by a group of Shades. Gage immediately yanked me behind a giant gravestone. We peeked around the edges to see what was happening.

"This is our turf, Lumens!" one of the Shades hissed. "Go back to wherever you came from, now."

Dash's and Jacob's wings snapped out and arched aggressively in the air as Drea pulled a longsword from the tattoo on her arm. Marlow already stood at the ready with an axe gripped in each hand.

I had no idea if the Shades recognized Indigo as one of their own, but Jacob and Dash both shifted so she was concealed behind their large white and gray feathered wings as the Shades stepped closer, brandishing weapons of their own.

I breathed a little sigh of relief, knowing that my friends had her back.

"We have business in town and will be leaving only when it's complete," Drea told them calmly.

There were over half a dozen Shades, but we had just as many Lumens. If a fight broke out, it would be evenly matched. But I hoped it wouldn't come to that.

With a scream of fury, one of the Shades ran at Drea and the rest of them followed suit. The clash of weapons ripped through the cemetery, and I gasped.

Okay, I guess there was going to be a fight.

Gage and I shared a look and then both pulled our own weapons, him from the sheath on his back and me from my forearm, before retraining our focus on the growing battle in front of us.

We still hadn't been seen, so we could easily sneak up from behind and surprise the Shades.

"Let's—" I turned to tell Gage something but stopped when I noticed he was staring transfixed at the swollen moon. His eyes… their once arresting green was threaded through with gold. What the…?

"Gage!" I hissed and shook him by the shoulders.

He growled, low in his throat, and looked at me. For a second it was as if he didn't know me, then the yellow retreated, and it was green again.

"Tate," he breathed, shaking his head as if trying to dislodge his thoughts.

"What was that?" I asked, completely in shock by the way he'd not seemed himself.

"Incoming!" Indigo yelled, and I spun, raising my weapon just as a Shade clashed his sword into mine.

There goes our element of surprise.

Throwing Gage's weird little, yellow-eyed freakiness from my mind, I fought the Shade.

Clack-clack-clack, our swords collided as I blocked every blow. I'd killed demons before, but Shades were different—could I kill a Shade? I knew they weren't all bad… this guy looked only a few years older than me. As I fought the dude, I snuck peeks around when I could to make sure my friends were still faring okay.

I lost track of Drea, but Dash was battling two Shades at the same time, using his wings to deflect a blow from one opponent while he hammered the other with an uppercut. Jacob was fighting a Shade with black shadow wings up in the air above the group. And Marlow and Indigo stood back to back as they deflected and delivered their own strikes. If the Shades didn't know Indigo was one of their own before, they certainly did now, because the dark-bladed shadow sword she fought with, much like the one Gage used to have, definitely gave her away.

I was just about to stick the Shade I was battling in the gut when Gage spoke behind me. "Thomas? Is that you?"

The dude I was fighting faltered, backing up as he lowered his weapon, and looked at Gage for the first time.

"Gage Alston?" the guy yelled, and the fighting around us halted. "We heard you were dead."

Gage shrugged. "Long story."

"What are you doing with a bunch of Lumens?" a girl growled from behind me, and I turned to see that she and Drea had swords at each other's throats. My heart hammered in my chest, refusing to calm down.

"An even longer story," Gage responded. "We will be gone in a few hours. We cool? Let us pass for old times' sake?" He winked at the girl.

Jealousy rose up and speared my heart like a hot poker.

I was going to kill him.

She rolled her eyes, but grinned after she lowered her blade and took a step away from Drea. "Fine, but we have to report you were here and got away."

"Understood. Can you wait until we've gone back to New York?"

The girl nodded, and the rest of the Shades backed off, stepping away and stowing their weapons. Drea looked at me and raised one eyebrow, but I shrugged.

"Let's go," Drea called to our crew and walked backward down the path. She wasn't going to give her back to a bunch of Shades no matter how cool they were acting, and I didn't blame her.

"Tatum, Dash, let's fly," Jacob called out.

Good idea. It would give us a good view of the entire cemetery and let us know if this was some bigger trap we were walking into.

I snapped my wings out behind me and looked at Gage, indicating with my head that he follow Drea, and then shot to the skies.

For old times' sake? What the crap did that mean? Jerk.

I scanned the cemetery for demon portals, random Shades, or anything that seemed dangerous, but saw nothing, not even a mourning family member.

Jacob and Dash flew on either side of me as we watched Drea and the rest of the non-flying members of our party make it safely out of the cemetery. The sun was just starting to rise, and if I wasn't on high alert for an ambush, I would have remained airborne and taken a moment to enjoy it. Instead I descended along with Jacob and Dash, and we landed on the cobblestone street right in front of the open gates.

"What was that? Shades guard cemeteries in London?"

Drea growled. Her hair was a mess, and she had a small cut on her arm.

Gage nodded. "It's common knowledge among the Lumens here that demons can't go to cemeteries."

"So the Shades in London patrol the cemeteries so Lumens can't go there for respite?" Drea asked, sounding disgusted.

"That, and the Lumens that are looking for safety because they are tapped of energy or injured are often easy pickings."

A look of hostility appeared on Drea's face, clearly conveying what she thought of the London Shades.

"Do you really believe they will just let us pass and not alert anyone until we've gone back to New York?" Jacob asked Gage.

Gage chuckled. "No way, they're probably running to call my father right now, but I've bought us some time. We'll have to use another cemetery to return home. This one will be crawling with Shades within the hour."

"Well, let's move." Drea started to walk away from the cemetery even though I was pretty sure she had no clue where we were going. The group followed and I moved next to Gage, shooting him a death glare.

"Old times' sake, huh?" I snapped, scowling up at him.

Gage reached out and pulled me even closer, squishing my head against his chest. He laughed and the sound in his chest rumbled against my ear. "Jealous Tatum is sexy."

I pulled back and smoothed my hair. "Not jealous." *Lie.* "Just curious who that was."

Gage slipped his hand in mine, lacing our fingers together, and it made it hard to concentrate on being mad at him.

"Hailey. She was my first kiss. I was twelve and visiting with my dad. It's not a big deal."

First kiss! That was like a super big memorable deal, but also not really a big deal since he clearly hadn't seen her in years.

Gage was wrong. Jealous Tatum was *not* a good look on me.

"Cool," I breathed, and pushed Hailey and the image of Gage kissing her out of my mind. I'd let the idea of Gage with Claire get in our way before, and I wasn't about to make that mistake a second time.

"What was with the moon staring thing?" I asked, dropping my voice so no one else could hear.

Gage's face fell and then he released my hand. "Oh, a taxi!" he yelled and then flagged down an old-school black car that looked like it was from the early 1900s.

Okay, he didn't want to tell me about that. Well, I was going to allow that, but just until we got back to New York, then I was getting to the bottom of it.

We hailed another cab and split into two groups. Drea and Indigo hopped in with Gage and me, and everyone else piled into the other car.

It was going to be a long ride to Brighton where Gage

had told the dude to go, like almost two hours, he'd said. We cut through the heart of London as we traveled south to Brighton, slipping through the city streets with ease at such an early hour. I leaned against Gage and looked out the window as he played tour guide, pointing out a number of London's iconic sights as we drove by.

When the big city had turned into rolling hills and then finally a small seaside town, the cabby stopped in front of a quaint little walk-up with a bright red door.

We shuffled out of the car after Gage paid the guy and stood before the building.

Marlow held her device up to the door and scanned it, her brows instantly furrowed. "There are some major wards protecting this house."

Gage nodded. "You guys might not even be able to knock on the door. I'm not even sure I can anymore to be honest."

Gage turned to face us, nervously chewing at his lip. "So, heads up, my aunt Vera is a little mentally unstable from years of using her gift and hates Lumens and Shades alike."

His aunt! Gage didn't mention the woman we were seeing was his aunt.

I frowned. *She hates both Shades and Lumens?* That was interesting.

"We're… estranged," he added. I reached out to squeeze his hand, and he offered me a weak smile of gratitude. Family stuff could be tricky, so I didn't envy him right now.

Gage cautiously climbed the steps and knocked on the red wooden door.

The door ripped open immediately as if someone had been waiting there, and a woman with messy dark hair and a wild look in her eyes stared at Gage. I remembered the photograph of Gage and his mother I'd seen in his Long Island bungalow, and even though the woman standing in the doorway was several years older, I could see the resemblance to Gage's mother immediately.

"Are you a ghost?" she asked, her British accent thick.

"No, ma'am," Gage said with a slight grin.

"I heard you were dead." Her voice cracked a bit like she wanted to believe it was really him.

"Lies," he stated.

Her brows drew together as she peered at all of us, and then focused her attention back on Gage. "What was your mother's favorite color?"

"Teal," Gage said.

"Favorite band?"

"Beatles," Gage shot back.

"First guy she kissed?" Vera asked.

Gage shivered. "Gross. I don't know."

Vera rapped her nails on the doorjamb. "If you're really my nephew, then prove it."

Gage stepped closer. "You two fought like cats and dogs. You're the messy one and she was clean. You were only ten months apart and called yourself twins. My mom once said you were the better part of her who got stuck with a gift so special that it was akin to a curse…"

Gage looked his aunt in the eyes as tears gathered and then spilled over and down her face.

"I miss her." She sniffled as the rest of us awkwardly shifted our weight and listened in on their private conversation.

"Me too," Gage told her.

"She was a horrible cook," Vera stated.

Gage grinned. "The worst."

That was enough for Vera. She stepped out onto the porch and wrapped her arms around her nephew. Their estrangement was clearly a thing of the past.

Swallowing hard, I blinked rapidly, noticing Drea and Marlow had to do the same. Today was really challenging my ability not to cry sappy tears. I was such a softy.

"Come inside." Vera waved to Gage, and we all moved forward. "Leave the traitorous trash out though," she said as she glared at the rest of us.

We stopped, shocked at her words.

Gage let loose a nervous laugh. "Auntie, this is my girlfriend, Tatum, and our friends."

My stomach dropped out.

Girlfriend.

He said it. He *totally* said it. Not *maybe*-girlfriend. Not *almost*-girlfriend. Just girlfriend, period.

The butterflies in my stomach multiplied then.

I gave his aunt a goofy lopsided grin and she narrowed

her eyes at me. "Fine. Bring the girlfriend, but the rest could be spies. They stay outside," she said sternly.

Muttering something under her breath, she fluttered her hands through the air and a green shimmer appeared briefly around her house and then it was gone.

The wards? Had she just modified them to allow me in?

"Go on," Drea said. "We can wait here."

Jacob, Dash, and Marlow nodded their agreement.

I cast a glance at Indigo, who looked anything but comfortable with the group of Lumens around her.

"Are you going to be all right without me?" I asked her.

She cast a side-glance at Jacob, who'd pulled a sword on her earlier, but then looked back at me and nodded. "No biggie. I got this," she said.

I knew she wasn't comfortable, but I also knew my friends would protect her like one of their own. I'd already seen it happen in the cemetery a few hours ago.

After casting her an apologetic look, I rushed forward, afraid his aunt would change her mind, and slipped into the open doorway behind Gage with no idea what lay beyond.

After I stepped inside, Vera quickly put the wards on her home back in place and slammed the front door shut on Drea and the rest of my friends.

Gage took my hand and walked me out of the foyer and deeper into Vera's house.

Holy glitter explosion!

It was like I'd walked into a craft store that had been bombed. The floors were hot pink with shellacked glitter, the walls quilted as if someone had painted glue over fabric squares. Each piece of furniture was a different color and size, and the coffee table was a pink wooden flamingo with a glass circle over its back. I spotted two paintings on the walls: one a two-tailed mermaid, another a bear with a teacup for a hat. The hallway was closed off with string lights and the ceiling had crystals hanging from it.

"Vera is an artist," Gage said proudly.

I knew I was staring at everything with rounded eyes

and my mouth hanging open, but there was too much to look at. I couldn't take it all in properly because it was so cluttered and eclectic.

"She hates my house," Vera growled, looking at me sternly.

I gulped. "No, I don't. I've just never seen anything like it. It's like an art museum." And it was. A really strange and almost psychedelic museum that made me feel a little queasy from sensory overload, but it was definitely something else.

She smiled at that, nodding as if I was excused for my wild gawking.

"Vera can sense truths from lies, pick up on people's thoughts, and also find lost objects," Gage told me. "Isn't that right, Auntie?"

Oh great, thanks for the warning! I immediately tried to focus my thoughts on something I liked about the house.

She nodded absentmindedly as if what Gage had just said was no big deal. "Would you like tea, dears?"

Gage smiled fondly at his aunt and inclined his head. "I wouldn't be a true Brit if I turned down a cup of tea."

Vera smiled back at Gage and then looked to me, waiting for my response as well.

"Yes, please," I said even though I'd rather have coffee. I was a New Yorker, after all. We lived on black coffee and pizza slices.

"She doesn't like tea," Vera observed, and my eyes widened.

"Can you stop reading her? It's not polite and you know that," Gage said sternly.

Vera shrugged. "So many liars in this world. Can't trust anyone," she mused as she started to make tea, but she also walked over to a coffeemaker and turned it on.

Wow. Okay. Note to self, don't lie while here, even if it's to be polite!

Gage tipped his head toward a delicate Victorian love seat in the living room that barely looked big enough for the two of us. As we took a seat and settled in, I noticed that the tufted fabric was once white, but now covered in intricate hand painted flowers. It was busy, but actually quite lovely. It was like she brought a bit of an English garden inside.

It wasn't a few short minutes before Vera returned, carrying a tray with a teapot and two teacups, and a mug full of coffee. She set it on the glass-topped flamingo table in front of us and then took a seat on a purple wingback chair across from us.

"I apologize for barging in on you like this, Aunt Vera, but we need your help," Gage said as he added a splash of cream to his tea.

"Hmm," Vera said as she brought her own teacup to her lips and took a sip. "That much I'd already worked out for myself." Another sip. "You know I don't get involved in Watcher business."

Setting his cup down Gage leaned forward, his gaze intent on his aunt. "I know that, but this is important."

"Important is relative," Vera said. "What's significant to one person is inconsequential to the next."

That was a rather obvious and noncommittal statement. I was glad Gage was leading this conversation because I didn't quite know what to say to that.

"This is important to every human alive. Past and present," Gage pressed.

Vera scrunched her nose like she smelled something off-putting. "I don't care for humans very much."

"You don't care for Watchers either."

"Exactly my point," she said with a cloyingly sweet smile, and then turned her sharp gaze on me. "I want to hear about this girlfriend of yours. When's the wedding?"

I had just taken a sip of my coffee and started to choke. I quickly set my cup down as I hacked and gasped for air.

Gage patted my back, trying to help me cough up the bit of liquid I'd inhaled. "Auntie, that wasn't nice."

She smiled broadly, looking nothing but pleased with herself. "So, Gage, you're dating a Lumen. How very progressive of you."

"How..." I started, and then clamped my mouth shut, coming to terms with the fact that Vera was picking up information from both Gage and me and was just going to know some things without us telling her.

"Is this just a rebellious phase?" she asked, "Or is this some sort of *Romeo and Juliet* situation?"

I winced. I'd always hated that play. Spoiler alert: they both die in the end. What's romantic about that?

"Tate isn't a phase," Gage said, sounding annoyed.

"We met before I chose my house affiliation," I added, as if somehow that made everything all right.

"Pity," Vera said, and then took another sip of tea. "Nothing good ever came from a Shade and Lumen pairing."

Err… maybe this was a good time to tell Vera that Gage wasn't a Shade anymore.

Without me saying a word, Vera's eyes widened and then fixed on Gage. She looked him up and down, as if seeing him for the first time. "She's right, you aren't a Shade anymore." Vera leaned forward, turning her head, and squinting her eyes. "But you're not really a Lumen either. But you are… something."

"Aunt Vera," Gage growled. "I asked you to stop reading Tate."

Vera waved her hand, brushing off Gage's admonishment. "Pish, you know I can't always help it. Tell me what happened? How did you lose your house affiliation? I've never heard of such a thing before."

Gage ran a hand down his face. "It's a long story, and unfortunately we don't have the time to get into it now. We need your help with something quite urgent. We need to find a talisman."

Vera slammed her teacup down on the tray hard enough that the remaining liquid splashed out and the handle cracked off. "I already told you, I *don't* get involved in Watcher business anymore," she said forcefully, and then grabbed the tea tray, stomping back toward the kitchen.

"Not even for your favorite nephew?"

"You're my only nephew," she grumped.

"Not even to stick it to my father?" Gage called after her, and Vera froze.

Turning slowly, she stared at Gage. "Come again?"

"If you help us, it hurts my father," he said. "Big time."

She set the tray down on the nearest piece of furniture, which happened to be a bookcase made out of branches and seashells, and returned to her seat.

"Well," she said almost pleasantly, "you should have led with that."

I was close enough to Gage to feel the tension leave his body. "Thank you."

Wow, Vera had been pretty adamant about not helping us before. She must really hate Arthur.

I didn't blame her though, and it made me trust her a tiny bit.

"So, whose talisman are you looking for?" she asked, folding her hands on her lap.

"Tatum's mother's," Gage said, reaching over to take my hand.

"That seems simple enough, but in order to find this talisman, I have to pick up on the owner's energy first. I'll need something of her mother's to do that." Vera's gaze turned to me expectantly.

My heart sank. I didn't have anything of my mom's.

But wait… maybe I did.

Leaning forward, I reached into my back pocket and pulled out the note my mom had left for me. I'd read it at least a dozen times and had taken to carrying it with me everywhere.

"Will this work?" I asked, handing the folded piece of paper over to Vera. "It's not one of her possessions, but she did write it."

"Hmm," she said as she eyed the note. "It's worth trying."

Opening the letter, she placed it flat on the coffee table and then put both her hands over it. She closed her eyes and her mouth started to move as she chanted silent words.

I caught my breath when a faint green glow emanated from the palms of her hands. Gage squeezed my hand, reminding me he was still there.

Suddenly, Vera's eyes popped open. A milky-green film covered her eyeballs. Her hand lifted and shot toward me as fast as a viper, latching on to my forearm. I gasped and tried to yank free.

"Auntie, let go," Gage yelled, as he tried to help me pull from her grasp, but her fingers were clamped around my arm like a shackle.

Vera looked right at me, or at least it seemed like she was, it was hard to know for sure since the white covered her irises and pupils.

"This power you carry might be too much for you in the end," she said in a strange monotone voice. "You may lose your soul before your next birthday."

A blast of green magic detonated from Vera, blowing my hair back and washing over and through me like I'd been plunged into a pool of ice. Goose bumps broke out on my arms and the hair at the back of my neck prickled. Once it passed, her eyes rolled back in her head and she let go, flopping back in her seat with closed eyes.

I panted as I stared at her slumped figure across from me.

What. Was. That?

Lose my soul? Did she basically just tell me I was going to die? Could she see the future as well as read thoughts? I wouldn't put it past her.

"Are you all right?" Gage asked me.

"Yeah, I'm fine," I said.

Gage looked down at my forearm where his aunt had grabbed me. At worst, it would bruise, but with my fast healing it probably wouldn't even do that.

He pressed his lips together, the corners pulling down in a frown. "You sure?"

I nodded.

After another glance at my arm, Gage got up, skirting the coffee table to check on his aunt.

"Aunt Vera," he said as he gently shook her shoulder, his brow furrowed in concern.

With a groan, she blinked her eyes open and then swatted him away. "Stop fussing over me," she grouched.

"What happened?" he demanded, crossing his arms over his broad chest.

"What happened is that you didn't tell me your girlfriend was a Shadowling," Vera snapped back. "It's dangerous to tap into someone with that much power. I almost blew up my house and all of us in it."

Shock rippled through me. "What?"

I wasn't sure which one of her statements stunned me the most. That she knew I was a Shadowling, or that because of it we were all almost blown to pieces.

"Are you really the daughter of Apollyon?" Vera asked, diverting her attention to me.

A deep growl rumbled in Gage's chest and a flash of yellow sparked in his eyes. Vera looked up at her nephew and frowned as he positioned himself in front of me protectively.

"Your Shadowling isn't the only thing you've kept from me, is it Gage?" She sighed. "Get yourself under control or you'll lose yourself forever," she said to him. There was a hint of sadness in her voice, almost as if she knew her cryptic warning was too late.

What's she talking about now? Lose himself how?

"Did you find the talisman?" Gage asked before I had the opportunity to question her. I had to lean to the side and peek around him to see Vera.

"I did," she said, notching her chin in my direction. "It's her."

Gage looked back at me, scanning for the talisman on me somewhere. "Tatum has it on her?"

"No. I mean it *is* her."

Gage snapped his head back toward Vera. "That's not possible."

"I didn't think it was either," Vera admitted. "Yet it's the truth. Somehow her mother figured out how to transfer the power of her talisman into her daughter. Bloody clever if you ask me."

"Is that bad?" I asked, and Vera just shrugged.

I was trying not to overreact to the news, but somehow this woman figured out I was a Shadowling and Apollyon's daughter through a single touch alone. I was inclined to believe she was right about my mom's talisman as well, even if that meant I'd somehow lived with, or maybe more technically *was* my mom's talisman for years and never knew.

Someone started banging on the front door and the sound made me jump.

"Tatum, are you okay?" Drea yelled. "We felt that energy release out here."

"Everyone is all right," Gage yelled back. "We'll be out in a few minutes."

I chewed on my lip, concerns swirling in my head. This was the craziest tea party I'd ever been to.

As if I needed another reason for Arthur and Apollyon to be after me. This only painted a bigger target on my back. The only good thing about me being my mother's talisman was that we wouldn't have to go looking for it. Well, that and we knew Arthur didn't have it.

"Thanks for the help, Aunt Vera, but we have to go. By now I'm sure my dad knows we portaled to London and is probably searching for us. We have to get back to New York."

After kissing his aunt on the cheek, Gage tugged me to my feet and practically hauled me toward the front door.

My mind was spinning with everything I just heard. I was my mom's talisman, and I had so much power that it might kill me. Oh, and my boyfriend was definitely hiding something from me.

Awesome.

Vera called to us when we were at her front door. Gage stopped and we both looked back at her.

"Be careful," she said as she wrung her hands. It was the first time since we stepped foot in her house that she looked concerned, and that worried me. "Your father's ambitions know no bounds."

"If anyone knows that, it's me," Gage said, but acknowledged her warning with a nod.

"Your mother would be proud of you. Despite her choices to the contrary, she did want to do the right thing."

Gage closed his eyes briefly at the mention of his mother. When he opened them, his gaze was filled with fiery determination. "Thank you," he said, and with a final look at his aunt, he grasped the door and hurried us out of her home.

Drea and the others were loitering outside on the street and looked up at us as we descended the steps to join them.

"How did it go?" Drea asked.

I exchanged a quick look with Gage. "We got what we came for."

Drea let out a sigh of relief. "Good. We'll head back to the Lumen Compound and make a plan on how to get your mom's talisman."

"Actually—" I started to say, and then Skye appeared.

"Apollyon knows you're the talisman and now he's planning to hide your mom, eat your soul, and then kill her. Come on, you gotta get to the Netherworld stat, before he stashes her somewhere you can never find her."

My heart jackknifed in my chest at her declaration. Okay, the universe just wasn't letting up today with the bad news.

"How did he find out?" I screeched at Skye while my friends stared at me in confusion.

Skye pointed to the house. "Whatever realm she taps into for her power, he was there listening."

Crap, crap, crap!

"How do you know all this?" I questioned, hoping it was some super unreliable source that I could immediately discredit because I didn't want it to be true.

"Aurum," Skye said while giving me a look that said, *"Duh, idiot."*

I growled under my breath, knowing I couldn't flake off her report.

Looking to my friends, I quickly filled them in. "I'm my mom's talisman and Skye just appeared and said that we have to get to the Netherworld right now to save her before

Apollyon hides her." The words rushed out of me in a jumbled mess.

"What?" Drea and Gage shouted at the same time. Similar shocked looks were splashed across everyone's faces.

"Meet me at the cemetery!" Skye called out, and then disappeared again.

This was crazy, everything was happening way too fast.

But I didn't care. I didn't need to process anything other than the fact that Apollyon was going to make it so that I couldn't get to my mom.

I spun, trying to figure out which direction the nearest cemetery was. "Guys, I gotta find the nearest cemetery so I can make a portal and get to the Netherworld. I understand if you don't—"

"Shut up, we're going. Stop talking and let's move," Drea cut me off and started to cross the street.

Gage's hand slipped into mine and he pulled me along. "The nearest cemetery is this way," he said.

"We'll scout the area," Jacob said, and then he and Dash released their wings and shot into the sky, heading in the direction we were all already moving.

"I'm in too!" Indigo yelled, jogging after us while Marlow brought up the rear. My friends' absolute willingness to just follow me into Hell to save my mom really hit me in the feels, hard. They didn't even know the details, but they had my back. How did I get so lucky?

"We got this," Gage assured me.

I wanted to stop and interrogate him within an inch of his life over what his aunt had said. He was clearly hiding something from me—definite weirdness going on with him and his yellow eyes—but it would have to wait for later. His strong hand in mine was an assurance that whatever it was, we would get through it together.

We ran across the street, down a cobblestone alleyway, and then across four more adorable stone cottage lined streets. Gage seemed to know right where he was going so we let him lead. When we finally ran up to a thick cropping of trees, he slowed. "This is it."

"Hang on." Drea pulled out her phone. "I'll see if my mom and some of the master Lumens can portal here and help us."

That would be amazing. The plan had been to bust into the Netherworld with an army, and so I was seriously freaking out about our small crew doing a last minute smash and grab under Apollyon's nose.

"Dad, I need to talk to Mom. It's urgent," Drea said into her phone.

She was silent a moment and then her face fell. "What? Is she okay?"

My stomach dropped at the shock in her voice. That didn't sound good.

What's wrong? I mouthed.

"I'm… in England and it's a long story, but Dad, go focus on Mom. I love you."

There was some yelling, but I couldn't make out the words and then she hung up.

"What happened?" Gage and I pressed her.

She swallowed hard. "My mom was attacked. Shades broke into the relic hall and stole the relic that keeps them from being able to use dark magic to make portals on campus. My dad said that my mom is in surgery. She'll be okay, but not for a few days."

"Oh my gosh, Drea. Go be with her." I pointed to a passing cab, but she shook her head.

"No, she would want me here. I'm with you," she said with tears in her eyes.

I pulled her in for a hug and then peered back to look at her. "Are you sure? Because I can totally do this with the others."

Drea wiped at her eyes, determination settling over her features. "We're going to get your mom back, Tatum." There was surety in her voice, and I knew she probably needed the distraction. Waiting in the healing center for a loved one was a dark place to be, I knew from personal experience.

With a nod, Gage guided us over to the front of the cemetery.

I felt a surge of power rush through me the moment I walked through the open wrought iron gates and stepped foot in the cemetery.

"Help us."

"Take us home."

"Save me."

Oh no, not again.

I glanced around the space and spotted Skye.

"This way," I called to everyone, and we sprinted to where Skye stood. Dash and Jacob landed next to us when we reached her.

"We spotted a couple of people headed this way from the south," Dash said as he readjusted the hood of his sweatshirt that had blown back during flight.

"We think they could be Shades," Jacob added, flexing his wings anxiously.

"They're right. They are Shades," Skye confirmed, and I told the group.

"You have to make a portal now, Tatum," Drea said. "We need to get out of here before they try and stop us."

Geez, no pressure. I hadn't been able to make a portal to the Netherworld when I tried in the past after leaving my mom there. The only portal to or from a different realm I'd ever been able to make was the one from the Netherworld back to New York, and I'm pretty sure my mom helped me somehow. But before today, I hadn't been able to portal to a different country either, so maybe I could do this…

I shook out my arms, trying to shake off my nerves, and Indigo stepped up and grasped my hands with a smile.

"You're a good friend," I told her.

She nodded. "I know."

That made me chuckle.

"Okay, so the last time I saw my mom she was in a black stone building that kinda looked like a modern-day castle in the middle of Shadow City. It was the tallest structure there, so I guess that's where we should look for her. I have no idea what I'm doing, but I'll try to open a portal there."

"Wait," Gage said, putting a hand on my shoulder. "You won't be able to portal straight into Shadow City. Apollyon has wards around it, preventing that. I've heard my father talking about it before."

"But I created a portal from inside the city back to New York," I argued.

"You can portal out, but not in," he said.

I growled in frustration. *Of course I can't portal right to the creepy castle to save my mom. Why can't I catch a break?*

"All right, form a line and let's be quick. I'll try to get us to the gates of Shadow City. I remember it well," I said, recalling the two demons that stood on either side and the way the lava seeped through the cracks in the ground.

Drea pulled a giant light sword from the tattoo on her arm and stepped forward. Dash and Jacob fell into line behind her, both pulling their own weapons and readying themselves for whatever they might face when they entered the Netherworld. Gage stayed next to me, but Marlow palmed matching daggers as she moved behind Jacob.

I took in a deep breath, pulling on the energy in the cemetery as well as Indigo's power, while simultaneously calling up my own. I imagined a portal forming right in front of Drea.

"It's working!" she yelled.

Relief rushed through me, but I kept my focus.

I'm coming, Mom. Hang on.

I took in another deep breath, channeling my power toward the portal while I siphoned from Earth and Indigo.

"It's creepier than I thought," Marlow said, and I popped my eyes open. There, just beyond Drea, was an open portal to the Netherworld. The Shadow City gates rose far in the distance.

I did it!

"Let's go. For Emery." Drea had more courage than anyone I'd ever met. She charged through the portal with her sword clutched in both hands, ready to cut down anyone who got in her way.

Dash, Jacob, and Marlow were next.

"I can't go there, or Apollyon could eat my soul," Skye said. "I'll see if there's anything I can do to help from Earth or Avalon though." She blew me a kiss and popped out of existence.

I turned to look at Gage, and he gave me a small smile as he jogged forward. "See you inside—"

He didn't make it far before he grunted and then stumbled forward, falling to his knees as blood bloomed on the lower half of his t-shirt.

I gasped, and then spotted Arthur standing about twenty feet away, wearing a grin. Several Shades I'd never seen before stood in a crescent around Arthur, backing him up.

"Gage!" I screamed.

A Shade suddenly dropped from the sky, tackling Indigo, and my hands were ripped out of hers. The loss of power, coupled with the sudden attack, caused me to lose control on the portal, and it fizzled to nothing, leaving Drea and the rest of the Angel Gang trapped inside, and Gage, Indigo, and me to face Arthur and his Shades alone.

Oh crap. Crap. Crap. Crap.

Pushing the fact that I'd just separated the group, I rushed forward and knelt next to Gage, staring in shock at the knife hilt sticking out of his side.

His father advanced on us, and two other Shades followed behind him.

Apollyon must have told Arthur where we were, and he had opened a portal nearby to come after us.

"Indigo, you are such a disappointment. Not as much as my son, but pretty close," Arthur drawled as he stalked toward us.

My wings snapped from my back, and a flood of anger rushed through me. How dare he!

Gritting his teeth, Gage ripped out the dagger embedded in his side and stood as if it were nothing.

"I'm *not* your son!" he growled—an inhuman sound that made chills crawl up my back.

"You're right. A son wouldn't betray me like this." Arthur threw his empty hand out and I braced myself, unsure what his powers were.

Gage stepped in front of me, and a black whip of inky dark magic flung from Arthur's hand and wrapped around Gage's torso, tightening like a rubber band and pinning his arms to his sides. He struggled against the restraints, looking super pissed but unfazed by the bleeding knife wound in his flank.

I sidestepped Gage and faced Arthur head on.

"Enough!" I shouted, throwing my arms forward. A shockwave blasted from my palms and slammed into all of them.

The unfamiliar Shades went down, but Arthur must have had some sort of protection field, because it didn't even blow his hair back.

"So it's true?" Arthur said to Gage. "You *were* bitten."

I risked exposing myself to attack and glanced at Gage, only to stumble backward when I looked into burning yellow eyes and fangs poking into his lower lip. Black fur crawled down his neck as his cheekbones became more pronounced.

No.

"Gage?"

I knew then. I knew what Arthur was talking about. What Vera had hinted at. What Aurelia had warned me about.

I'd been so blind. Maybe I just didn't want it to be true, but I couldn't deny it anymore. Gage jumped in front of the hellhound that Apollyon sent to bite me, but instead it bit Gage. That bite had changed him. I didn't know how extensively Gage had been affected except that he looked as much beast as man right now.

Those black bands. Were they forcing this change on him? Or was he doing it himself?

With one swift motion, I pulled a light weapon from my arm and slashed through Arthur's inky black magic, careful not to cut Gage. The bands fell to the ground and Gage bolted forward like a wild animal freed from a cage.

Indigo was locked in battle with the winged Shade who had dropped on her, and one of the Shades that I'd knocked over with my power rushed to meet me as the cemetery was plunged into chaos.

Our swords clanged back and forth as the Shade tried to gut me. He wasn't trying to knock me out or kidnap me, he was going for the kill. He lunged at me again, and in a moment of panic I spun, thrusting my sword into his chest.

He went down on his knees; mouth open in shock.

Bile rose in my throat as I realized I'd delivered a death blow.

I'd never killed anything other than a demon. The Shade on the ground in front of me was about twenty-five, with blond hair and kind eyes, and when he looked up at me I saw so much regret.

I wasn't prepared for that. I wasn't prepared to kill a guy. He could have been like Indigo, a lost soul with a horrible leader.

"I'm sorry," I whimpered, reaching out to him as he tipped over.

"Tate, look out!" Gage's beast-like voice startled me, and I spun just as Arthur's giant sword was coming down at my head.

I didn't have time to block his blow; my sword was still embedded in the chest of the dying Shade at my feet.

There was a blur of black hair and then Gage rushed between us, grabbing his father by the neck. His fingers transformed to claws, and I gasped as Gage ripped his father's throat clean out.

Blood spurted from the hole in Arthur's throat, splattering Gage's face.

Arthur went down on his knees, his eyes wide in disbelief as he brought his hands to his neck and tried to cover the wound, but there was no staunching the river of blood pouring from the opening. Arthur's lips moved, but only a gurgling noise came from his mouth. He lifted a hand toward Gage, his red lifeblood dripping from the tips of his fingers as his black magic sparked, dimmed, and then fizzled out.

I looked away from Arthur and over at Gage as he stood above his father's body. He looked almost normal. The only remaining evidence of his beastly transformation were the bright streaks of gold that ran through his wintergreen eyes. But with red dotting his face, and his chest heaving like he'd just run a marathon, he still reminded me of a feral animal.

My instincts were all over the place. I couldn't decide whether to step closer and offer comfort or run away. My heart urged me to make sure he was all right, but another part of me recognized the predator in Gage and screamed at me to flee.

"We have to get rid of the body."

I started at Indigo's voice, temporarily having forgotten she was with us because of the enormity of what had just happened.

Gage freaking transformed into a beast and killed his dad! I could not deal right now.

"What?" I blinked back at her, my brain still taking a moment to catch up.

Gage didn't even acknowledge she'd spoken; he was looking at me expectantly.

Indigo's short hair was disheveled, and she had a cut on her cheek, but other than that she seemed unharmed. "Arthur," she said, and then also pointed at the guy I'd run through with my sword, who was slumped on the ground a short distance away. "And him too."

There was a female Shade on the ground next to a cracked gravestone a little ways away. She lay on her side with her back to me, and I couldn't tell from this distance if she was breathing or not.

"Did you…?" A knot formed in my throat, and I couldn't get the words out.

Indigo shook her head. "No. I didn't kill her. I kicked her and she smashed her head on the gravestone. The others ran away."

I nodded, feeling a little relieved. I wasn't sorry Arthur was gone, but I was glad Indigo didn't have the death of a fellow Watcher on her hands like I did.

I killed him.

"I'll need to figure out what to do with her too," Indigo

went on, pointing toward the unconscious girl, "but for now you and Gage have to get to the Netherworld to save your mom."

"You're not coming with us?" I asked.

"Someone needs to stay and clean all this up. Listen to me, Tatum, the Shades are going to find out that Arthur is dead, and there will be hell to pay when that happens. They might go as far as to declare all-out war on the New York Lumens. If I can burn his body, then that will at least buy you some time before that happens."

Gage finally turned from me and looked to Indigo. "We can't leave you here to do that alone," he argued, and I nodded my agreement.

"You can and you will. I can take care of this," Indigo said sharply enough that I knew there was no room to debate.

Gage pressed the heel of his hands into his eyes and groaned. When he dropped his arms, the look on his face said he was resolved. "Go back to my Aunt Vera's. Tell her I sent you and that my father is dead. She hates him enough to help you cover up his death."

Yes, that was a good idea. Vera definitely gave off the vibe of being resourceful, so I had no doubt that if anyone knew how to dispose of or hide a body, it would be Gage's eccentric aunt.

I grabbed Indigo's hand. "And then get yourself to the Lumen Compound in New York and see Aurelia. Tell her what happened and where we are. And tell her I'm bringing everyone back, including her daughter. That's a promise."

Looking into my eyes, Indigo nodded. She was with us now, like Gage was. I knew Aurelia wouldn't turn her away.

The next couple of minutes passed in fast forward. We bound the unconscious female Shade's hands behind her back with Indigo's shoelaces. It wouldn't hold her for long, but hopefully long enough for Indigo to run and get help from Vera. We had no idea if more Shades were on the way or if the ones who ran would come back, so I needed to make this portal quickly and rejoin Drea and the others in the Netherworld.

"Get rid of the bodies, and then get your butt back to New York. Aurelia will protect you," I reiterated to Indigo as we held hands.

"I will," she said and then I immediately pulled on the energy from the cemetery and her to create a portal.

My mind was a mess. Gage killed his dad after he went all beasty, and he'd barely said more than two words since he told Indigo to find his aunt. I was super concerned about not only Indigo, but also my friends who I'd stranded in the Netherworld.

"Concentrate. You can do this," Indigo encouraged me after I felt my power flare and then sputter out two times.

Taking a deep breath, I closed my eyes and did all I could to lock my concerns away and focus on creating a portal like Aurelia had been teaching me. When I smelled the sulfuric stench of rotten eggs, I knew I'd done it.

"It's large enough for me to go through," Gage said.

I opened my eyes and stared at the opening between

worlds my magic had created. I couldn't see the landscape through the thick smoke seeping out of this portal, but from the strong scent of sulfur and heat coming from the smoke-filled opening it was obvious it led to the Netherworld.

Gage cast a final look at his father's crumpled form on the ground. I couldn't read his expression. It wasn't sadness or regret, but it wasn't satisfaction either.

"I'll wait for you on the other side," he said to me, and then stepped forward and disappeared into the smoke.

I gingerly released Indigo's hands, concentrating on still siphoning energy so the portal wouldn't collapse before I could get through. I didn't give myself any time for doubts to creep in, and instead ran forward and was swallowed into Hell.

I landed in the Netherworld on shaky legs and fell to one knee. Gage was there in an instant to help me up. Just like last time I traveled to the Netherworld, it felt like I'd been spun in a dryer before landing on solid ground.

I glanced around as I got to my feet, immediately on alert. The Netherworld was just as I remembered: black ashy ground as far as I could see, broken up by veins of orange that cut through the landscape. But one thing was glaringly missing: Shadow City.

My stomach dropped at the realization.

"The portal didn't take us to the same location as it did the others," Gage said, voicing my fear.

Oh, no.

"Where are we, then?" I asked as I scanned the area.

"Shadow City is that way, over that mountain range," Gage said as he pointed over my shoulder.

I spun to see what he was talking about and caught my

breath at the rock formations in the distance. They shot up from the ground like jagged shark teeth. Shiny red dripped from the top of each peak, leaking down the sides of the black rock.

"What is that?" I asked. "Lava?"

Gage was silent a moment, and I turned back to him. "Not lava… blood. Those are the Blood Mountains."

Holy creepy Nightmareville.

"How do you know Shadow City is on the other side of those nightmare mountains? Have you been here before?" My boyfriend of all of one hour was just full of surprises today.

Gage shook his head. "No, but I've seen a map on my father's desk. It was a while ago. It's been years since he's let me in his office unsupervised, but I had enough sense to memorize it while I had the chance."

I took in a calming breath, gathering my thoughts while also trying not to freak out that I'd locked four of my Lumen besties in Hell and we were now miles away from them. "Okay, then we head that direction. By now Drea and the others must realize something has happened and we're not coming through. The plan was to head toward the black castle in Shadow City, so you and I will still do that. We'll find them on the way."

"According to the map, there should be a tunnel through the mountains, so we don't have to scale them," Gage said.

At least that was one thing we didn't have to worry

about. I didn't know if I could have climbed a mountain that was drenched in blood.

No, that's not true, for my mom and friends I would have, but I was glad that I didn't have to.

"All right, let's go," Gage said, and then turned toward the Blood Mountains.

"Hold up," I said, and Gage stopped, glancing over his shoulder at me. When he saw the look on my face, he turned fully in my direction.

My mom needed me. My friends needed me. I knew we didn't have a moment to spare, but this couldn't wait either. I couldn't go a minute longer without knowing what was going on with Gage. He'd kept secrets from me for days, but that stopped now.

"What's going on with you, Gage? And don't even try to play it off as nothing. I heard what Arthur said. I *saw* what happened to you. Were you bit by the hellhound you saved me from?"

I knew he had been. I'd already seen the evidence, but I needed to hear him say it.

Gage just stood there staring into my eyes, expression-less, almost as if he wasn't sure if he wanted to tell me the truth or not.

"Yeah," he finally said, and gazed to the side. "I was bit."

I brought my hand to my mouth, emotion clogging my throat. There must have been a small part of me that was still hoping it wasn't true, that there was a different explanation for what I'd witnessed in that cemetery. "And what does that mean?"

Gage looked back at me and softened his expression. He took a step forward and then stopped himself almost as if he was unsure if he should touch me or not. His hands turned to fists and he jammed them into his pockets. "Dash knows a little about hellhound bites. His uncle was bit by one, but apparently every person presents symptoms differently based on the bite. According to Dash, some of the changes can even be reversed. I haven't fully transformed, so there's hope all this could be temporary."

My heart skipped a beat at the words *fully transformed.*

I swallowed hard, finding my voice. "Fully transformed?" I tried to sound nonchalant, but it came out panicked. I thought back to the hellhound who'd shoved me out the window. The one that had bit Gage. It had stood on its hind legs and my first thought was that it had been a werewolf. "Do you mean to say that hellhounds used to be people, and that you might turn into one?"

Don't freak out. Don't freak out.

Gage was silent for several heartbeats, and then he sighed and ran an agitated hand through his hair.

"Yeah, it's a possibility," he admitted, looking ashamed.

"And you've kept this from me!" It was a statement rather than a question and one I shrieked in a crazy high-pitched voice that I wasn't super proud of.

This whole time he'd known something this serious was

possible and hid it from me? How was I supposed to trust him when he obviously didn't trust me with the truth?

"I didn't even know what was happening, not for sure, so I didn't want to worry you. You had your mom to worry about, and I've caused enough trouble for you. It might be nothing. It might—"

"Nothing?" I laughed, and it even sounded bitter to my own ears. "I just watched you grow fangs and claws and rip out your father's throat. I don't call that *nothing*."

Gage flinched and I immediately wanted to take the words back, but I didn't know how. He killed his father to stop him from stabbing me, and I just threw it in his face. He also jumped in front of that hellhound for me, but the words were out there, and the damage was done.

I didn't know how to handle this situation. I was a mix of emotions and too shook up from this entire day to be normal or think rationally. I was both scared for Gage and furious at him. I couldn't reconcile those feelings.

Gage turned to keep walking when it seemed like I wasn't going to say anything more, and I reached out and grasped his hand. He looked over at me hesitantly, and I pulled him closer.

"I'm sorry." My voice cracked. "I just want you to trust me with tough things. That's what you do in relationships. I can handle it, I promise."

Dash's words came back to me then, about he and Gage not having normal childhoods and how that affected them. I had come to terms with the fact that Gage wasn't going to be boyfriend of the year, and I was going to have to walk him through how to have a normal relationship—not that I was an expert. But his heart was in the right place, and that counted for something.

Gage nodded. "I'm sorry I didn't tell you. To be fully honest, I'm freaked out myself and would rather ignore it until we know whether it's permanent."

I could understand that. How many of my own emotions had I shoved into Pandora's box the last week alone? But some things couldn't be ignored. Shifting into a hellhound was one of them.

I tugged him forward until the tips of our shoes were touching. I knew he didn't exactly love his dad, but it was still his father he'd just killed for me.

"I'm sorry about your dad, and I'm sorry you were bit trying to protect me." I reached up and wrapped my arms around him, and he nuzzled his face into the side of my neck. I felt his entire body relax now that we were holding each other.

"I'm not sorry about any of it. I would do it all over again to protect you, Tate." His voice was gruff and what he said made my heart grow wings. When he pulled back, things felt better between us. Not perfect, but better.

We started off toward the Blood Mountains, in search of my friends who I'd trapped inside this nightmare realm.

"Gage, we've been walking for hours." I stumbled as my foot snagged on a rock. Gage's arm reached out and caught me, pulling me upright.

We might be angelic beings, but we still needed sleep. I'd lost count of how many hours I'd been awake. Twenty four? Thirty-six? Being in New York felt like days ago. The Blood Mountains in the distance looked deceivingly close, but the more we walked toward them, it was like the farther they got away.

Gage scanned the open landscape and nodded, pointing to a small hill. "We'll make camp over there."

Make camp. With what? All I had on me was some lip gloss, and I was starting to get thirsty and hungry. I pulled out the tube of gloss and stared at it. It *was* watermelon flavored...

"I need water," I told him as we clambered over some rocks. We luckily seemed to be in an uninhabited portion of the Netherworld, for which I was grateful.

"Me too." Gage hiked up to what looked like an empty shallow cave. It wasn't a deep one, but it went in about four feet, which was enough to give us shelter if it started raining blood or anything crazy.

We both collapsed onto the ground of the cave, panting, and I moaned, "Water."

Gage sat up. "I know of some storage facilities near Shadow City where Apollyon keeps food and water for him and the Shades who live in the city. But that's like a day's walk away, so for now..." He let that sentence linger in the air.

What, starve? Die of thirst? If only Indigo was still here to help me stabilize a portal. I'd try to get us closer to Shadow City. I'd already tried once but failed miserably. I couldn't get the portal large enough for Gage and me to pass through, so walking was our only option.

I couldn't help but think of what Drea and the others must be doing for food and water. I just hoped they'd either made it into the city or one of those storage houses he spoke of, because I already felt enough guilt for trapping them there.

"How's your wound?" I indicated his bloody shirt from where his dad had stabbed him. He hadn't complained about it at all the entire walk, but he was a tough guy like that. If Gage needed medical attention, maybe I should create a portal into a hospital in New York or the healing center and push him through. Then I could go on the rest of the way by myself. Sure, he'd be mad, but he would be alive.

He lifted his shirt and I gasped. There was no bloody wound, just a faint pink scar where it used to be.

He looked down at it, then over at me. "Dash said his uncle had healing powers too after being bitten..."

I was grateful he was sharing this hellhound stuff with me, and so I didn't want to react too strongly and scare him from sharing future things with me.

"It's not a bad power to have," I said nervously.

Gage side-eyed me and then put his head into his hands.

When he lifted his face, I couldn't help but note how gorgeous he was. Even now, looking stressed and with dirt and sweat on his face he was utterly kissable.

"Tate, I should tell you something else Dash told me."

I braced myself. I'd wanted him to hit me with the tough stuff and now he was going to. I just needed to prove to him that I could handle it. Reaching out, I slipped my hand in his. "Whatever it is, we can get through it together," I told him.

He nodded, squeezing my hand. "Dash said that if enough venom got through the bite to make me fully shift, I would automatically be sucked into a portal to the Netherworld for a full day every full moon."

It was like time stopped. I stopped breathing, stopped blinking. Everything just froze as I processed his confession. When it finally seeped in, I sucked in a lungful of air.

"Okay… so when do we find out if that's happening or not?" My voice shook.

I'm cool. You can trust me with your darkest secrets, and I won't run away screaming.

"You're totally freaking out," he chuckled nervously.

"I am not." I tried to school my expression as Gage looked down at our clasped hands. I followed his gaze and realized I was squeezing his so hard my knuckles were white.

Oops.

Letting his hand go, I smoothed my sweaty palm on my jeans. "Sorry, just processing if my boyfriend will be a hellhound for Halloween. Could be cool. You wouldn't need a costume."

Gage laughed, and I was glad it had lightened the mood a bit. Leaning closer to me, he raked his hands through my hair and down the side of my neck. "Say it again," he whispered.

It took me a second to realize what he was asking, and when I did I couldn't help but smile. "Boyfriend."

Gage smiled back, shaking his head. "Never thought I'd see the day."

"You said it first," I joked, and then poked him in the side.

He captured my fingers and brought them to his lips for a gentle kiss. "I sure did," he said.

I held up my hands and made air quotes with my fingers. "I don't do relationships, I have a reputation, blah, blah."

Gage tickled my side, and I jerked my arms down, laughing.

"You're never going to let me live that down, are you?"

I grinned at him. "Probably not."

He groaned, but the smile he couldn't wipe from his face said he didn't care.

My grin grew wider. Even trapped in the Netherworld I could be at ease with this man. My relationship with him was a great comfort right now, and I was glad I wasn't down here alone.

"I have an idea to get us dinner," I told him suddenly.

The thought of making a portal to a New York hospital to shove Gage in if he was injured gave me an idea.

He perked up. "Whatever it is. Yes."

That made me smile. Gage was equally as food motivated as I was.

"Okay, in my experience, it's easier for me to make a portal into New York than it is to make one from New York and *into* the Netherworld. I won't need a cemetery or a boost from a Shade, and I could open a small portal into a grocery store in New York City."

"Brilliant. Let's give it a try. If you keep the portal open the whole time, I'll run through and grab the food. That way there is no chance we'll get separated."

I nodded, my tongue feeling swollen and thick in my mouth for the lack of water. Hopefully it was the middle of the night in New York, because I was about to raid a grocery store and I didn't want anyone to have a heart attack when they saw a smelly Netherworld portal open up in the middle of it.

Standing, I cracked my neck, closing my eyes to get a visual of where I wanted to portal to. There was a really nice Whole Foods at the corner of 9th Ave and 58th Street that I ate at with Gran once. I could clearly picture it in my mind, the rows of apples and oranges so neatly stacked. The cases of water and the hot food bar. My mouth watered as I pulled on my power and held out my hands.

Gage crouched on his heels, ready to jump into whatever portal I created.

"Just stay calm no matter what happens. I don't want to be locked away from you," Gage told me.

I nodded. I found that the best way to stay focused was for me to keep my eyes closed. I did that now, and envisioned the shelves lined with food. Pulling on my power, I breathed in and out slowly.

"You did it. Be right back!" Gage said.

I debated between opening my eyes and keeping them closed but decided not to open them and just focus on my breathing, envisioning the portal remaining open. When I heard a crash, I couldn't help but look and the portal shrank in half.

"Everything's fine!" Gage yelled, and my heart hammered in my chest as I peered at him standing over a broken jar of pasta sauce. "Accidentally knocked into it." He looked back at me.

He had taken off his shirt and made a makeshift mask to cover his face and identity from the security cameras they no doubt had. Clutched between his hands, I noticed he was holding a purple and pink tribal print backpack with the tags still on it as he shoved food into it quickly. It was kind of comical.

"Water!" I whisper-screamed, and he jogged down another aisle while I pumped my purple magic into the portal to make it bigger.

We will totally pay them back for this, I told myself.

One day.

It was dark inside the store, but when Gage disappeared

from view I could still hear him rustling around. Finally, after a few minutes he walked toward me with two backpacks full of items slung over each shoulder *and* a twenty-four pack of bottled water in his hands.

Yes!

Holding my concentration, I sighed in relief as Gage stepped back through into the Netherworld just as an alarm sounded inside the store.

"Close it!" Gage yelled, and I let the vision in my mind's eye fall away as I retracted my magic.

Gage pulled the shirt off his face and then handed me a bottled water and an identical pink and purple backpack. Reaching out, I unscrewed the cap and chugged the contents, moaning when the lukewarm water hit my parched throat.

Gage watched me, unmoving for a moment, his searing green eyes piercing into me.

"What?" I pulled the water away from my lips.

He cleared his throat. "Nothing. Open your bag. I got you a clean shirt, toothbrush, and some toothpaste."

I opened the backpack and pulled out the soft blue cotton shirt. Peering down at the bold lettering, I laughed.

Hot Vegan Chick.

Gage grinned. "It's all they had."

"Fine, but the second we get back to New York I'm buying a shirt that says, 'I Love Bacon,'" I told him.

He pulled out his new shirt, which was just a solid green color, and slipped it over his head.

I cleared my throat. Gage and I had had some pretty steamy kisses, but I hadn't exactly been topless in front of him and sitting on the dirt ground in the Netherworld wasn't the way I wanted to do that.

Turning to give him my back, I pulled off my gross blood-splattered and dirt-streaked shirt and slipped on my new one. It was so soft and a perfect fit. By the time I turned back around, Gage had opened a bunch of food for us to share.

"Dinner is served." He gestured to the unwrapped protein bars, chips, sunflower seeds, and even crackers with peanut butter.

We ate the meal in companionable silence while looking out onto the desolate landscape.

"Can you believe my mom has lived here for almost eighteen years?" That fact hit me like a punch in the gut.

He nodded. "Can you believe my dad is dead?"

I froze, a peanut butter cracker to my lips. But Gage just shrugged. "I've dreamed of it for so long and now... he's gone."

Silence descended between us, and I didn't say anything more. What was there to say to that? Gage and his father had a super toxic relationship, and Arthur had tried to kill me. But Gage was now completely parentless, and that had to have him feeling a certain type of way.

When we were done eating, fatigue pulled at my limbs.

"I'm beat." I yawned.

"Me too."

He reclined in the dirt, putting one arm behind his head, and tapped his chest. Scooting over, I leaned so that my head was resting on his right peck. Gage's free arm came around my lower back and I sighed in contentment. With each breath he took, my head slowly lifted, and I could hear the constant rhythmic thump of his heart.

Boom. Boom. Boom. It was soothing, and before I knew it, I was asleep.

Something roused me, and the heavy feeling in my limbs told me I'd only been asleep a few hours. Opening my bleary eyes, I sat up, blinking out into the dark distance as I tried to get my bearings.

I was in the Netherworld, and I'd fallen asleep on Gage, who was still asleep next to me.

I peered down at him. He looked so peaceful.

What had woken me? My mind was so foggy with sleep I couldn't remember.

A thump on the ground had me more alert. There were shadows at the mouth of the cave.

I was just about to shake Gage awake when the shadow nearest me turned into a hellhound.

"Gage!" I yelped as it barreled for us.

Reaching onto my right arm, I grabbed for a weapon hidden on my skin, but before I even had it halfway into my hand, Gage stood and rushed the beast. They crashed into each other like two football players and went tumbling down the side of the hill.

Holy crap.

I stumbled to my feet, light weapon in my hand, and made my way outside to see that Gage had already shifted into half a beast. His chest was still man, but his arms and face were like a demon. Black fur wrapped down his arms, which had bulked in size, and his fingertips were pointed to claws. From the neck up was like looking into the face of a demonic wolf.

I whimpered. Seeing him like this killed me. After everything he'd been through, how could Avalon strip him of his powers and send him back to Earth helpless? He wouldn't have been bitten by the hellhound if he'd had his wings and his old Shade powers. He'd chosen the good side and was punished for it, and that pissed me right off.

Gage and the beast grappled with each other while I tripped down the hill and then snuck around behind the hellhound. Gage was holding it by the throat as it snapped in his face, baring its sharp teeth at Gage, whose beastly face was covered in short black fur, below yellow glowing eyes.

Beast or not, I realized in that moment that it didn't matter, because even now I didn't want to walk away. I just wanted to draw closer to him and help him through this.

With a battle cry, I leapt forward, stabbing the hellhound in the back, right where I thought its heart was. I was careful not to go too deep and stick Gage.

When the beast howled, its legs collapsing, Gage released its throat.

I twisted my knife and the hound shuddered before going limp. I waited for him to turn to ash, but it never came. Maybe that wasn't something that happened in the Netherworld?

Yanking the light weapon out, I looked up to make sure Gage was okay, but he just stared at me with those glowing yellow eyes, and I couldn't interpret the look.

When he was in this form, did he still know me? Would he ever hurt me? More importantly, was he hungry and did he like blondes?

So many questions went through my mind. From his head down his neck was covered in black fur. He looked even more transformed than when his dad put those shadow bands around him in the cemetery. Each shift seemed to be bringing him closer to being fully consumed.

"Gage, it's Tate." I started to grow nervous with the way he was staring at me like he didn't recognize me, but when I said the pet name he called me, he turned his face to the side and looked down, as if ashamed.

Slowly, the black fur retreated along with the animal-like nose, and then the eyes returned to their bright green. When he was back to his normal self, he glanced down at the hellhound in shock. "I would never hurt you when I'm like that, Tate."

It was like he'd read my mind. Now I felt so guilty.

Rushing forward, I threaded my hands through his. "I believe you."

He nodded. "I was just staring because I was processing what the hellhound said."

I frowned. "What do you mean what it said? I didn't hear any words."

Gage swallowed hard. "Apparently hellhounds can speak into each other's minds." He looked at me then, absolute desperation in his gaze. "It said that it could smell me. That every hound in the realm could *smell* me."

My stomach bottomed out. "What does that mean?"

Gage chewed at his bottom lip. "Dash told me that hellhounds are all alphas, and they compete for territory and power. I think they see me as a threat."

Well, I wasn't going to be able to sleep after that newsflash. I'd rather brave the Blood Mountains at this point.

"Let's find Drea and the gang, get my mom, and then get the hell out of here," I told him.

He nodded, giving me a small smile, but it didn't reach his eyes.

"This is disgusting!" I shivered and then gagged for the tenth time as the blood trickled down the walls of the tunnel we were walking through. We'd been hiking ten, maybe twelve hours, and my boots were soaked with blood and my feet felt like they were going to fall off. I would have just flown but there was no way I could carry my gigantic boyfriend, so we were relegated to walking through the Blood Mountains, which, spoiler alert, dripped blood.

"Whose blood is this? Why is it here? I have so many questions," I said.

I think Gage had tired of my chattiness hours ago, because he'd stopped answering me.

"It can't be much longer," was all he said, and I wanted to believe him, but he'd said that two hours ago and I was starting to get tired, and worried sick about Drea and the others.

On the plus side, I discovered that I had light powers and could basically turn my hand into a light bulb, so that was cool.

I was just about to ask another question when I heard talking up ahead. Both Gage and I froze.

"Master said to keep the tunnels clear. He's moving the wife," a male with a growly voice said.

The wife. Master Apollyon's wife, AKA my mom?

I inched forward.

"That wench is more trouble than she is useful. Given him hell over the years with her tantrums. I've never understood why he doesn't just kill her. She ain't that pretty," another voice responded, and anger flared inside of me.

I quickly pulled two weapons and handed one to Gage, who took it silently. I wasn't sure if he even needed weapons anymore since he was a weapon at this point, but until he rejected the swords, I was going to keep giving them to him.

Moving forward, I peeked around the bend and saw two figures leaning up against the sides of the blood walls. They were framed in a bit of moonlight that shone in from the tunnel entrance just past them.

Yes, the end is in sight. I couldn't wait to get out of this creepy blood-drenched tunnel.

I crept toward the pair in ninja-like silence.

"Where's he moving her?" the one asked, and I froze again. If we didn't find my mom in the castle, I would need a second place to look.

"Devil's Meadow," the other replied.

I looked at Gage, praying he knew where that was, and he nodded once.

Time to die, bastards.

Leaping out toward the entrance, I slashed the level six demon right across the throat as Gage took care of the other one. They both went down quickly, and I did a full three-sixty to get my bearings and make sure there weren't any others.

We were alone, halfway up the mountain. I could see Shadow City in the distance.

Thank God.

"*Help us*," a voice whispered, and I spun but nobody was there.

"*She's here to save us*," a female said, and my heart hammered in my chest.

"Do you hear that?" I asked Gage.

He frowned, looking at me like I'd grown an extra head.

Awesome. That was a no.

"*Free us*," a woman said, this time closer, and I spun around to come face to face with a ghost.

A shriek tore from my lungs, and I stumbled backward. The woman was see-through like Skye, but unlike Skye she looked ill. Okay, she was dead, so of course she wasn't healthy, but her cheeks were sunken in and patches of her hair missing. Parts of her transparent form were missing, like holes in Swiss cheese.

"Are you here to help us?" she asked me.

I swallowed hard.

"You okay?" Gage stepped protectively closer to me.

"I'm seeing a ghost," I reported to him, and the woman frowned.

"Skye?" Gage asked.

I just shook my head. The woman was looking at me like I'd shot her dog.

"He's killing me," she sobbed, pulling at her hair. "Each day I feel myself wasting away. He feeds on us until there is nothing left. So many have already been lost." Tipping her head back, she wailed into the dark night sky.

Geez. She had to be talking about Apollyon.

I did not want to deal with this kind of ghost drama right now, but the woman didn't seem to be in a hurry to leave and I felt really bad that she was sick or disappearing or whatever. As she drew closer to me, I caught movement out of the corner of my eye and looked over to see several other shadowy ghosts clambering up the side of the mountain toward me.

"I'm sorry," I told her, "I wish I could help you all, but—"

"Please!" She lunged, her bony fingers wrapping around my wrist.

I hissed when the cold rushed through my system, but the second she touched me a jolt of power left me and bled into her. Her ghostly form wobbled and wavered, and I yanked away from her.

The woman gasped and I stared at her in shock. She was

more solid now, a full ghost like Skye, and her hair had grown back, as well as fat put into her cheeks.

Holy ghost rejuvenation!

"I'm so lost here," Gage muttered.

I ignored him, because now the spirits that had been climbing toward us had arrived. There were half a dozen, and they all looked at the woman in shock.

"Mina! You're whole again," an older woman said. She had the Swiss cheese spirit form going on as well.

"She healed me! Took power back from the dark master," the woman, Mina, said.

I held up my hands. "I didn't do anything on purpose."

The older woman looked at me and then inhaled. "You smell like him. Like that festering demon pustule, Apollyon."

Well, it was clear my biological father was not loved in this realm, and I didn't blame them.

"I—well, I…" I was scared to tell them who I was for some reason, like they might attack me, which was stupid because they were dead. What could they really do to me anyway? "I'm Apollyon's daughter," I finally said.

A dawning came over the older woman and Mina's faces, and they both nodded. The other spirits shifted behind them anxiously. They were even less corporeal, and I wondered if maybe they weren't strong enough to communicate with me.

"We know who you are, and we've been expecting you," Mina said. "Your mother spoke about you."

My throat constricted. "You've, you've seen my mother?"

They all nodded. "She can use his power sometimes. She speaks with us, tries to help us hide from him."

The more I learned about my mom, the more I loved her.

"What's going on?" Gage grumbled.

I quickly brought him up to speed.

"They've seen your mom? Have they seen Drea and the other Lumens?"

That was a brilliant question that I'd been too shocked to ask.

I quickly rattled off my friends' descriptions and Mina and the old woman shook their heads. My heart fell, but a young teen spirit in the back, a boy, pressed forward. He opened his mouth to speak, and his voice was so quiet I almost couldn't hear him. "I saw them. They're in Shadow City, on the roof of the big nightclub building."

The roof? Of course. Jacob and Dash can fly, so they would have gotten Marlow and Drea up to safety as well. They would have known that from a high vantage point they could see the whole city. They were probably even watching for us to arrive. Just like I knew they would never abandon me, they knew I would be on my way to join them.

"Thank you." I reached out and touched his arm and a pulse of purple light went through me and into him, strengthening his spirit.

The other souls gasped, and I beckoned them forward. Clearly the mere act of touching them helped them, so I was going to try and do my best to give them a boost. What was a little energy exchange if it helped them not disappear?

After I'd touched each one and made them as strong and healthy as possible, I promised them I would come back to free them at another time. It was my purpose after all, I was just hoping that Aurum knew how to transport souls from the Netherworld to Tartarus, because right now I had no idea.

I took a step forward and dizziness washed over me. I stumbled, causing Gage to reach out and steady me. I engaged my strength angel marks and they lit and swirled white as a punch of energy returned to me.

"Whoa, whoa. What just happened?" Gage eyed the place the souls had been, but they weren't there anymore because they'd already floated off into the distance.

I peered behind me and swallowed hard. "They were disappearing. Apollyon was feeding on them, and I strengthened them."

Gage frowned. "But at what cost to you?"

It was a good question, one I hoped I'd find a good answer to, because my gut told me that what I'd just done was an appetizer for the main course when I'd set all of the souls trapped here free.

When the dizziness subsided, I stood taller. "I'm good, let's get in there," I said, nodding toward Shadow City in the distance.

Gage pinched his mouth shut and I could tell he was worried, but he didn't voice his concerns. Reaching down, he started to pull the cloak off of the demon we'd killed, and I quickly caught on to what he was doing.

"Brilliant," I said, and pulled the cloak off of the other demon as well. The material was strange, like a scaly leather. Mine was charcoal gray and Gage's was a deep hunter green. I was pretty sure they were made from the hides of some long-dead demon, but I pushed the gruesome thought from my mind, not wanting to obsess over whose skin I was wearing. Once we had them fastened around us, with the hood pulled up, we set off.

We traversed the rest of the mountain in silence, but Gage stuck close, and more than once I felt his concerned gaze settle on my face. When we reached the base of the mountain, we headed in the direction of Shadow City, keeping a keen eye out for any demons.

"What's the plan to avoid the two guards at the gate?" I asked Gage, peering across the distance at the faint moving blobs that were demon guards. The cloaks were a good disguise as long as no one looked too closely, but I didn't think they'd fool the guards at the gate who were trained to keep lower demons out of Shadow City.

"I'll take on my partial hellhound form and attack them while you sneak past the gates and into the city. Then once I've taken care of them, I'll meet you inside," Gage said.

I didn't love that idea, but I nodded anyway. As much as I would like to fight by his side, he had his hellhound form to disguise him, and I did not. I had no idea how many of my father's demons knew who I was or if they could smell me like the spirits did. Best to stay out of it and keep a low profile.

"Be safe," I told him.

He took off his cloak and handed it to me.

Leaning in, he gave me a quick peck on the cheek and then stalked toward the gates. When his body started to hulk out, contorting as he grew black fur, I ran to the side, ducking behind some big rocks.

Gage started howling and moaning, making a big scene to draw attention. The two guards in front of the gate stepped away to investigate while I waited in hiding.

Don't get hurt. Don't get hurt, I chanted as I watched the scaly demons, one with a snakelike head and the other with a long slick tail and black membranous wings, approach Gage.

Standing on the sidelines was not my jam, but Gage had strength from being bit by a hellhound and so he totally had this handled.

As if proving my point, Gage went for the demon nearest him, his movements blurring, and in the time it took me to blink he'd ripped out the snakelike demon's throat with a clawed hand.

I cringed, torn between being excited Gage was an amazing fighter and horrified he was, in fact, more hellhound than man right now. The second demon flapped his wings and landed on Gage's back and the breath caught in my throat. I was about to run out and help him when I remembered that I was supposed to be sneaking inside.

He's got this. Trust him.

This attack might draw notice. I needed to get inside quickly. Gage pitched himself forward; the demon on his back flew off, and that was all I needed to feel better about the situation.

Running from my hiding spot between the large boulders, I bolted for the gates of Shadow City. It was difficult to tell if it was night or day since the Netherworld didn't have a sun and moon, but whatever time it was, it was gloriously not an active part of the day.

I slipped inside the gates, making sure my head was deep within my hood and then slunk behind an empty market stall. Standing there, I caught my breath, watching a few demons mill about. A female that had long squirming worms that hung to mid-back instead of hair walked across the street, leaving what looked like a tattoo parlor and sauntering into a bar. Two male demons gestured wildly and spoke in grunts and grumbles as they unknowingly passed in front of me to go into a shop down the block that had an all-black door with no sign.

My gaze flicked to the roofs of the nearby buildings, but I saw no demon guards, nor my friends from this angle. I was just starting to worry about Gage when he strolled in through the gates shirtless and covered in black blood, still in his furred form. His upper body looked even larger than the last time he partially transformed, which would account for the missing shirt. He must have busted right out of it.

"Psst!" I hissed, and his head snapped in my direction, yellow eyes flashing.

Slipping into the shadows beside me, he took a moment to get back into his human form. As I watched, the fur on his face and upper body retracted, and the bones in his face reformed.

Once that was done, he grabbed the cloak from my outstretched arms and put it on. "We good?" he asked.

Beside the fact that you just basically turned into a hellhound and killed two demons without breaking a sweat... yeah. Instead of voicing that thought, I just nodded.

We darted across the road, looking for any large buildings that might be the nightclub the spirits had described. I scanned the tops of the buildings looking for any humanoid figures that might be my friends.

Where was the club? We'd passed a bar when Trilok had brought me in, but I didn't know if that was considered a nightclub here. Some buildings were old and crumbling, some were modern and new, and from the street it was hard to tell if anyone was up on any of the roofs.

My options on how to find my friends were dwindling, so I decided I had to risk being seen and take to the skies.

"I gotta get higher to look for them," I told Gage.

He paused, not looking happy about me leaving his side, but eventually nodded. We slid into a little alcove at the side of a big building that resembled a library, though probably wasn't. I doubted demons were interested in their intellectual growth. What would they even read? *How to Torture Humans? 101 Watcher Recipes?*

I handed Gage my cloak and wasted no time releasing my wings. The moment they snapped out, I flapped wildly. It took almost no effort to fly now, it was as easy as breathing. I went straight up, higher than I'd ever gone before, trying to use altitude over Shadow City as camouflage. When I was high enough, I looked around quickly, inspecting every rooftop. When I got close to the giant black castle that I knew Apollyon lived in with my mother, I hesitated. It looked out over the entire city. What if Apollyon was there right now looking out and saw me?

Demons lingered below, and I held my breath as I flew high above them.

Don't look up. Don't look up, I silently pleaded.

Circling back, I went to the edge of the city, and that's when I saw it: a giant warehouse type club with a flat roof and music blaring out of its open doors. Huddled in one corner of the roof were four people I loved very much. Knowing Gage was safely tucked away in the alcove of the building below, I headed for my friends.

They all looked a little worse for wear, and by the dry cracks in their lips I worried they hadn't found water or food. Tears filled my eyes, but I blinked them back as I lowered myself until I was descending right in front of them.

"I'm so sorry," I immediately said when I landed before them, unable to hold back a few of the tears born from both relief and guilt. Some great friend I was, locking them in Hell.

Drea saw me first and lurched forward, yanking me into a hug. When she pulled back, she looked me in the eyes. "Please tell me you have water."

Crap.

I nodded. Retracting my wings, I lowered the backpack from my shoulders. When I opened it, she reached in and grabbed four of the six water bottles I had and tossed them to Marlow, Dash, and Jacob. One by one, they cracked the lids off and then moaned as they drained the bottles.

"Take them all. We can get more." I pulled the other two out and gave them to her. "And here are protein bars." I gave them those as well.

After the water had been drained and Marlow and Drea were tearing into the protein bars, I looked at Dash and Jacob. "Could you fly Gage up here? He just partially shifted into a hellhound and took out the guards at the gate. He's waiting in the alcove of that library-looking building over there." I pointed to the one I meant.

Drea coughed on her protein bar and a piece flew out, landing near my shoe. "What did you just say?"

Shame and guilt played out on Dash's face, and I nodded to him. "I know everything. Please get him up here."

Jacob just stared wide-eyed at me but nodded.

"Come on, I'll fill you in on the way," Dash told Jacob, and they took to the skies.

Sitting before Marlow and Drea, I told them quickly

what had happened with Gage. He and I had agreed on the way over here that we needed to tell our friends what was going on with him; this wasn't a secret he could keep anymore. When I was done, I looked at them both, waiting for their responses.

"I think it's romantic. He threw himself in front of the hellhound and took a bite that was intended for you," Marlow reminded me.

Well, yeah, when she put it that way…

Drea cleared her throat. "I'm not sure I would call it romantic, but we will support and accept Gage no matter what form he comes in," she declared.

I hit the lottery with these friends. "I'm beyond sorry I left you guys here. Arthur showed up and threw a knife into Gage's side. My mind blanked and the portal closed."

Drea nodded. "We saw. I knew you'd make it back eventually, but the hillside was crawling with level two demons by nighttime, so we decided this vantage point was safer. Did Arthur get away?"

I shook my head and lowered my voice. "Gage killed him. To protect me."

Marlow made a swoony face. "Okay, that's *definitely* romantic."

Drea's mouth dropped open in shock. "Holy crap. Arthur is dead? That's a huge deal." If any one of us could fathom the impact Arthur's death would have on the Watcher community, it would be Drea.

Personally, whenever I imagined a New York City

without Arthur it brought a smile to my face. It was going to be nice.

Footsteps sounded behind me and I turned to see Jacob and Dash lowering Gage onto the rooftop. Gage joined us, sitting next to me with his head low. The cat was out of the bag, and I was sure he didn't know what everyone thought of him now.

Drea reached across the space and grasped his hand lightly. "We know and we don't care. You're still with us."

Gage gave her a small smile, and my heart felt lighter knowing there were no more secrets between any of us. "Okay, we know where my mom is. A place called Devil's Meadow."

Gage nodded. "It's north of the city. On the map I saw, it only had a single tower to denote what it was."

Before we did anything else I wanted to make sure we had a solid exit strategy. I'd already stranded my friends in the Netherworld once. I didn't want to accidentally do it again, or worse, decapitate one of them with a collapsing portal.

"Drea, what if I made a portal to New York and we tried to see if your mom was recovered? I can open a portal from the Netherworld back home pretty easily now, but Indigo's not with us, so keeping it open if things go sideways is another story. I would feel better if I knew we had someone else with us to get you guys home if things get dicey."

Drea shook her head. "My dad said she was in surgery and had quite a recovery ahead of her. It would only worry her. Besides, your mom is a Shade, so once we find her you can link with her to make a stable portal. We can do this."

In theory, that was right, but it still made me nervous.

Drea handed Jacob and Dash a protein bar. "Eat up and then we'll head to this Devil's Meadow place, but we need a plan."

Right. A plan. But you needed to know what you were walking into in order to have a plan, and I'm not sure how much we really knew about what we were about to face.

Gage cleared his throat. "When we get there I'll shift into… you know… and fight that way, carve a path for you to wherever they're keeping your mom."

Jacob and Dash nodded. "We'll fight any flying demons they have."

Marlow puffed up her chest. "I'll watch your back."

Drea placed a hand on my shoulder. "And I'll be right at your side."

I breathed out a shaky breath. "Thanks, guys. Who knows, this may go really smoothly. Apollyon shouldn't be expecting us and might only have a few demons guarding her."

At least that was the hope keeping me sane right now.

CHAPTER
SEVENTEEN

Getting out of Shadow City was way easier than getting in since Gage had killed both of the guards. We slipped out of the gates unseen, but in order to get to Devil's Meadow we had to cross some pretty treacherous landscape. The really lava-ish parts were impossible to cross on foot, so we had to fly over them. With the help of my strength angel marks I could fly over those parts with Marlow hanging onto my front like a monkey. Jacob carried Drea, and Dash struggled with Gage, barely getting a few feet off the ground.

Marlow and I snickered at the sight of Dash cradling Gage like a baby as his wings furiously beat against the air.

Gage shot us a glare. "We will never speak of this again."

"Bro, could you eat less? You weigh as much as a small elephant," Dash growled as he set Gage down on the ground. Dash's strength marks were swirling and lighting up his biceps.

"It's called muscle," Gage griped, looking highly offended.

"Shh. Is that it?" Drea pointed ahead of us.

We were behind an outcrop of huge black lava boulders, and I had to move to where she was to peek through two of them. When my eyes landed on a giant black stone tower in the distance, I felt in my gut that we'd found what we were looking for.

"That's it," Gage confirmed.

I peered at the desolate wasteland around it and a thrill went through me. "There's no one here. Let's go."

Gage's hand shot out and grabbed me. "Hold on, something doesn't feel right." His nostrils flared, and the normally sharp green of his eyes turned yellow. "I smell them," he growled, his voice barely human.

My stomach dropped. I still wasn't used to him like this, and by the way everyone else took one giant step backward, neither were my friends.

"Who?" I asked.

"Hellhounds. Hundreds of them," Gage said, fur rolling down his neck, his fingers sharpening to points.

I peered around the rocks again. Spread out in front of us was cracked dry earth, lava rocks, and nothing more.

"Where?" I asked, not seeing a living—or dead—soul anywhere.

Gage cracked his neck, yellow eyes glued to the horizon. "I don't know, but I can feel them."

"Okay, well, I don't see anything, and my mom is in that

tower." It was almost as if I could sense her energy, as if she was reaching out to me, letting me know she was there.

"I'm going first," Gage said. "Tate, you take to the skies and get your mom. We need to make this a very fast rescue."

Trepidation skated down my spine. I took another look at the empty land between us and the jutting monolith in the distance. Were hundreds of hellhounds on their way here? Would they crest the horizon at any moment? I hoped not.

Maybe Gage's senses were just going a little haywire, or he was picking up on hellhounds from all over the Netherworld, but in the event he was right, I agreed with him, we needed to make this a fast rescue.

"I know I haven't linked with my mom yet, but I'm going to open a portal behind these rocks and do my best to try to keep it open. I need to know there's a way for you all to get to safety if things go south. If that happens, run back here and return to New York. Promise?"

I looked each of them in the eye, and one by one they all nodded. All except for Gage.

"Gage," I growled.

He sighed. "I'm not going through until you are."

Drea pointed at him. "Tatum's a flyer who can open portals. She could easily fly to safety and open another portal home. But she won't if one of us stays back and gets injured. Your inability to cooperate with the plan could actually get her killed."

And that's why Drea was our leader.

Gage's beast was partially to the surface. Drea's redress had clearly angered him, but they also made sense.

"Fine. I'll go through if things go sideways, but you better make it home, Tate," he growled.

"I will. *With* my mom," I told them all.

Now that I had all of their agreement to safely flee the scene if things went crazy, it was like a weight had been lifted from me.

Turning around, I took in a deep breath and imagined the cemetery in New York City. It was hopefully a non-busy place to put an open portal for the next half hour or however long this took. I would open it and then fly up to my mom and hopefully use her power to stabilize it and keep it open. I was encouraged by the fact that I'd been able to keep the portal into Whole Foods open by myself when Gage got the groceries. Granted, I wasn't fighting for my mom multiple feet away from the portal, like I would be now, but it was something. Maybe my power was growing.

I gave myself a little pep talk: *Breathe, concentrate, you can do this.*

The mausoleum popped into my mind then, the tiny stone room where we'd hidden to listen in on Apollyon and Arthur's conversation. It was the perfect place to hide a portal.

Pulling on my power, my marks swirled and glowed, and then without even needing to close my eyes like I normally did, the portal began to open. It was the size of an orange first and then grew to a basketball, before finally widening to an opening over six feet tall. The familiar stone walls of the mausoleum as well as the four sarcophagi came into view, and I grinned. I'd only had a few training sessions with Aurelia, and not yet learned or mastered many of the portal making skills, but clearly I was in the "good enough" category.

B- for me, and I'm happy with that!

I yelped as a figure suddenly stepped in front of the portal, and I nearly closed it until I recognized her.

Indigo. It was as if my thoughts alone had conjured her.

She stepped through, hair a wild mess, her under eyes lined with dark circles. I wondered when she'd last slept.

"Indigo! What are you doing here?" I asked in surprise.

"Your dead friend Skye got a message to me through Gage's psychic aunt, Vera," she huffed, as if she'd run here. "I needed to be here and help you hold open a portal?"

Who knows how Skye knew where we'd be. At the moment I certainly didn't care. Sweet relief washed over me. As annoying as Skye was sometimes, that girl always had my back, and I was forever grateful.

"That would be great. We're about to go save my mom." I indicated the tower beyond.

She nodded, looking around the Netherworld a little uneasily. Then she planted her feet and rubbed her hands together. "We got this. Just connect with me and then I'll join with the portal so that no matter how far away you are, you can feed me energy like refilling a battery and it will stay open."

I frowned. "Where did you learn that?"

"Skye," she said.

Marlow and Drea were both grinning. I think we all missed our brunette Angel Gang member. I owed her, big time.

Gage cleared his throat and Indigo looked at him, her eyes widening a little at his beastly appearance.

"I took care of the bodies," was all she said, and Gage nodded.

Friendship goals.

"Okay let's do this!" Lifting the hem of her shirt, Drea pulled two light weapons from the tattoos on her midriff.

Marlow, Jacob, and Dash pressed their palms to various parts of their bodies and followed suit.

Gage made fists of his monster hands and his face shifted into that of a beast.

"I'm coming, Mom," I muttered.

Indigo reached out, keeping one hand inside the portal as if touching New York, and then I connected our energies and began feeding her my power.

This had to work. It *would* work.

Gage gave me a nod, and then slipped through the opening in the boulders and onto the dry cracked earth of the flatlands in front of the black tower.

Without a speech, or any fancy words, we all followed suit.

Gage growled, and I didn't get more than ten feet before everything around me changed.

Oh no. Oh, please don't be real.

It was as if we had crossed some invisible shield that was hiding a full army of demonic warriors. Gage was right, there must have been over a hundred of them, mostly hellhounds. They'd been lying in wait this entire time, protected by some ward that we had just crossed through.

"Gage! Turn back!" I screamed, but he didn't listen to me. He was already in a battle with two hellhounds, and dozens more were running at him.

I looked at Drea, panicked, hoping to see strength in her gaze.

I didn't find it. Instead my panic was mirrored on her face.

"Do something before they rip him apart!" she told me.

Jacob and Dash had taken to the skies, and I froze, unsure what I could do with such a large number of demons.

"I… I can't…" My hands shook as I tried to pull on my power, thinking of what to do. In the back of my mind I was still concentrating on the portal and Indigo and feeding her power to keep it open.

Drea grabbed the base of my chin and forced me to look at her. "Do you know what my mom said about you the day you got back from Avalon?"

I shook my head.

Drea looked at the marks swirling on my arms. "She said she'd never seen a warrior with so much power at their disposal. That we could support you and build your confidence, but in the end you probably wouldn't even need us. You've. Got. This."

Her words shocked me. I didn't even know what half of the symbols and marks all over my body meant, but if Aurelia said that about me, maybe I could do something. If I directed a blast of energy to the hellhounds attacking Gage to the right, and then the ones to the left, it would give him enough time—

"Gage!" Marlow's scream of terror ripped me from my thoughts.

I followed her gaze just as half a dozen beasts piled onto Gage and he fell to the ground, disappearing under them.

Something within me snapped. One second I was staring in shock at my boyfriend being no doubt ripped limb from limb, and the next it was as if I had touched a live wire. A current ripped through my body and I screamed as everything in front of me was swallowed up with purple light.

This power was raw, unbridled, and somewhat dark. It wasn't my portal power, this power sought to destroy, to kill, to have revenge. It flowed through me effortlessly, and in that moment I didn't think about anything else. It was as if the very flow of time had stopped and all that existed was this power.

It spread throughout the field, consuming everything in its path, and pride swelled in my chest.

Kill them all. My revenge will extend to anyone who even looks at Gage wrong. Every single hellhound, demon, or person who has ill intentions for him will burn alive.

Pure, unbridled rage consumed me as I stared at the ocean of purple flooding the valley, and grinned.

"Tatum, enough! You'll kill us all!" Drea's voice pierced the power that held me enthralled and I gasped, realizing that something had taken over me.

Shaking myself, I tightened every muscle in my body as if turning off a tap, and the power shut off all at once, leaving behind an emptiness in my chest.

When the purple glow was gone, I blinked at the carnage of Devil's Meadow.

Every single hellhound was incinerated. All except for Gage, who lay panting on the ground now in his human form. Large gashes raked along his back, but he otherwise looked okay as he lumbered to his feet.

I glanced at Drea with excitement over what I'd just done and recoiled when I saw the fear in her gaze. She was holding her arm to her chest. Along the top was a red blistering burn.

A gasp ripped from my throat as guilt threaded through me. "Did I...? I'm so sorry," I whimpered.

She nodded, curtly. "It's okay. Go get your mom. I'll get Gage through the portal back home." Her words were reassuring, but her voice held reservations. I'd hurt my friend.

I looked over at Marlow and she couldn't meet my eyes. The tips of her boots were smoking. I felt sick. I'd almost burned my friends alive. Dizziness washed over me, and my strength marks lit up, but I was disgusted with myself and the way I'd almost allowed my power to hurt people I cared about.

"Marlow… I—"

"It's fine. Go get your mom!" Marlow reached out and shoved me, and I pushed the guilt about what I'd just done into the Pandora's box deep inside me, and kicked off the ground, heading into the skies.

Peering behind me, I saw that Indigo still had the portal open, and relief washed over me. When Dash and Jacob flew next to me, they both wore curious looks. They'd seen everything, and I felt like a monster. This was probably how Gage felt in the courtyard after he had returned, and the Lumens looked at him like he was a demon.

For a split second it had felt like the power was controlling me… versus the other way around… and that was terrifying.

"Go through the portal! I'm right behind you," I told them. I couldn't let anyone else get hurt. What if I did that again and killed my friends?

"No, we'll go with you, you might need help," Dash pressed as he continued to fly alongside me.

"No. I can't do this if I have to worry about you guys. Just go. Make sure everyone gets through the portal, including Indigo. I'll make a new one and get my mom back to Lumen Academy."

I didn't wait for a reply. I zoomed through the sky toward the top floor of the tower, where a single light was on.

CHAPTER

EIGHTEEN

I touched down on an open balcony that was hewn into the side of the tower. Up close, I could tell that the tower wasn't constructed from black rocks, but rather was carved from one mammoth stone that shot skyward like an oversized pillar. It was like the old-fashioned cousin of the modern black tower in Shadow City.

Without a thought, I sucked my wings of mist and smoke back into my body and rushed through the open archway and into the interior of the structure.

"Mom!" I called as I took in the room before me. There was one tiny window on the other side of the room, which wasn't big enough to exit out of. A cloaked figure stood in front of it and turned toward me. Just like the last time I saw my mother, her cloak covered her from head to toe, but she was fast to pull back the hood this time and show her bruised face.

"Tatum," she said, shock apparent in her voice. "You can't be here!"

I ran to her side, tugging her into a quick hug and ignoring the twinge of hurt at her immediate dismissal. She was stiff in my arms for only a single breath before she wrapped her thin arms around me and returned the gesture.

I pulled back from our hug with a smile on my face. I'd found her, I'd actually done it. I was standing before my mom, and in a few minutes we'd be back at the Lumen Compound with all my friends. I almost couldn't believe it.

"Mom, I'm here to take you home," I said, my grin so wide my cheeks were starting to ache.

My mom's eyebrows furrowed, and she shook her head. "No, Tatum. I can't go."

"The hell you can't," I argued. I'd fought my way through the Netherworld for her. I wasn't taking no for an answer, even if I had to swing her over my shoulder and carry her through a portal back to New York.

"Sweetie, you don't understand." Her eyes pleaded with me. "I can't leave. I'm tethered to Apollyon and this place. As long as these chains link me to Apollyon, I'm as much a part of the Netherworld as he is, bound by even stricter rules to remain in it."

I looked down, seeing the length of chain that peeked out from under my mom's cloak and snaked across the black stone floor, leaking wispy shadows.

She cupped my cheek with infinite care. "That's why I didn't go with you last time. I'm stuck here. Until death."

Shock ripped through me at her words. "What? How?" We didn't have time for a long conversation, but I needed to know what I was dealing with. She couldn't leave? Like at all?

My mom swallowed hard. "I came to kill him all those years ago and I failed. Instead he dragged me down here and tortured me for your whereabouts."

Anger rose up inside of me as I looked at the bruises on her face. I was going to kill him.

"When he realized I wasn't going to give you up, he tried to kill me." A darkness passed over her features. "I panicked and did a very dark spell. One I didn't know I was even capable of; one I don't know how to break. I bound myself to Apollyon in an effort to survive, and now I can't leave, and he can't kill me unless the spell is broken."

My heart sank. She really was bound to him. Bound to this place. Forever.

Break the spell.

But that's why Apollyon was looking for her talisman. *Me.* To break the spell over her and kill her. But what if I could break it first and get her out of here?

"No, Mom, *you* don't understand. I'm getting you out of here right now. Apollyon is looking for your talisman so he can break the spell and then kill you."

My mom's eyes flashed, and a look of guilt swept over her face before she cleared her expression. "As long as you leave now and never return, that won't happen."

"Yes, I know. Because *I'm* your talisman," I said boldly.

My mom gasped and brought a hand to her throat. Her head bobbed up and down a few times before she found her voice. "How did you find out?"

"It's a long story. We have a lot to fill each other in on, but that will have to wait until we're somewhere safe."

A bolt of lightning cracked somewhere outside, and I glanced over my shoulder toward the balcony opening. Dark clouds had formed in the distance, they sizzled with red fire, rolling and undulating as they headed straight for us.

"He's coming," my mom said, a wild look in her eye. She dragged her gaze off the sky and pinned me with it. "You have to leave. *Now*."

She'd told me to leave without her once before, and I regretted doing so. I wouldn't make the same mistake twice.

"No. I'm not leaving without you." I just needed to figure this spell thing out.

My mom shook her head so violently that loose hair smacked her cheeks. "If he captures you, you'll never escape this place. We'll both die."

Right, I'd never escape because Daddy Dearest wanted to slurp my soul down like a smoothie. Revulsion rolled in my gut over the atrocities Apollyon was willing to commit to gain power.

"Then I guess that's our cue to blow this popsicle stand." I glanced down again at the smoky chain hooked to my mother's ankle, momentarily wondering how it connected her to Apollyon. It was obviously some sort of black magic, because the chain remained even when Apollyon wasn't near my mom. I remembered how she'd used it to yank Apollyon back into the Netherworld right before I ascended to Avalon.

"It's time to break some chains," I muttered as I slapped a hand to my bicep and peeled a long light sword off my arm. The handle was heavy in my grip as the blade separated from my arm and elongated. Light pulsed from the sword, but I didn't think that a light weapon would be enough to break the length of inky links that slithered across the ground. If I wanted to be sure I could sever the connection between my mom and Apollyon, I would have to use *all* my power.

Grasping the sword in both hands, I reached deep, plunging straight into the wellspring of power inside of me and called it forth. Not only was I blessed with powers from Avalon, but I was also my mom's talisman, which meant somewhere inside of me was the key to breaking this spell.

In an instant, purple fire erupted on my arms and ran down them, twisting and licking over my blade from hilt to tip, casting the room in a lavender glow. These flames were slightly different though, they were black at the tips.

My mom's eyes widened as I continued to unleash my power, creating my own spinning tornado as I pumped more and more into the blade, not willing to take the chance that I'd come up short.

"Tatum, no!" my mom yelled. "You'll be giving Apollyon

just what he wants. Right now I pull on his power. If you break this bond, he'll be unstoppable."

I gritted my teeth, not bothering to argue with her. She'd done the best she could to help protect me from my father, but I was past caring if Apollyon became more powerful. That was an issue for another day. This was a no-win situation. If I left without her, he would just hunt me down eventually and kill both of us. Right now I just wanted my mother back, and I wasn't leaving this place without her.

The purple light built so strong that my eyes watered from the intensity of it.

Suck it, Apollyon.

With a warrior cry, I swung the sword down, arching it toward the smoky chain in front of me. When the blade connected with the black links, it caused a detonation from the point of impact, and I was tossed backward. My back smashed into the rough stone wall, the wind knocked from my chest, and I fell to the floor in a heap.

Coughing, I struggled to my feet and felt the tower shudder. In fact, it felt like the *entire* Netherworld shook in that moment. The ground beneath me swayed and quaked. I didn't know if that was from the spell being broken, or if Apollyon was here and flexing his restored powers, but I wasn't going to stay and find out.

A maniacal scream echoed all around me and my blood ran cold.

Apollyon.

I searched the room and found my mom crumpled on

the other side, her black cloak spread out underneath her like a blanket, her blonde hair tossed over her face. My gaze fell to her skinny ankles and relief poured through me.

They were chainless.

My excitement was short lived, since she was unconscious.

Sprinting to her side, I fell on my knees next to her. After quickly brushing her hair back, I ran my fingers over her throat, searching for a pulse. My own heart rate kicked up as the moments passed and I couldn't detect a steady beat. Then, finally, I felt a small flutter under my fingertips. It was weak, but it was there.

"Mom..." I tried to gently shake her awake, but it was useless. She was out cold.

Calling upon my power once again, I held my hand up in the direction of the middle of the room. I imagined the courtyard in the middle of the Lumen Compound and released my magic. Purple fire shot from my palm, and ten feet away a rift appeared in the air and a portal began to open. A few seconds later, I could see the sanctuary sitting in the middle of the manicured lawn inside the round opening.

A guard inside of the Lumen Compound spotted the portal and left his post and jogged toward me, his face lined with concern.

"Hello, daughter." Apollyon's voice growled from behind me, and I was spurred into action.

Engaging my strength marks, I reached down and

scooped my mom up, lifting her fragile body with ease. She was so small and frail it was almost like carrying a child, but I pushed concern for her out of my mind. She was going to be fine. I wouldn't allow any other outcome. Apollyon was my bigger worry now, I needed to get both of us out of here ASAP before—

Something wrapped around my ankle, and I yelped, nearly falling over with my mother's weight in my arms.

No.

The guard from the Lumen Compound had reached me, and he was someone familiar. I couldn't remember his name, but I recognized him as one of the sanctuary guards from the day of my Ascension. The pressure on my ankle cinched tightly, and my panicked look to the guard was the only warning I gave before I tossed my mother out of the portal and right at him.

"No!" Apollyon growled and yanked me so hard by the leg that I fell on my face and the portal snapped shut, but not before I saw the guard catch my mother in his arms.

I was dragged backward, but without taking a moment to catch my breath, I rolled over and pulled my sword out in front of me. This was now a fight for my life. I'd broken the bond that my mother had to Apollyon which kept him weak, giving him exactly what he wanted... a chance at freedom.

Apollyon grinned, and the mere sight gave me chills. I risked one glance at my ankle and the thick black smoky rope that was tightened there. I was pretty sure I wasn't strong enough to fight him, so instead I was going to have to run. I needed to sever that rope and find some space to create a portal he wouldn't be able to follow me through, but the only problem was that he was standing in front of the balcony, blocking my exit to this crappy tower.

"You're welcome." I tried to bait him into talking to buy me some time to think of a plan to move him away from the opening.

"Shut up," he spat, not taking the bait. He flicked his wrist, and I was thrown into the wall. My shoulder crashed into the brick and pain shot down my arm as I slumped to the ground. The wind was knocked out of me, and before I could even breathe he yanked the rope and I slid across the stone floor toward him.

I could see where this was going. He was going to throw me around this room like a ping-pong ball and kill me slowly.

I pulled for my power, but immediately felt it sizzle to nothing as the cord around my ankle seared with heat. He'd capped my power!

Bastard.

As he pulled me near him, I tucked my knees into my chest, and when I was within kicking range, I kicked up, connecting right with his balls.

The ruler of the Netherworld was a powerful dude, but he still screamed like a little girl and crumpled forward.

Using the distraction, I pulled my sword in front of me and hacked at the black spelled rope holding me captive.

The moment the blade sliced through the bond it fell away.

Apollyon stood to his full height. His wings snapped out, and black wafts of smoke began to fill the small space. His eyes glowed red.

Oh crap.

Good news: I'd maneuvered him away from the opening that led to the outside.

Bad news: He was totally going to kill me.

I quickly stood, praying that I now had access to my power, and inhaled deeply, pulling from the open well inside of me. A surge of raw magic filled my veins, and as Apollyon lunged for me, I unleashed it all.

Purple flames engulfed the room, but immediate fatigue pulled at my limbs. I'd just done this to save Gage. Now it felt like the well had run dry. My strength marks swirled on my arms, but the purple fire sputtered out and I surged forward, ready to flee.

The purple flames now gone, I ran for the window, but stopped when I spotted an untouched Apollyon. Not a hair was burned, not a feather ruffled.

I'm so screwed.

He cocked his head to the side and inhaled deeply, as if smelling me.

"Is that all you have?" he chuckled. "To think I was actually a little afraid of the power you might wield."

I pulled for more power and the purple flames came, but unlike before my legs quivered with fatigue, and I wanted to cry as a helpless feeling settled into my bones.

Apollyon raised his hand and an unseen force gripped me. It was as if a giant vise had wrapped around my body and squeezed.

A scream of terror ripped from my lips as I pushed against the power that held me. Purple and black sparks shot off my body and ricocheted off the walls like bullets.

Apollyon growled, seemingly frustrated, and threw another hand out; the pressure around me intensified. I tried to fight it, I did, but it was too much. I had used up my power, and my will to live began waning as my bones felt like they were going to snap. The pressure in my head alone was enough to make me break out in a cold sweat. It was as if Apollyon was trying to crush me alive.

A minute passed, maybe two. Apollyon groaned and then screamed in frustration. I was trapped, but still alive.

Something was wrong. Could he not kill me?

I stared at Apollyon, falling to my knees, and was shocked to see beads of sweat running down his face. A black rope flew from his hand and wrapped around my neck, but then a purple spark shot from me, and it fell away.

Finally, Apollyon dropped one hand and the pressure eased but didn't leave. I was still rooted to the spot, and he shook his head. "I knew having two of you was a mistake." He nodded as if confirming something to himself. "Sometimes our backup plans become burdens. Now I'll need to get her too. I see that now."

What the what? Was he getting dementia or something. Two of what?

I tried to move but it was like walking through quicksand. His other hand came up, and again that agonizing pressure enveloped me. "Oh no. I'm not letting you go. I'll get your sister and bring her here and then finish you both off," he sneered.

Sister. He said… *sister*.

My brain was still processing his words when the room exploded with golden light. One second I was looking at Apollyon, locked in some invisible vise, and then the next Aurum appeared before me and everything fell away. No more pressure. I could finally move.

"Run!" Aurum bellowed, and I was so relieved to see him I nearly burst into tears.

Without wasting any time, I ran and leapt out of the window, watching as Apollyon's face contorted from disappointment to rage. A black whip shot from his hand, reaching for me, but Aurum's golden light filled the entire tower, and then I was falling.

I had to believe Aurum wouldn't have beamed down here if he couldn't handle himself. So I envisioned the beautiful blue sky above Lumen Academy and pushed my power beneath me, opening a portal in midair. My wings snapped out of my back, but then one of Apollyon's black ropes wrapped around one and I fluttered as I fell. A sharp pain laced up my shoulder and then there was a snap.

I screamed, rolling over in the sky, peering down at the

portal I'd made. I could see the green lawn of Lumen Compound; a few guards were clustered around my mom. It was all from a bird's eye viewpoint, and I realized I'd opened a portal in the sky. No time to fix that.

Reaching behind me, I hacked the black whip with my light blade and Apollyon's bellow resounded through the sky.

With one useless wing, I fell through the portal like a stone and sealed it shut immediately behind me. I flapped madly with my good wing to slow my descent, but it did nothing but make me spin in the air.

Looking up, the guards on the ground shouted, and I did the only thing I could think of. I braced for impact.

The ground came up to meet me and I collided with it. My forehead slammed against the ground, and everything went black.

I came to and immediately remembered everything.

"Mom…" I moaned, pushing through the fogginess and peeling my eyelids open. Drea's face swam into view, then Gage's, then the rest of the Angel Gang, including Indigo.

I nearly sobbed in relief at the sight of them all safe and sound. I was in a recovery room at the healing center.

"My mom…?" I said again.

Drea put her hand on mine, smiling. "Alive. Healthy, and with your gran in the next room."

I sat up and hissed at the pain in my shoulder and head.

"Wing fracture," Drea told me, "that turned into a dislocated shoulder. Even though your wings are made of smoke, they still carry an energy that's connected to your physical form. It will take some time to fully heal."

Gage leaned down and kissed my cheek. "You did it," he whispered. "You saved her."

It hadn't really hit me until that moment that he was right. I did save my mom from almost two decades of imprisonment in the Netherworld. I couldn't help the smile that graced my face then.

"We did it. All of us," I said loud enough for everyone to hear.

They all looked tired and battle weary but were wearing matching grins.

"Help me see her?" I asked Gage.

He nodded, holding out an arm. With my right hand pinned to my chest by a shoulder sling, I took his outstretched arm with my other one as I got to my feet and started to slowly shuffle out of the room.

"See you guys later," I told my friends.

They nodded and waved, urging me on with smiles. This was as much their win as mine, I couldn't have done this alone.

I hobbled next door and Gage knocked on it for me.

"Come in," Gran's familiar voice called from behind the door.

Gage moved to let me go in alone, and I shook my head. "I want you to meet them first."

He swallowed hard but nodded. Besides Gage, these two women were the most important people in my life. It was time we all got acquainted.

Gage opened the door and helped me inside. When my gaze fell on my mother who was freshly showered and eating a sandwich, I sighed in relief. There was color in her cheeks and her bruises were already fading. She still looked too skinny, but we could fatten her up in no time.

Gran pushed off from the bed and pulled me into a fierce hug. "You've got to stop doing this to me or one day I'm going to have a heart attack."

I chuckled, pulling back from her. "Don't say that!"

She smiled and smoothed my hair before turning to Gage and looking at our interlocked arms.

I cleared my throat, suddenly nervous. "Gran, this is my boyfriend, Gage. He helped us rescue Mom."

With my crazy training schedule and the fact that Gage had been in the healing center most of the three days after he'd returned to the Lumen Compound, Gran had yet to meet him. I'd told her all about him though, and we'd planned a dinner, but our impromptu trip to the UK got in the way.

I had no idea what to expect. Gage wasn't technically a Lumen, especially not now. And even if he had swirling white tattoos all over, he still gave off a bad-boy vibe. I wasn't sure if Gran would pick up on that.

Instead, she surprised me. Moving quickly, Gran pulled Gage into a hug. "Thanks for helping my Tater Tot get her mama back. It's nice to finally meet you."

I groaned. "Tater Tot, really, Gran? You haven't called me that in ten years."

Gage hugged her tightly and grinned. "I'm so calling you that now," he told me.

I pointed sternly at him. "You are *not*."

Gran snickered. "What are grandmothers for if not to embarrass their grandchildren a bit?"

My mom cleared her throat then and Gran stepped aside. When I looked down at her, I wasn't prepared for the expression of shame I saw.

"I'm sorry I put you and your friends' lives at risk like that. I'm sorry for a lot of things, Tatum." Her hands were clasped in her lap, head bowed.

It was weird because technically I didn't even know this woman, and yet I was part of her. I felt like I'd known her my whole life and that we'd somehow grown close in our absence. Pulling Gage to her bedside, I sat in a chair next to it.

"Nonsense, no one was hurt," I told her.

She looked at my arm cupped to my chest, and the white shoulder sling, and raised an eyebrow.

I waved her off with my good hand. "I'll be good as new in a few days." I hoped that was true.

My mom inhaled suddenly and then looked up at Gage. "Honey," she said to me, "why does your boyfriend smell like a hellhound?"

Gage and I winced at the exact same time, and Gran let a colorful curse word fly as nervous laughter pealed out of me.

"Well, it's a romantic story actually," I started, and then launched into the story of how Gage jumped in front of a hellhound for me the night Aurelia contacted my mom to tell her to hang on.

"That *is* romantic," Gran agreed, making goo-goo eyes at Gage.

My mom frowned, looking at Gage. "How deep was the bite, did it hit bone?"

I peered at Gage, who nodded.

"How long until your first symptom appeared?" she asked with all the emotion of a medical doctor. My mom spent so much time in the Netherworld around demons, maybe she could help us figure out what to do about Gage.

"Within hours," Gage admitted.

My mom whistled low. "Have you fully shifted yet?"

Wow, she was totally taking the my-daughter-is-dating-a-hellhound thing in stride.

Gage shook his head. "Not fully. My friend Dash says it might not happen, and then things will be better for me. Only if you fully shift do you have to go to the Netherworld for the full moon."

My mom nodded. "That's true, but you haven't had a full moon here yet, right?"

Why was she saying it like she fully expected him to shift when the moon went full? I didn't like this. I didn't want to be talking about this anymore.

"Tomorrow," Gage croaked, and my mom nodded solemnly.

Tomorrow? There was a full moon tomorrow? We'd find out then if Gage was going to fully shift?

I hated that. I hated everything about that.

My gaze caught on a gold bangle around my mom's

wrist. It looked like there was angelic script etched into the metal. "What's that?" I asked, sure she hadn't been wearing it in the Netherworld.

"Oh, this?" my mom asked as she gently shook her hand, jiggling the bracelet. "The wards went crazy when you threw me through the portal, shocking me, until they slapped this on my wrist."

I winced. That sounded painful, and I immediately felt bad that I'd been the cause of it, but I couldn't regret my actions because at least she was alive. If I hadn't tossed her in the portal and gotten her out of there, Apollyon definitely would have killed her.

"This bracelet conceals my Shade magic so I can be here within the Lumen Compound," she continued. "I think your friend, Indigo, has been given one as well."

For a minute there I'd forgotten my mom was a Shade, but the truth of it hit me like a tidal wave, reminding me I had no less than five hundred questions for her.

Reaching out, I rubbed Gage's arm. "Can you give us some alone time now?" I asked, partially to stop talking about this hellhound stuff, but also because some of the questions I had for my mom were really personal, and I felt like she wouldn't want to talk about it in front of Gage.

He leaned in and kissed my cheek. "Nice to meet you both." He dipped his head to my mom and Gran and then left, shutting the door behind him.

My mom smiled. "I actually like him." She sounded surprised, which made me chuckle.

"Me too," Gran chimed in.

That was good, but I needed some answers and I'd waited long enough.

Turning, I faced my mother, and by the look on her face she knew what was coming.

"Mom, how? How could you marry and have a kid with him? He's a fallen angel and the ruler of the Netherworld. The worst, darkest soul there is. He betrayed Avalon. He's evil. *How?*"

I hadn't meant to say it so passionately, so judgmental, it just came out that way.

"I'd like to know that too." Gran pulled up a seat and my mother nodded. Her face was devoid of all emotion as she inspected the thread count of the sheets.

"How did you fall for Gage? The son of a Shade leader?" my mom asked me, and my mouth popped open in surprise. She knew exactly who Gage was the entire time. "I imagine you found a spark of light in him that drew you to him."

I just nodded. It was only a spark when we first met, now it was a roaring fire. Gage was a good man, an even better one now that he was in the right environment.

My mom sighed deeply and lay back on the pillow, staring up at the ceiling. "It was like that with Apollyon, except that the spark of light I saw in him was fake."

That caught my attention, and both Gran and I leaned closer.

My mom reached up and ran her fingers through her damp, blonde hair. Looking at her now I got a glimpse of what I might look like in my late thirties. She was beautiful despite the bruises and being underweight.

"That entire first year with him was a blur." She met my gaze and years swam in her eyes. "He put a spell on me, similar to a love spell you see in the movies."

Gran and I both gasped at the same time. Like an *actual* love spell? She'd mentioned she'd felt like he'd cast a love spell on her in her letter, but I assumed she was joking.

"What do you mean?" I asked.

My mom chewed the inside of her cheek, looking lost in a distant memory. "That first day I went to Shade Academy for my tour I had *zero* intentions of becoming a Shade. He was waiting for me. He projected himself as a Shade in his early twenties with a rich family. Told me his name was Aaron. He took me to lunch, and the more he spoke and the more I fell in love, the more what he said made sense. He could have told me that my foot was on fire, and I would have laughed and smiled."

He spelled her! That bastard!

I balled the sheet in my fists as she went on.

"I chose to become a Shade to be with him, unaware of the consequences of that action. I fought alongside them, protecting portals, killing—" Her voice cracked. "Lumen hunters."

Gran reached forward and massaged my mom's leg.

A single tear slid down my mother's face and she swatted it away. "I didn't recognize myself, but at the same time I was happy. Aaron came and went at odd hours, and I didn't question it. He was a powerful Shade with business all over the world."

So that's how he explained his absence. He was really in the Netherworld. Lying douche.

"Then…" My mom looked at me with a small smile. "I got pregnant with you, and all at once the love spell started to wear off. I started to question why I was doing things. Aaron became less funny, less charming, and I began to notice the workings of a spell."

A sob escaped Gran's throat. "I should have known. I should have helped you."

My mom reached out and grasped Gran's hand, "How could you have known? I didn't. And by then I'd completely cut off contact with you and everyone from my old life. It took my pregnancy with Tatum to dilute the spell. Tatum's life force merged with mine and his spell didn't account for that. It was weakened and I was able to see through it. I saw the ugly monster I'd married," she growled. "I still had to act the part of brainwashed wife when he was around, but when he left I started to follow him. I learned where he went and who he really was, and that's when I realized what I was up against."

"Oh, Mom." My heart broke for her. I couldn't imagine finding out the man I was married to and pregnant with his child was the freaking ruler of the Netherworld.

My mom picked at her fingernails. "I was so close to my due date when I figured it all out. I knew I'd only have one chance to escape, but it would have to wait until after I gave birth. I wouldn't be physically strong enough to leave him before then. I also wasn't willing to risk a potential confrontation with Apollyon and jeopardize your life, Tatum. So I had to wait. He wasn't physically abusive back then. It was a safe environment."

Back then. I ground my teeth together hard enough that my jaw ached.

Gran patted her hand. "It makes so much sense now, why you came to me that day with baby Tatum… the things you said."

My mom looked at her mother and it really hit me in the feels how much Gran must have agonized over all of this too.

My mom nodded. "Once I learned why Apollyon even wanted a child, you were the only one I trusted to keep her safe if I wasn't around to."

"And you tried to kill him?" I asked.

My mom laughed, "Like an idiot, yes. I was a powerful Shade, but not *that* powerful. I'd studied some dark magic at Shade Academy in the hopes to use it against him, but it backfired. It created the spell that linked us together, which actually ended up saving my life. It made it so I was able to siphon some of Apollyon's power, and if he tried to kill me, which he did try, it hurt him."

I realized then that I'd judged her. I'd assumed she just chose Shade to rebel and fell for Apollyon because he was good looking and charismatic.

"I'm sorry," I said, even though she wouldn't know what

I was even apologizing for. She just shook her head as if rejecting my apology, and it was in that moment that I remembered the shock of Apollyon telling me I might have a sister up in the black tower on Devil's Meadow.

My concussion must have been worse than I thought, because that entire conversation came back to me now, as well as Aurum saving me, and I sat up straight.

"Mom…" My voice shook.

Gran seemed to catch on that something was wrong, because her hand came to rub small circles on my back. "What's wrong?" she asked.

I looked at my mother, my heart pounding in my throat. "Why did Apollyon say he had to go and get my sister so he could kill us both?"

Both my mom and Gran wrapped their hands around their mouths at the same time and I could tell by the shock that it was news to them.

My mom sat up fully and winced as if it caused her pain. "What do you mean? What exactly did he say?"

"He said his backup plan had backfired. It was almost as if he was trying to kill me but couldn't. Then he mentioned a sister."

Her chest heaved as she stared at me quietly for a full minute. "He said backup plan?"

I nodded and my mom swallowed hard. "Apollyon would occasionally mention some sort of backup plan that he had, but I never knew what that was. He let it slip once that it was in Los Angeles, but I don't know more than that."

She looked deep into my eyes. "He never mentioned another child. I can't imagine he has one, but he was always good at keeping secrets."

My head started to pound. Trying to process the possibility that I had a secret sister stashed in Los Angeles on top of everything that had happened today was just too much.

"I'm going to make us all some fresh cookies," Gran piped in and stood. I guess she agreed with me that this conversation had gotten too heavy for one day.

My mom lay back on the bed and patted her stomach. "We will be right here, Mom. Chocolate chip please," she said, and I relaxed.

Leaning forward, I placed my head on my mom's lap and she played with my hair. Operation Find Out if I Had a Secret Sister was going to have to wait. I wanted to just be with my mom. I grew up my whole life without one and we needed to make up for lost time.

Drea peeked her head into the dining hall and I waved her over to our table. The full moon was yesterday and a fully man Gage was still with us, so we were celebrating. An official my-boyfriend-is-not-a-full-fledged-hellhound party. Unconventional, but totally happening.

Indigo raised her glass of soda and cheered me with a grin. Theo was acting on Aurelia's behalf while she healed and had permitted Indigo to live on campus while we figured out if we could chuck her in the portal to Avalon or not. Apparently, we needed permission for that type of thing, and I wasn't keen on breaking it again, so we were waiting to hear back from Cael if she could ascend.

The bracelet on her wrist that allowed her to walk freely within the Lumen Compound shone under the overhead lights as she brought her drink to her mouth. It was a relief to know she could take refuge here and that she wasn't under the Shades' thumb anymore.

Skye had popped in yesterday to tell me Aurum was okay after the fight with Apollyon, and I'd told her about my sister. She nodded as if she knew about it already and said she was on it. Then she'd poofed out of the room before I could ask anything else. Typical Skye behavior.

Gran and my mom were getting settled in their new two-bedroom apartment they were going to share. I had taken my lunch break to eat with them earlier in the day and helped them move some furniture around. It was so amazing to be with both of them and to all be safe that I had a permanent smile on my face for the rest of the afternoon.

Things were definitely looking up.

Drea joined us, and everyone went silent as we waited for her to update us about her mom. We all knew she'd just gotten back from checking on her. She gave us two thumbs-up and we whooped and cheered.

"She'll be out of the healing center and back home day after tomorrow." She grinned, but then her smile faltered.

"And we're all getting reamed for going to the Netherworld without taking a team of master Lumens."

The cheering stopped, but then everyone burst into laughter.

"All's well that ends well, right?" Gage asked.

"Yep, let's party." Dash pulled back the cardboard box top to reveal a steaming hot pizza.

Gage was the first to grab a slice, but instead of taking a bite, he set it before me.

"Awwww," Drea and Marlow said in unison, and I turned beet red.

Indigo just chuckled and said, "Never thought I'd see the day."

A sudden motion to my right caused me to swivel, and when I saw that it was Skye, I grinned.

"Skye's here!" I announced, and the table broke out into cheers again.

But the smile fell from my face as I examined the horrified look she wore. Was she crying? Could ghosts cry?

"I'm so sorry, Tatum." she said, her voice breaking with emotion. "There's nothing you can do, and I'm so sorry."

Chills rose up on my arms at her words. "Wh—"

A popping noise, a crash, and a growl all sounded at the same time, and I spun.

No!

A black and red smoking portal to the Netherworld swirled in the middle of the cafeteria. Gage was bent over in front of it, growling as his body hulked and changed. His back snapped in half, and I ran to his side, tears streaming down my face.

"Dash! Help him!" I yelled, casting a frantic glance at the other Lumen, unsure what to do.

Familiar dark laughter filled the room. Apollyon stood in front of the portal with his fist raised. He twisted his wrist and Gage howled as if in pain.

I looked down at my boyfriend to find that none of the Gage I knew and loved was left. There was no more man. He was completely lost to the beast. He'd fully shifted.

"I own him now. He's mine," Apollyon said with a sadistic grin, waving Gage forward like you would command a pet. Gage moved to go toward him, but I reached out and grasped his fur to stop him. His animal head whipped around, teeth bared, and he snarled at me. I didn't see an ounce of recognition in his yellow hellhound eyes.

Shocked, I let go with a yelp, and Gage walked on all fours through the portal and into the Netherworld to his new master. In that moment my soul shattered.

This isn't happening.

It was like Drea, Dash, and I had one mind in that moment. We all burst forward collectively, intending to pull Gage back. I lashed out with my magic, trying to keep the portal open, but it was no use. Apollyon flicked his wrist, a shockwave burst outward; Drea, Dash, and I were thrown off our feet, and the portal snapped shut before we hit the floor, landing in a heap. My shoulder was still injured, and the hit caused fresh pain to shoot up my elbow.

How the hell was Apollyon able to make a portal on school grounds? But then I gasped, remembering Aurelia had been injured because a group of Shades had stolen the relic that was supposed to strengthen the wards ensuring no one could open a portal on campus with dark magic. We still had our regular wards, but Apollyon must be too powerful for them now. I couldn't help but think that I had done this by breaking the spell that weakened him.

The cafeteria went into panic mode. Students and teachers ran in and out, yelling commands and pulling weapons off their tattoos. Indigo was crying and the sound made my heart hurt.

I stood, my heart pounding in my chest as my hands shook.

Gage is a hellhound. Apollyon controlled him like a master controlled a dog.

A sob ripped from my lips, and I fell to my knees crying.

No. No. No. This wasn't fair. Not Gage.

Holding my hands together, I pulled on my power, the purple magic forming a ball between my palms. I wasn't going to let Apollyon take him like that. I was going after him like I did my mom. We would figure the whole beast shifter thing out later.

"Tatum, no." Dash fell to his knees before me, agony in his gaze.

"Move!" I growled.

The portal was already opening behind him. I didn't need a cemetery right now. I didn't need Indigo. I was never more powerful than I felt in this moment. Gage was mine. Not his. *Mine!*

Dash reached up and grabbed my shoulders, squeezing so hard that I hissed, and I met his gaze.

"Listen to me, Tatum. My uncle told me that once they are lost fully to the beast they don't recognize family. Gage would rip you in two right now. You *have* to let him go."

My power left me in that moment and the purple magic in my hands sputtered to nothing as I looked at Dash in desperation. "No, Gage promised he would never hurt me when he was like that. I can find him and—"

"He's right," Skye's voice came from over my shoulder. "Gage isn't Gage anymore."

Those were the final words that broke me.

Gage isn't Gage anymore.

What were they saying? Leave him there?

"I can't leave him like that," I told Dash.

Dash nodded. "It's only twenty-four hours. He'll be back and in his human form by tomorrow night. Trust me."

I looked in Dash's eyes, needing someone to be held accountable. "If he's not, I'll tear this world and every other one apart looking for him."

Dash swallowed hard and nodded.

The next twenty-four hours were literal Hell on Earth. I didn't eat, I didn't sleep, I did nothing but envision Gage snarling at me and then walking to Apollyon on all fours. I was pacing the garden with the Angel Gang plus Indigo exactly twenty-four hours later.

And nothing happened.

"Maybe we need to be in the cafeteria. Maybe he'll show back up there," I said, consulting my watch.

My mother had confirmed what Dash had said. Once a bitten person took the full form of the hellhound, they wouldn't remember their loved ones. All I could do was wait in agony for—

"There!" Drea pointed to a portal opening in the court-yard. It widened to a six-foot oval, spit someone out of it, and then snapped shut quickly.

What the...?

"Gage?" I recognized the dark hair but that was all. He was naked, covered in black blood, and completely unconscious.

I froze, unable to tell if he was breathing.

Dizziness washed over me as Dash pulled off his hoodie and covered Gage's waist, shaking him gently. Only when Gage coughed and I was sure he was alive did I run forward, spurred on by hope.

I fell to my knees beside him, searching his green eyes for any memory of me.

"Tate?" He looked confused but thank God he wasn't confused about me.

He looked down at his hands and I noticed he was holding a note of some kind. The black paper was blotched with dried blood.

"What the? Why am I—" The color drained from his face as I pulled the note open.

When I read it over his shoulder, all hope fled.

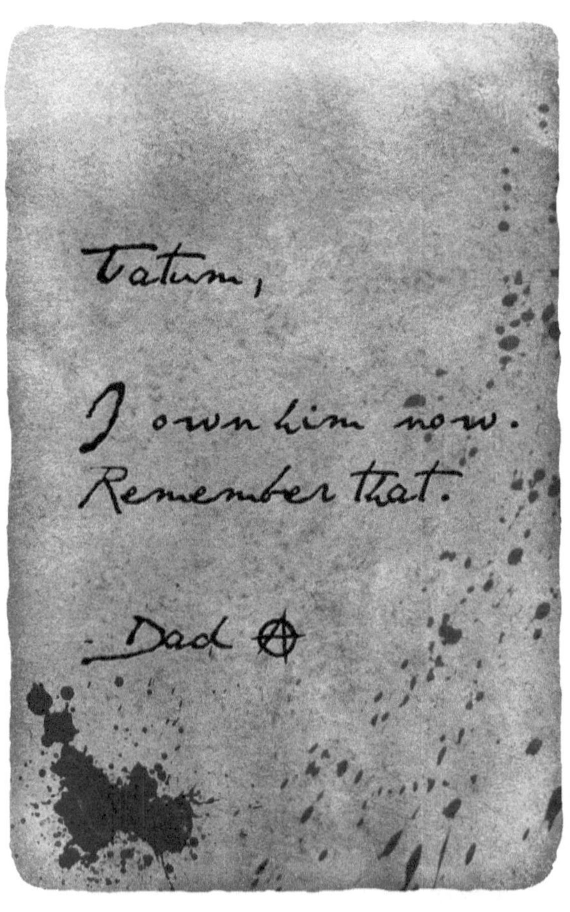

SHADOW ANGEL: BOOK 3

Don't miss Tatum and Gage's epic conclusion.

www.ShadowAngelBook3.com

PLEASE WRITE A REVIEW

amazon   goodreads

Reviews are the lifeblood of authors and your opinion will help others decide to read our books.

If you want to see more co-written books from Leia and Julie, please leave a review on Amazon.

http://Review.ShadowAngelBook2.com

JOIN THE FAN CLUB(S)

Get involved, make some friends, and get exclusive sneak peeks before anyone else.

🤍 Leia & Julie

ABOUT LEIA STONE

Leia Stone is the USA Today bestselling author of multiple bestselling series including Matefinder and Wolf Girl. She's sold over two million books and her Fallen Academy series has been optioned for film. Her novels have been translated into five languages and she even dabbles in script writing.

Leia writes urban fantasy and paranormal romance with sassy kick-butt heroines and irresistible love interests. She lives in Spokane, WA with her husband and two children.

www.LeiaStone.com

ABOUT JULIE HALL

Julie Hall is a USA Today bestselling, multiple award-winning author.

She writes YA paranormal / fantasy novels, loves doodles, and drinks Red Bull, but not necessarily in that order. Julie's daughter says that her superpower is sleeping all day and writing all night . . . and well, she wouldn't be wrong.

Julie currently lives in Colorado with her four favorite *people* - her husband, daughter, and two fur babies.

www.JulieHallAuthor.com

BOOKS BY LEIA STONE

LeiaStone.com/books

BOOKS BY JULIE HALL

Fallen Legacies Series

www.FallenLegacies.com

Life After Series

www.LifeAfterSeries.com